1 007712 36

SAFEKEEPING

"Wha_____ Thadeus?"

"F_____ school, said Thadeus.

"Quite right. There must be a public school nearby. Well, that's settled. Is tomorrow a school day?"

"Tomorrow is Thursday."

"People go to school on Thursdays, Robby," stated Mrs. Lowry.

"Yes, ma'am."

"The trick is," advised Thadeus Lowry, "to leave the apartment in the morning and walk around the blocks in ever widening squares until you find a school."

"We'll set you off with a nice warm breakfast in the morning," proffered Mrs. Lowry. "I'm sure you'll have a lovely adventure..."

"S-sir?"

"Yes, Robby. What now?"

"Can I take your gun to school with me?"

"A *gun!*" gasped Mrs. Lowry.

"Good heavens, no," chuckled Thadeus Lowry. "What could happen to you on the streets of New York?"

D0813107

Also in Arrow by Gregory McDonald

FLETCH
FLETCH'S MOXIE
FLETCH, TOO
FLYNN'S IN

SAFEKEEPING

Gregory McDonald

ARROW BOOKS

1 007712 36

In Memory of M.A.M.,
who told me to close my eyes,
then asked me what I saw.

Arrow Books Limited
62-65 Chandos Place, London WC2N 4NW

An imprint of Century Hutchinson Limited

London Melbourne Sydney Auckland
Johannesburg and agencies throughout
the world

First published in Great Britain by Victor Gollancz Ltd 1986
Arrow edition 1989

© 1985 by Gregory McDonald

This book is sold subject to the condition that it shall
not, by way of trade or otherwise, be lent, resold,
hired out, or otherwise circulated without the
publisher's prior consent in any form of binding or
cover other than that in which it is published and
without a similar condition including this condition
being imposed on the subsequent purchaser

Printed and bound in Great Britain by
Courier International Ltd, Tiptree, Essex

ISBN 0 09 949130 3

RENFREW DISTRICT
ARTS
AND
LIBRARIES
COUNCIL

1 In Which Noses and Other Outstanding Matters
  Are Discussed 1
2 Water Is Crossed and Thadeus Lowry Is Met........9
3 Penetrating the Frozen Tundra by Foot............17
4 Thadeus Lowry Offers an Explanation 24
5 Advent 28
6 Thadeus Lowry Does a Day's Work................34
7 Held Up on the Way Home 40
8 Care, Feeding and Education Are Discussed 48
9 The Streets of New York 55
10 Kidnapped 62
11 Worthiness 70
12 A Man of Peace 77
13 In Durance 82
14 With the Aid of the Law 87
15 The Power of the Press 96
16 Philology 109
17 Taking Stock 120
18 The Odor of Sanctity 129
19 Tempest in a Bathtub 134
20 A Congressional Bill 141
21 Pushing and Shoving 148
22 In the Lap of America 158
23 The Charitable Lady............................168
24 Trapped! 181
25 *Mort à Guerre* 187
26 "Allow Me to Explain." 195

1

In Which Noses and Other Outstanding Matters Are Discussed

"Burnes?" Mrs. Jencks enquired generally of the small room filled with six beds, six eight-year-old boys scurrying to get dressed, and odd pieces of clothing on the beds, on the boys, in the air, on the floor, underfoot and in hand as weapons.

"Yes, sir?"

"Headmaster wants to see you straight off."

"I can't find my stocking, sir."

In the doorway, Mrs. Jencks still couldn't be sure which boy had answered her and thus identified himself as Burnes. All the youngest gentlemen at Wolsley School called everyone over five feet in height *sir*. At their age everyone, including the gardener and the imbecile from the village who collected the wash, was in a position of authority over them, by size if not by rank, and if there was a word to placate authority, *sir* was the word.

Wisely, Mrs. Jencks maintained her expression of benign maternity while waiting at the door. It was this expression of bemused patience, and her ample, maternal dimensions, which had won and kept for her the job of matron of Wolsley School. Parents and faculty both perceived Mrs. Jencks as a bosom into which anyone

1

would be happy to sob. Three decades of students, however, had penetrated Mrs. Jencks' placid expression and knew it to connote nothing more than painless indifference to the world at large. They also knew that nothing had nestled against her bosom in all those years except crumbs from her tea cakes.

"Hurry along," Mrs. Jencks said, as a general admonition.

Eight-year-old boys haven't that many years' dressing practice behind them. When given a square foot of cold floor on which simultaneously to hop and execute one of life's First Things, including shoe strings and ties, the result is similar to that of any great, unexpected human undertaking: confusion, consternation, and disputation. Out of that room, in twelve minutes, six eight-year-old boys were expected to march, toileted, washed, brushed, dressed identically in kneepants, kneesocks, shoes, shirt, tie, the Wolsley School blazer and cap, six made beds behind them. Occasionally, it almost happened; expectations were almost fulfilled, but never, of course, with more than two of the six dressed entirely in their own clothes.

Doubtlessly, parents are smarter now, but in the early 1940s they sincerely wished to believe, or wished their friends to believe, or wished their children to believe, that they sent their children off to school or camp with some continuing sense of identity. Name tags were sewn into every article of clothing with thread staunch enough to do its umbilical duty. Traditionally, parents need to believe something of the sort when, in truth, they are throwing their children to the public, their clothes after them.

Jaime Pomfrey, two beds west of Burnes', had name tags in his stockings stiffer than the rest, and placed uncomfortably below the fold. This was one lad at school who seldom forgot his mother. He wrote her each Sunday and cursed her each morning. Very shortly he became adept, via diversionary tactics, argument, offers to dispense bloody noses, at getting anyone's stockings but his own on his legs. His own stockings remained balled neatly in his drawer.

"Burnes," said Mrs. Jencks. "Headmaster wants you before Chapel."

"Yes, sir, but I can't find a stocking."

"Hurry along."

At the shrill sound of a bell, the future of Britain agitated each other to the door, narrowly circumnavigated Mrs. Jencks, and threw themselves suicidally down the stairwell. Left amid the confusion of the room, one bare foot elevated from the cold floor, was—as marked in the school register—Robert James Saint James Burnes Walter Farhall-Pladroman, S.Nob. To this son of a nobleman, Mrs. Jencks' girth appeared to be holding the door jambs at a distance from each other wider than normal. On the high plateau of her bosom sparkled a necklace of early morning toast crumbs.

"You are Burnes, aren't you?"

"Yes, sir, ma'am."

"You little ones confuse me the first year or two. Until your noses grow."

"Noses, ma'am?"

"Find a stocking somewhere, Burnes. Headmaster's waiting."

As "Headmaster's Waiting" was a disaster on an all-school scale comparable only to the Union Jack's touching the ground, an element of such magnitude that it was capable of causing faculty as well as students to rush from playing field and classroom, even of causing parents to rush from London, Robby was forced to accept the inevitable: that Pomfrey had won again. He went to Pomfrey's drawer and pulled on one of Pomfrey's stockings.

Hopping in a fruitless effort to adjust Pomfrey's identity against his shin, Robby Burnes (as he was generally known by people who had something other to do with their lives than remember all his names) followed Mrs. Jencks down the stairwell, across the courtyard, through the smells of hot chocolate, past the cough-filled, sneeze-filled chapel, and into Admin. Wing, wherein Headmaster had his study. Seeing Mrs. Jencks hurrying from behind over a long course distracted Robby from speculating what difficulty he had caused, precipitating his impending interview with Headmaster. Mrs. Jencks achieved forward motion by the action of each cheek upon the other: The right would rest against the left, which would contract and propel the right outward and onward again— which was intensely interesting to Robby. He wondered if such an athletic device would survive a long scrimmage.

"Aha, there you are, Burnes! That is Burnes, isn't it, Mrs. Jencks?"

"Yes, Headmaster. I have trouble with them, too, sir, until they get noses. A bit slow dressing this morning. Missed breakfast altogether, he has."

"Tadpoles will be tadpoles, Mrs. Jencks."

On Headmaster's desk was a finished breakfast tray.

Headmaster, Robby knew, divided the world between *tadpoles* and *honored parents*. Parents considered him England's greatest boy handler. Boys considered him England's greatest parent handler. He achieved these reputes mainly by keeping a threadbare nine-by-twelve Persian carpet on his study floor. The rug served the double purpose of giving the tadpoles a touch of home (as all, typically, thus far in their lives had been brought up in the back rooms of their parents' homes, those rooms relegated to servants, worn-out rugs and boys) and thus suggested to the boys they could speak freely, confidentially, to Headmaster, as they had been in the habit of speaking at home only to Nanny and Cook. To honored parents, the worn carpet bespoke Headmaster's selfless, soulful dedication to the education of boys. Over the decades, the worn carpet in Headmaster's study had attracted contributions to the school's endowment many, many times its own original worth. Headmaster himself, as he paced restlessly in his black, academic robe, seemed oblivious of the magic carpet beneath his feet. Headmaster's eye, Robby noticed, repeatedly checked the decanter of sherry on the sideboard, as if the rate of evaporation was a cause of concern to him.

"I went to the funeral yesterday," Headmaster said. "Very nice. Although, I must say, two coffins in the one aisle were a bit much, even in this day and age."

"Sit down, Burnes," Mrs. Jencks suggested.

"Yes, yes, sit down, Burnes."

"Funeral, sir?"

"Good heavens. I always start at the back of things. Comes from being a Latin scholar, my wife used to say. She's dead, too, of course."

"Sorry, sir."

"Years ago. Do enough Latin and see what happens to you. Begin starting everything at the wrong end."

"Sir?"

"Latin's the curse of the English school system. Never understand why your honored parents keep expecting us to ladle it out. They conquered Britain, you know."

"Our parents, sir? Did they need to?"

"The Romans. Why should we spend centuries learning the

language of a bunch of beasts we spent centuries throwing off the yoke of? Tell me that."

"I'll look it up, sir."

"I daresay if the Germans conquer us, two thousand years from now English schoolboys will be translating *Mein Kampf* as reverently as they're made to swallow Caesar's *Gallic Wars* today. It's all the same bully rubbish, you see."

"I see, sir."

Mrs. Jencks cleared her throat. "Very instructive, sir. I'm sure."

"People wonder why I accepted the position of Headmaster of Wolsley School, ur . . ."

"Indeed I did, sir."

". . . ur. What's your name?"

"Robby Nose, sir."

"Burnes, Headmaster."

"Burnes, yes, of course. The funeral. I accepted the position of Headmaster simply to get away from the teaching of Latin. Can you understand that?"

"Oh, yes, sir."

"How many times can a British subject read the reports of legions of Roman jackanapes marching up and down our green hills, laying waste our villages, slaughtering our young males and despoiling our virgins?"

"I haven't read that book yet, sir."

"No. And it's a jolly good thing you're not going to. You're off to America this afternoon, and the best thing about America is they've never been conquered and therefore have no regard for anyone's language, including the one they pick-pocketed from us. You'll never have to know Latin in America, lad. Or English."

"Sir?"

"Is he sniffling, Mrs. Jencks?"

"I think he's confused, sir, what with the Romans and all."

"Your parents, Burnes. Their London house was in Mayfair?"

"Yes, sir. Mayfair."

"A direct hit. Damned foolish of them, too, I might say. If they ever conquer Britain, they'll want those Mayfair houses, mark my words."

"Who, sir? The Romans?"

"Am I not being clear, Mrs. Jencks?"

"It's the shock, Headmaster. It takes a moment."

"Ah, well, yes. Cheer up, Burnes. Things could be worse, you know. You could have been at home with your honored parents getting bombed instead of enjoying the safety, the staunch peace, the security we provide here at Wolsley School."

"Thank you, sir."

"Any questions?"

"Give him half a moment, Headmaster. He'll understand."

"Chapel," Headmaster said "Must go do my Christian duty . . ."

Robby's eyes followed Headmaster's to the sherry decanter, then through the window to the chapel spire. Robby looked at the school emblem on the wall behind Headmaster's desk and at the desk itself. He then studied the threadbare carpet on the floor.

"Are my parents dead, sir?"

"Yes."

"I see, sir. Thank you, sir."

"A bomb. I passed the ruins of your home yesterday, in the taxi on the way to the funeral."

"There was a camera in my room, sir. I got it last birthday. Moms made me leave it home."

"What's he saying, Mrs. Jencks?"

"Something about a camera, Headmaster. But he's not sniffling."

"That's good."

"Did you happen to see my camera?"

"Rubble, my boy, all rubble. Pladroman House is rubble. End of an era and all that. Funeral yesterday."

"Why didn't I go to the funeral?"

"Lord, no place for a tadpole. All that sniffling going on. Press photographers buzzing about, trying to catch someone with her hanky down."

"Sir?"

"Yes, Burnes?"

"Deepest jungle or frozen tundra?"

"I don't get you, my lad."

"You said I'm going to America."

"Yes. You're being evacuated. Cheer up. Plenty of chocolate in America. No Latin."

"But am I going to the deepest jungle or the frozen tundra?"

"I don't know. Never been either place. Never been to America at all. You're going to an uncle in New York."

"But, sir?"

"Yes?"

"I haven't an uncle in New York."

"Of course you have."

"I have a grandaunt, in Scotland."

"Several of us decided yesterday in a meeting after the funeral that you have an uncle in New York. Name of ... let me see ... Lowry. Thadeus Lowry. Must be an uncle somewhere on your mother's side. A newspaper publisher someone said. Probably publisher of *The New York Times*. Anyway, that's where you're going."

"Yes, sir."

"Safekeeping."

"Yes, sir."

"There's my brave lad," said Mrs. Jencks.

Headmaster said: "The Evacuation Lady is coming for you at noon. Mrs. Jencks will help you pack while the other tadpoles are in class. We try our best, you know, to keep the war away from the tadpoles at Wolsley School. One only gets to enjoy childhood just so long. Tuition refund will be made to your family's solicitors."

"Thank you, sir."

"Now I really must go give Chapel."

Thus it was Robert James Saint James Burnes Walter Farhall-Pladroman, S.Nob., found himself seated on his cardboard suitcase the other side of the groundskeeper's lodge at ten o'clock in the morning, as shunted from his mates' view as World War Two itself.

Robby thought of the camera he had never gotten to use. The two coffins in the church aisle. Would his mother have liked the flower arrangements? Mr. Colmap, the butler, would not appreciate the silverware he had polished all those years ending up in rubble. Cook probably wanted to grab her favorite saucepan when she heard the noise of the bomb. Boots was as lucky as Robby to be away from the house when it received a direct hit. Boots was in France with the army. Nanny would not have liked falling down through the whole height of the house in her nightgown. It would have scared her.

Safely out of view of Wolsley School and of everyone left in the world who knew him, Robert James Saint James Burnes Walter Farhall-Pladroman, S.Nob., discovered himself sniffling. All these people who had been good to him were dead. No longer alive. No longer to be seen, heard, smelled, touched. Never.

At first, Robby tried rubbing from his face that offending sniffling instrument, his nose. Then his hands seemed better employed as fists stuck in his eyes to dam the water which wanted out through them. All the rhetoric that had resounded in his head these eight years past—and which he had always supposed had been instilled in his head for just such a moment as this—bounced from one side of his head to the other, trampolined in his throat to hit the roof of his skull. The clearest maxims collided, wrestled with each other, broke each other into a jumble of disjointed syllables. They needed clarifying now. The water which is tears cannot be contained, even by fists. For a long while, the heel of one hand dammed an eye, the other hand rubbed his sniffler; for another long while, the heel of the other hand dammed his other eye, and the hand that had failed so miserably at eye-damming was set to the task of sniffler obliterating. Robby wondered if it might be just such sad exercise that made noses grow, and thus distinguish us.

Robby had missed breakfast. Mightily he came to miss luncheon. Fiercely he came to miss tea.

The Evacuation Lady arrived alone at dusk in a Morris Minor with the news that they were late and had to drive straight through to Southampton, if Robby were to make his ship for America on time.

Voraciously, he missed his supper.

However, by the time the Evacuation Lady arrived, Robby was no longer sniffling. His two eyes and his nose had ceased their mad competition for the attention of his fists. The center of his attention, the center of his being, had slipped millimeters toward his mouth. A single piece of Resounding Rhetoric had won the jumble in his brain. His upper lip was stiff.

2

Water Is Crossed and Thadeus Lowry Is Met

A lifetime later (or so it seemed to him), Robby found himself sitting on his suitcase on a misty, blowing dock in New York Harbor. He had been sitting there since before dawn. Of course he had missed breakfast, and of course he had missed lunch. The past ten days his relationship with food had become strained. He had seen food seldom, and what food he had seen had parted from him quickly. He no longer *missed* his meals; he was simply hungry.

H.M.S. *Scaramouche* had waddled into the harbor at three in the morning. She leaned, wheezing and sagging, against the dock as if hoping never to be asked to confront the sea again. The evacuated children were roused *en masse* for the last time, put together with their belongings, shouted into a double line and marched, slipping, stumbling, staggering down the gangplank, half asleep in the dark. Women with clipboards, in charge of sorting them out, awaited them on the dock. Robby was identified as someone to be picked up by a Mr. Thadeus Lowry. Mr. Thadeus Lowry was paged. Mr. Thadeus Lowry was not present. Robby was told to "Go over there, dear, and sit on your suitcase, out of harm's way," which he did. Other names were paged and women came forward from the

9

group waiting on the dock: women in fur coats, women in cloth coats, women in nuns' habits. Each greeted a child, or two, or three, and took her, or him, or them, off with her, doubtlessly to warm rooms and steaming breakfasts. Men, too, took some children: a man in a homburg, a man in a fedora, two men in yarmulkes. None identified himself as Thadeus Lowry. Each found it possible to leave the dock without Robby Burnes.

After the sorting-out apparently had been fully accomplished, a lady with a clipboard walked over to Robby, said, "You're Burnes, right? Waiting for Mr. Lowry?" The clipboard had told her so. "He must be delayed. Send him to me when he arrives. I'll be in that little office over there."

Robby's eyes followed her to a small, lit office on the side of the dock. Through the wide window he watched her sip a cup of coffee. He had never had coffee, having been assured by Nanny it would stunt his growth, and therefore did not want it now. He thought his recent diet had been sufficiently stunting.

So he sat on his suitcase, scratching at Pomfrey's name tag on a kneesock, then on Robby's left leg. The wind from under the dock whipped up his short pants. His overcoat was precisely the length of his trousers. His blazer was a few inches shorter. Both his overcoat and trousers stopped three inches above his knees, and six inches above the tops of his kneesocks. Schoolboy fashion at that time required that he have a cap, undervest and drawers, a shirt, necktie, blazer, overcoat, shoes, kneesocks and blue knees.

Buses and ambulances pulled onto the dock at dawn. Still keeping out of harm's way, Robby watched as the war wounded, some on stretchers, some on crutches, some hanging on others' shoulders, were unloaded from the ship. It was a silent operation. Except for the wind, and the engine of a bus or ambulance starting off, hundreds of people were moving, being moved on the dock, wordlessly, noiselessly. It took until well past noon to unload the wounded from the ship.

The first Evacuation Lady had taken Robby by car from Wolsley School to the train and then by train to H.M.S. *Scaramouche* in Southampton. "Poor tyke," she announced to the other passengers in the compartment as soon as the train began moving. "Orphaned by one of those nasty bombs. This is the Farhall-Pladroman boy, if roiling New York Harbor, Robby Burnes reflected that before leaving Wolsley School, he really had seen his suitcase only once before—the day he left home for Wolsley School.

Nanny, sniffling, carrying the small, black, empty suitcase, appeared in the doorway of Robby's bedroom shortly after breakfast. She put it on the bed, and opened it.

Nanny was hugging Robby when Robby's mother appeared, carrying six school uniforms, including shirts, socks and ties in her arms. Five were to go into the suitcase; one was to be worn. Her disapproval of Nanny's expressions of sorrow made Robby's mother firmly cheerful.

"Here, here, now. Robby will love Wolsley School, won't he?"

Robby was studying the school emblem on the cap and on the blazer: a stag butting its head against an oak tree.

"Robby's been looking forward to going to Wolsley School ever so long now, hasn't he?"

Mothers, universally, when afraid of receiving an unsatisfactory answer, have a way of putting a question into the air. The air never answers, and thus equilibrium is maintained.

"How do you do the tie, Moms? I'll need to do it myself."

"Here, silly."

Robby's mother brought Robby to the mirror and taught Robby the Windsor knot. Thus, with loving hands, was one more colt bridled.

Robby's father stood in the library of Pladroman House, which is what he normally did while at home, awaiting the moment to go off and sit in the House of Lords.

"You're off, are you?" he said, brusque and clubby with his only son newly emblazoned with stags butting their heads against oak trees. "Building blocks behind, balls in front?"

"Yes, sir."

"Any patter at Pater before handing over the sovereign?"

"Yes, sir. I'd like to take my new camera to school. The one I got for my birthday."

"Ah!"

"Moms says I mustn't. Nanny says it will be on the mantel in my room when I get home for Christmas hols."

"I expect Mother's right. I'm sure your teachers won't want you running around snapping at them. Shy lot, teachers—especially in a strong draft."

He rubbed his hands together and then drew a gold sovereign from the pocket of his waistcoat.

"There we are, then." He handed it to Robby. "Traditions must be kept."

"Thank you, sir."

"A sovereign and a few words of wisdom from Pater. Deuced world we live in, Robby, especially at this moment. Your greatest joys, and your greatest hurts, will come from other people. Try to be interested in your fellow creatures, son, and try to be kind."

"Yes, sir."

"Off you go, now. I'll go upstairs and try to cheer up old Nanny."

On the dock Robby's hands were in his pockets for what warmth they provided. The fingers of his right hand were closed tightly around the sovereign.

During the morning the sole remaining Evacuation Lady had looked at him through the window of the dock shed several times. Robby had looked back. No further words had passed between them.

In what Robby knew must be the early afternoon, even for America, a portly man carrying a walking stick in a jaunty manner ambled onto the dock from the street. He stopped, looked this way and that along the cavernous, roofed dock. He apparently did not see the lit window of the little office. He approached Robby as the only animate thing in sight.

Half a meter from Robby, he crouched on his walking stick and peered into his face. "What are you?"

"Cold, sir."

The portly man had a puffy, red face, spotted with razor nicks and most veins showing.

"Did anyone ever suggest within your hearing you're a Robby Burnes?" the man asked.

"Yes, sir. That's what I am. A Robby Burnes."

"God love a goose." The man stood up for a fuller view. "Certainly your legs aren't long fellows."

"Are you my uncle, sir?"

"Did anybody say I am?"

"I think that's the expectation, sir."

"You're not at all what I was expecting, are you?"

"What were you expecting, sir?"

"Approximately nine paragraphs for the morning edition, easily written, gracing my byline, I," the man said rather archly, "go under no name but my own, and that name is Thadeus Lowry. Of *The New York Star*, I might add."

"You're to pick me up," Robby said.

"Pick you up?" said Thadeus Lowry. "Why would I do that?"

Thadeus Lowry's protruding eyes stared down at Robby and watched the boy shrug not once, but twice. Robby finally turned his head away and looked at the hull of the *Scaramouche* leaning against the end of the dock.

The Evacuation Lady, having spotted Thadeus Lowry through the window, approached.

"Are you Mr. Lowry?"

"I am," Thadeus Lowry said, turning himself and his walking stick in a half circle. "Thadeus Lowry of *The New York Star*."

"We tried to phone you at the newspaper. No one there seemed to know where you were." The Evacuation Lady straightened her hat. "In fact, some we talked to there didn't know who you are."

"You must have been talking to the advertising department," said Thadeus Lowry. "Those who sell space for the dollar feel my writing intrudes upon their displays offering hair restoratives."

"Well, if you'd come this way and sign forms . . ."

"Forms? For what?"

"For Burnes, here. He's an orphan, Mr. Lowry. Don't you understand? He's been evacuated from England."

Thadeus Lowry looked at Robby as if Robby suddenly had grown larger. "An orphan. Oh, yes."

"There's a war on, Mr. Lowry. We all have to do our bit."

"Oh. And what are you saying is my bit?"

The Evacuation Lady jerked her elbow toward Robby Burnes. "That's your bit. Take him along with you."

"Oh, yes," said Thadeus Lowry. "Take him along . . ."

"He's been here, you know, waiting for you since before dawn. The others were picked up before seven this morning."

"Ah. Well. You see, this way the boy and I will be able to appreciate a timely and leisurely lunch."

"Come into the shed."

Robby picked up his suitcase and followed them into the shed. The office was not much warmer than the dock.

The Evacuation Lady put a sheet of paper on a grimy counter and said, "Have you a pen?"

"Is a carpenter ever without his saw, or a plumber without his wrench? The answer to both questions, of course, as these poltroons of the lower classes are now paid by the hour, is yes. The pen, however, is the tool of my trade, and I know no hours."

"Apparently not. You're a reporter?"

"A man of letters, ma'am, a writer, a journalist . . ."

"Would you sign the forms, please?"

"Let me see, now: Robert Burnes, male, age eight, English, good God," said Thadeus Lowry, looking down at Robby, "is that all they have to say for you? They ask me to acquit myself little better. Married, yes, American citizen, yes; yes, I promise to run him 'round to the post office to get him stamped English, send him to school, keep him out of the pool room, provide him with clean hankies . . ." Thadeus Lowry's voice dwindled as he signed the paper with a large hand.

Putting his pen back into his pocket, he said more loudly to the Evacuation Lady, and more precisely: "And now, where is his leash?"

3

Penetrating the Frozen Tundra by Foot

"**W**hat a journalist needs most, Burnes, is a good set of legs."

Thadeus Lowry, his walking stick preceding him, and Robby Burnes, running behind, dragging his black suitcase, set off briskly from the customs shed into America. As they stabbed and dragged their way along the sidewalk several taxicabs passed, honking their horns, their drivers shouting through their windows offers of quick, warm, comfortable transportation. The mist had turned to light, blowing snow.

"Am I to be a journalist then, sir?"

"I should certainly hope so," said Thadeus Lowry into the wind, "if you take proper advantage of being under my influence. There's no higher estate to which one may aspire. We're all reporters, one way or another, in life. We'll turn up this street. But only those of us who make a fine art of observation and have good legs are privileged to be employed as the minds and the hearts of The People, as journalists."

"Observation, sir?"

"Observation and legs: the foundation and erection of a noble

17

career in journalism. Look at The People, young Burnes. A story in every one of them. Up this way."

"Look at all the taxicabs, sir."

"Things aren't so easy in England just now, are they? Around this corner."

Robby's legs were still wobbly from his sea voyage. His school shoes were not much good on the frozen slime of the sidewalks. His suitcase was as heavy and as disobedient hanging from his left arm as from his right. And the only area of his body which was partly warm was the section of his left leg being abraded by Pomfrey's kneesock's name tag.

"I daresay you'd like some lunch."

"I'd like anything, sir."

"Something warming."

"Yes, sir."

"Melted cheddar cheese over crackers. A mug of chowder. A warm egg sandwich in the fist. Just the morning for it."

"It's afternoon, sir."

"I know a place just up this street."

After another block or two, Thadeus Lowry opened a recessed brown door. Flashing red neon lights on each side of the door warned MEN ONLY.

Thadeus Lowry was holding the door open. Inside was darkness. The same smell of wetpine-tree disinfectant and vomit emanated from the darkness as had from the ship.

"Is this place called Men Only, sir?"

Thadeus Lowry pointed with his walking stick to three golden orbs stuck together, hanging over the door. "It's called The Three Balls," he said. "It's named after the entire Nazi High Command."

"But, sir, the signs say nothing about small boys."

"That," said Thadeus Lowry, "is because there is nothing to be said about small boys. Will you come in?"

The floor was a pentagonal tile. Green sawdust collected in piles and swirls on it.

Along the right-hand wall ran a tall, brown, wooden bar. A brass rail ran along its base. Half the men at the bar had one foot on the rail.

"Lowry!" shouted one of them. "Great story this morning. Great human interest."

"My byline wasn't in the morning newspaper," Thadeus Lowry said with dignity.

"That's what was so great about it," the man said. "In behalf of human interest, the editors threw your story in the wastebasket!"

Along the wall across from the bar were brown wooden booths with tables in them.

"Who've you got carrying your suitcase now, Thadeus?" asked a man breathing on Robby.

"This is Burnes. My bit for the war effort."

"He's rather short, Thadeus."

"I expect so. It's all right. I'll pay."

Thadeus Lowry raised his stick and called at someone over the bar.

"Solomon! A drink!"

A voice said, "What will you have, Mr. Lowry?"

"A double whiskey for me, please, and a proper Guinness for my friend here."

"What friend, Mr. Lowry?" said the voice. "Are you seeing the small, crawly things again?"

"My friend," said Thadeus Lowry, pointing his stick at Robby. "My friend. Down here."

"Can you spell your name backwards for me, Mr. Lowry?"

"Solomon, if you'd just look over the bar, you'd see my friend. Indulge me this much."

The top of a head, eyeglasses, and a nose appeared over the edge of the bar and peered down at Robby.

"You see, Solomon? A person."

"He drinks Guinness?" asked the head.

"Never touches a thing stronger before lunch."

"He hasn't had lunch?"

"We're coming to that."

"It's quarter to three in the afternoon, Mr. Lowry."

"As long as you're bringing the drinks over to a booth," said Thadeus Lowry, "you might save yourself a truss by bringing me two double whiskeys."

"And two Guinnesses?"

"And two Guinnesses."

"And how many straws?"

After Thadeus Lowry had hung his overcoat and his hat on a peg and propped his walking stick against a wall, he conducted Robby to a booth.

Robby continued wearing his overcoat, as he had since leaving Wolsley School.

"Is this a gentlemen's club, sir?"

"Yes," said Thadeus Lowry, looking at Robby carefully. "It is. In a way."

"And are all these gentlemen members?"

"They are. But in this country we call them regulars."

"Is it terribly difficult to get into a club like this?"

"Allow me to explain," said Thadeus Lowry. "In England, the expression is, you have to stand for a club. In America, being more of a democracy, all you have to do to be admitted to a place like this is to stand."

"You mean: stand up?"

"Yes. That's what I mean. Things are more democratic here."

"Is your newspaper office near here?"

"Not far, not far. We'll go there after lunch. Ah, here's lunch."

On Solomon's tray were two glasses of whiskey, the two glasses of beer, and a bowl of chowder crackers.

Solomon waited at the edge of the table until Thadeus Lowry paid him.

"This is the American bookkeeping system," said Thadeus Lowry. "Nothing on the cuff. Simplifies things."

"It's the only way of getting paid regular," said Solomon, thus allowing Robby to understand why the club members were called regulars. "I brought you some *hors de saison*," Solomon said, pushing the bowl of chowder crackers nearer to Robby.

Thadeus Lowry saluted Solomon's back and drained one of the glasses of whiskey. "Now I'll show you how to drink the Guinness." He took one of the glasses of stout, drained it, wiped his mouth with the back of his hand, looked at Robby and said, "Ah, the first drink of the day. Makes sleeping late worthwhile."

Robby was eating the chowder crackers by the fistfuls. "Is that why you missed the boat, Mr. Lowry? You slept late?"

"'Missed the boat!' I never missed the boat in my life. A true journalist, Robby, strong in the thigh and quick of eye, never misses a story within his purview."

"Am I a story, sir?"

Thadeus Lowry sipped from his second glass of whiskey. "There was a moment, there, when I thought you might be. Why else would I have shown up at the dock this morning?"

"You didn't, sir. You showed up at the dock this afternoon. Everyone else showed up this morning."

"A story, Robby, doesn't happen until a journalist arrives."

"Yes, sir."

"You must learn these things, if you're to take advantage of my influence upon you."

"Yes, sir."

"I received a cable, from London, saying, 'Meet Robby Burnes, H.M.S. *Scaramouche*, New York,' etc., etc. The spelling of your name puzzled me, somewhat, your extra *E* in Burnes, but then again the cable company had managed to spell New York with three *A*'s. Now, I ask you, what journalist in his sane mind wouldn't put in an appearance having received such a cable? As a journalist, Robby, one must consider the best uses of one's valuable time. At best, I reasoned, a dead poet would appear; at worse, a smokeable cigar. A story. You must always think in terms of the story, Robby."

"You're not my uncle, sir."

"Hardly likely," said Thadeus Lowry. "I had only one sibling I knew of, a sister. An impatient child, she was crushed by an ice-cream wagon at the age of six. Story was she was in a mortal rush for a chocolate ripple cone."

"Honorary uncle, sir? Lots of lads have 'em."

"My name must have entered your life, somewhere, been mentioned somehow in your family's progress. Of course, it's entirely possible your parents were admirers of my journalism, perceived my wit, wisdom, sagacity, and agreed between themselves that, should anything befall them, the best thing that could happen to their son would be to be brought up under my tutelage."

"I don't think my parents read *The New York Times*, sir."

"Actually, I don't write for *The New York Times*. I write for *The New York Star*. *The Star* is somewhat smaller than *The Times*, but a livelier newspaper. It has a reputation for attracting the more imaginative writers."

"Is *The New York Star* read in London, sir?"

"Who knows how far the written word flies? Sagacity cannot be confined within borders."

"Could there be some other explanation, sir?"

The redness of Thadeus Lowry's face had increased greatly since coming into the warmth of The Three Balls after his brisk walk in the snow from the dock. His eyes, coursing over the various glasses on the table, had softened. He reached into a pocket. "One thing you can say for your family's attorneys is that they do not fritter away your shillings by being garrulous in a transatlantic cable."

Thadeus Lowry unfolded a yellow rectangle of paper and read from it. " 'Meet Robby Burnes, H.M.S. *Scaramouche*, New York.' It's addressed to me at *The Star*, and it's signed 'Pollack, Carp and Fish, Solicitors.' " Thadeus Lowry dropped the sheet of yellow paper onto the wet table. "Someone at Pollack, Carp and Fish has missed a wonderful career as a headline writer. Or maybe they have T. S. Eliot on retainer to do their cables for them. I could have used a column or two of information. At least a sidebar. And note if you will, young Robby, the cable does not conclude with the usual, forward-looking phrase, *Letter following*. In truth, it doesn't even indicate—at least to the guileless and unwary—*Boy following*."

Robby did not pick up the cable. He said, "Our house was bombed."

"While you were away at school?"

"Yes."

"Good for you. Is that your school uniform?"

"Yes, sir."

"I like the school emblem," Thadeus Lowry said, looking at Robby's cap. "How many years has that moose been sharpening his horns against that tree?"

"Is that what it means, sir? No one ever said. The school is three hundred years old. We're celebrating this year with a special Games Day."

"Sounds drafty."

Robby picked up the cable from where it had been lying wet in a beer ring and handed it back to Thadeus Lowry.

"I've been left in your charge, sir."

Thadeus Lowry studied the cable further. "H.M.S. *Scaramouche* is clearly a ship. Normally, it would have been a simple matter to look up ship arrivals in *The New York Star*, and thus find when, and particularly where, the self-same *Scaramouche* was to dock, but something Pollack, Carp and Fish failed to realize, in their red-hot desire for terseness, is that that sort of information, concerning the comings and goings of ships, is not published information in these dark days of World War Two. It took my best reportorial instincts until late last night to discover against which dock, out of seven thousand miles of New York docks, the *Scaramouche* would nestle this morning. Throughout this entire intellectual exercise, the thought never entered my head—not once—that a small boy was being sent to me for safekeeping."

"I feel rather dizzy, sir."

"I am similarly overwhelmed."

"My stomach, sir. And my head."

"Drink up your stout," said Thadeus Lowry, quaffing the last of his whiskey. "Lots of vitamin P. The thing is," he said, "lots of you children are being shipped over to dodge the bombs."

"You don't have bombs here?"

"Only those we set ourselves. They're all right, if you're careful where you step."

"I'll be careful, sir."

"I spent a few days with an Englishman, once," Thadeus Lowry ruminated. "And got decorated for it. Maybe the occasion meant more to him than it did to me." Thadeus Lowry signalled Solomon for more service. "Allow me to explain."

4

Thadeus Lowry Offers an Explanation

"Twenty-five years ago," Thadeus Lowry explained, his fingers warming a fresh, iced double whiskey, "when I was not that much older than you, it now seems, although three times your size and doubtlessly possessing ten times your wisdom, there was another world war raging—a war now referred to as the First World War, as if we plan a steady succession of them, which probably we do. At that time it was called the Great War; some benighted politician referred to it as 'the war to end all wars.' It wasn't great, in the preferred definition of the word—it was nasty and mean and stupid, and nothing nasty, mean and stupid can be great. It wasn't the war to end all wars, either, as present evidence indicates. In fact, it (and its settlement) went a long way toward causing the present altercation. It will be a lark, I expect, to see what the present war causes."

In the big brown booth of The Three Balls Tavern, Robby Burnes began to feel warm and drowsy. Thadeus Lowry's voice was a sonorous, gravelly growl. Listening to himself, he smiled at certain points he made, and at certain pleasing, well-lathed phrases.

"You see, no civilized adult really likes the young. Whenever you have a universal consensus on such topics as *the loveliness of*

24

youth you know profound feelings run dialectically opposite. The young human being is like a kitten: Everyone thinks kittens are cute and one should have one, but, as the kitten grows and gets older and reveals more and more of its own cold, churlish, independent, insolent, destructive, demanding, and otherwise quite human nature, the more one devises ingenious means to get rid of it. Notice what happens to the human child: Immediately it begins to assert itself, yowling and thrashing, it is put behind bars in something called a crib, or a playpen; as soon as it is able to escape the playpen successfully, it is imprisoned in a building, usually made of stone, brick or concrete, called a school; and once the child grows to the point where school can no longer physically or intellectually confine it, and its own human nature becomes frighteningly assertive, adults arrange a war for it, and off it is sent to destroy itself and other youth. Nothing threatens older people more than the existence of youth. If you ever meet an adult, my boy, who genuinely loves the young and does not fear and resent youth at all, if not murderously, send him or her to me, and I'll see to it a statue is raised in his or her image.

"It was this revelation which allowed me, in all good conscience, to desert."

Thadeus Lowry, smiling, swallowed a fair portion of his drink.

Robby asked, "Aren't deserters shot, sir?"

"Under circumstances then prevailing"—Thadeus Lowry smacked his lips with his tongue like an old cat—"everyone was being shot. Every day, sometimes twice a day, with our officers' handguns at our backs, we were forced to rush forward into the rifles of our enemies. The enemies would push us back with their bayonets. We would go five trenches forward and five trenches back. In the stink and the dust and the smoke of the battle I came to recognize in which trench I was by the bodies in it. I was only sure time was passing in this nightmare by the decomposition of these same bodies—each time I jumped back into a trench, the flesh of these bodies separated more easily from the bone.

"Now, at twenty, one is willing to put up with anything for a while—which is why wars are possible.

"However, after days of this back and forth I aged to the point where I realized there were no grown-ups in these trenches, no one very old at all, no politicians, statesmen, church leaders, captains of industry or officers over the age of twenty-five. There were none of that generation who staunchly had erected the issues, drawn the lines of contention, given the speeches of denouncement and uttered the challenges. In those trenches were youth whose faces had been shot off before being permitted to say anything.

"So, one morning, in a lovely acrid fog, in a comparative silence, with no one pushing me forward or back at the moment, the *we* became *I*. I climbed out of my trench and, hands in pocket, head down to avoid stumbling on felled youth, I walked north.

"After only two or three hours of walking there was a puff of wind, enough to raise the fog like a lady's dress, and I saw a small, stone village. I entered it. The windows of the houses and stores were shuttered. The village appeared abandoned. But I smelled food cooking. I followed my nose to a red plank door, and knocked on it.

"A voice from inside said, '*Entrez! Willkommen! Ich dien!* Come in!' Deciding that anyone who could issue such an invitation, in those languages, under those circumstances, was a man who had made similar peace with himself, I entered without hesitation.

"Inside this cottage, there was a tall, skinny Englishman in an apron standing between a stove and a kitchen table. He gave my muddy uniform a perfunctory eyeing, and said, 'I've just basted the lamb. About to attack the potatoes and onions. Do you know what to do with turnips? Here, a glass of this will make you a more amiable dinner companion.'

"He poured me out a cognac, and brought it to me. I said, '*Mort à guerre*,' and drank it down.

" '*Mort à guerre*,' he said.

"We had lamb basted in *rosé*, potatoes and onions basted in *blanc*, turnips basted in cognac. A meal to remember. You can have no idea how great that meal tasted."

"Are there more biscuits, sir?"

"We kept a fire going on the grate. We ate until we could eat no more, slept, ate some more, rested. We didn't talk much—left the fighting to the soldiers and the talking to the politicians. Ah, you can't imagine what a time that was."

"There's Mr. Solomon now, sir. He might have some more biscuits."

"We spent three or four days there, eating, sleeping, being warm. *Death to the war*."

"It sounds a very good supper, sir."

Rousing himself slightly from his nostalgia for past comforts, Thadeus Lowry said, "Within three or four days our own British and American armies caught up with us and were most pleased at our having pacified this village ahead of their advance. We were each sent back to our general headquarters, highly decorated, and sent home to heroes' welcomes." Thadeus Lowry laughed. "To answer your earlier question, young Robby Burnes: Armies have a far greater need to acknowledge heroes than deserters."

"My father was decorated during World War One," Robby said. "For capturing a forward village almost single-handedly."

"That was the only Englishman I ever really knew," Thadeus Lowry continued. "If you can say spending a few days with someone eating, drinking, resting, makes for true acquaintance. For obvious reasons, we did not correspond. We both accepted our decorations, I expect, with the silence of due modesty."

His glass of whiskey finished, Thadeus Lowry sat back in the booth, and said, "A tale as good as any other, sufficiently ironic and spotted with proper moral instruction for the young—but I don't see the connection between that Englishman in France, and you. He had sort of an Italian name, as I remember, Romani, or Something-Roman . . ."

"Pladroman?"

"Yes," Thadeus Lowry said, his voice still somewhat absent. "That was it. Pladroman."

"My father's the Duke of Pladroman," Robby Burnes said.

On the table, Thadeus Lowry's hand jerked and knocked over an empty beer glass.

"That's all right," Robby rushed to say, "we're not royal. Just noble."

He set the glass upright.

"What the hell's the son of a duke?" Thadeus Lowry shouted. "A count? A baron? A marquis? What's the son of a dead duke?"

Robby lowered his eyes. Regulars at the bar had turned to stare at them. "An S.Nob., sir."

"God love a goose!" Thadeus Lowry's eyes were suddenly as tall and wide as if he were seeing heaven open before him. "You're a story!"

5

Advent

"**W**e have plenty of time to catch the first edition," Thadeus Lowry announced after glancing at his pocket watch, which he did after he had put on his hat and his overcoat and picked up his walking stick.

Outside The Three Balls, the wind had increased its bluster. There were two inches of snow on the sidewalks and streets.

"A brisk walk 'round to the office," Thadeus Lowry said, "will help settle lunch."

However, even with the aid of his walking stick, Thadeus Lowry fell against the wall of the recessed doorway when the wind blew the door against him. He grabbed his hat and almost lost his footing.

"You must be tired," he said to Robby, once he had collected himself.

Robby hung onto his suitcase so he wouldn't blow away in the wind.

"There's a cab, now." Thadeus Lowry raised his walking stick to an approaching taxi as if anointing it.

Robby walked into the backseat, dragging his suitcase with him, and sat in the far corner. Through the open door, he watched

Thadeus Lowry apparently proceeding to sit down in the street. He
was holding his hat on his head against the wind with one hand,
his walking stick into the wind with the other. At a certain point in
his crouching, when his hat was below roof level, he backed up
suddenly and landed cater-cornered on his back on the seat of the
taxi.

"The offices of *The New York Star*," Thadeus Lowry spoke up to
the driver. "I have a story to write."

"Close the door, willya, Mac?"

"My feet are still out."

"You're in charge of 'em, arncha?" the driver asked.

Thadeus Lowry finally got himself upright on the seat, his hat
deeply in place, scrunching his ears, his walking stick between his
knees.

Thinking that somewhere in the world there might actually be
melted cheddar cheese over crackers, a mug of chowder, and a
warm egg sandwich—that such images had not risen entirely from
Thadeus Lowry's imagination—Robby tried to complete the image
by confirming, "You have a wife, Mr. Lowry?"

"I have," said Thadeus Lowry. "But you won't like her."

"I see, sir."

"She drinks too much," opined Thadeus Lowry, "and cooks too
little."

The taxi began to pass department stores with large, brightly lit
windows. Robby looked at the Christmas displays. In one window
was a manger with Mary and Joseph and the infant, Jesus, and the
three adoring Magi. In the next was a lady in a red bathing suit
trimmed with white fur.

"Sir?"

"Yes, Robby?"

"Will I grow up in America?"

"No."

"I won't, sir?"

"No one grows up in America."

"What, sir?"

"In America people don't grow up. They just get bigger."

"Yes, sir."

The air of Thadeus Lowry's belch made the atmosphere of the
taxi similar to that of The Three Balls Tavern.

"Well," Thadeus Lowry said with contentment. "That was the

best interview I've had since this blasted war started. We'll get a good story out of it, never fear. Need a photographer. Put your hat on straight."

"Yes, sir."

The taxi slid sideways to a stop at a red light.

"How does the driver know which red lights to stop at?" Robby enquired. "He drives past most of them."

"Like everyone else in America," intoned Thadeus Lowry, "our driver is an executive. He makes executive decisions instead of doing his job."

On the sidewalk, a Salvation Army band was playing "O, Little Town of Bethlehem."

"Now that," said Thadeus Lowry, nodding through the window toward the band, "is a perfect example of an exception that proves a rule. No matter how much a Salvation Army band plays, it never, never gets better. Practice, in their case, does not make perfect. In fact, it appears to do no good whatsoever. Perhaps if they would take their minds off the serenity of God, and demonstrate mercy for the ears of the general populace, we would all smile more benignly upon them."

The taxi slid forward again.

The sidewalks, and most of the street, were clogged with people carrying gaily wrapped Christmas packages.

"Goddamned people," said the driver. "Why don't they all fall down the sewer?"

"Some of us," sniffed Thadeus Lowry, "apparently already have."

"You bein' wise, mister?" Driving forward, the taxi at an angle to more sedate traffic, the driver fixed Thadeus Lowry, through the rear-view mirror, with a hard stare. "You don't like my cab? You can walk."

"I don't like your cab," said Thadeus Lowry. "And I shall not walk."

"Any more your lip," screamed the driver, "I'll give you a shot in the mouth."

" 'Don't Tread On Me,' " said Thadeus Lowry, fluttering one gloved hand in the air.

A line of nine Christmas shoppers jumped in sequence back onto the sidewalk as the taxi ran through a red light and sprayed their knees with slush.

"Stupid sonsabitches," said the driver.

"Driver?" Thadeus Lowry began enquiringly. "Why aren't you at The Front?"

"I am in the front. What are you, stupid?"

"I said *at* The Front. Where the war is."

"Why aren't you at The Front, you lousy sonofabitch," the driver yelled at his rear-view mirror, "instead of running around in the snow with a little boy in short pants?"

"I'll have you know," announced Thadeus Lowry, with firmness and dignity, "I am a highly decorated veteran of World War One."

"Yeah?" The driver took a more comprehensive look at Thadeus Lowry through the rear-view mirror.

"Yeah."

"Whacha do?"

"I, together with the father of this lad here beside me, went behind enemy lines and held an entire town—just the two of us, mind you—for three days and three nights."

The driver whistled appreciatively through his teeth. "Wow."

"Therefore, I have every right, as a citizen, a taxpayer, and as a highly decorated war veteran, to ask you, an aggressive youth, why you are not at The Front."

"Aw," said the driver. "I have a bad knee."

He rubbed it.

"A bad knee, is it?"

"Terrible right knee. Hurt it when some clown ran his Ford into me just before the war."

"Then," said Thadeus Lowry conclusively, "be apprised that if it is, was, or becomes your intention to assault me once I get out of this cab, it is my intention to kick you in the right knee."

While the driver was staring at Thadeus Lowry through the rear-view mirror, his mouth slightly open, the taxi slid against the curb and bumped to a stop.

Through the windshield Robby saw a Santa Claus, who had been ringing a brass hand-bell on the sidewalk, look at the approaching taxi with alarm. He jumped back out of the way. The taxi's bumper nudged one leg of the tripod holding Santa's charity bucket. Dropping his bell on the sidewalk, Santa tried to catch his bucket. All the coins spilled out of the bucket and scattered in the slush of the gutter.

Santa Claus waved his fist at the taxi driver. "You sonofabitch!" yelled Santa Claus.

"What's that sonofabitch shouting at me for?" asked the taxi driver indignantly, his left hand going for the doorknob.

"That son of a bitch," said Thadeus Lowry, "is the Spirit of Christmas."

"Yeah? Well, I don't give a shit who he is. Nobody's gonna call me a sonofabitch!"

Through the snow-streaked windshield, Robby watched the taxi driver approach Santa Claus and hit him in the mouth.

"Thadeus Lowry!" Robby Burnes shouted. "The sonofabitch hit Santa Claus!"

Santa Claus was sitting on the sidewalk, feeling his mouth with a gloved hand.

"He did," agreed Thadeus Lowry.

The driver had turned back to get into the taxi when Santa Claus rose up from the sidewalk with murder in his eye. Blood dripped from his mouth onto his white beard. He took a long step and belted the taxi driver on the back of his head.

"Never," clucked Thadeus Lowry, shaking his head, "turn your back on the Spirit of Christmas."

The driver bounced off the hood of the taxi. He went after Santa Claus with both fists. Never, in Robby's peaceful weeks at Wolsley School, had he seen fists fly so fast.

"Thadeus Lowry, our driver is beating up Santa Claus! Do something!"

"You must be drunk," said Thadeus Lowry. "Otherwise you wouldn't want to get into it."

Fists and fur flying, the combatants sank out of sight below the hood of the taxicab.

"I suppose we ought to do something," said Thadeus Lowry. He began to get out of the cab. "Leave the meter running."

Robby ran around to the front of the taxi.

The taxi driver was sitting astride Santa Claus, snapping his head up and down on the street. Each time Santa Claus' head hit the street there was a splash of blood and slush. People were standing on the sidewalk, clutching their Christmas packages, watching.

In the middle of the street, Thadeus Lowry flagged another taxi with his walking stick.

"Somebody, please!" Robby cried. "Somebody please stop him! He's killing Santa Claus!"

"Robby! Robby Burnes!" In the middle of the street Thadeus Lowry held open the back door of another taxi. "Come on! I'm on deadline!"

Near blind with tears, Robby walked into the backseat of the taxi.

Thadeus Lowry entered as before, that is, after making his lap in the street.

"*The New York Star*," he announced loudly. "I have a story to write."

"Close the door," the driver said.

"My feet are still out."

Immediately the door was closed and Thadeus Lowry had regained his balance in general, he rolled down the window and shouted through it, "Kick him in the right knee!"

He rolled up the window and settled back in his seat, his walking stick once again between his knees. The taxi started off, at first sliding sideways through the snow.

"Ah, this is a cruel world," Thadeus Lowry observed. "A violent, heartless, indifferent orb." He handed Robby his handkerchief. "Hard it is, to keep childish illusions for long, in this indifferent world."

6

Thadeus Lowry Does a Day's Work

"I'll be ready to take you home in a minute," said Thadeus Lowry, "as soon as I write my story."

Being in the city room of *The New York Star* was rather like still being outside in the street. It was cold. It was dark. And it was noisy. It was a huge room with wet stone walls and a linoleum floor. The windows in the walls were as filthy gray as the snowing sky outside. The floor was strewn with crumpled balls of paper, through which paths had been trampled.

Men in green eyeshades were sitting at desks placed in no discernible order, banging on typewriters hard enough, one would think, to quell them for good. On each desk was a telephone. At any given moment, half the telephones were ringing. About half the ringing phones were being answered. Much noise came from teletypes and police radios along one wall, clattering and squawking like an unpaid chorus line.

In the front of the room, standing in the middle of a U-shaped desk, stood a white-haired, red-faced man shouting huskily at the room at large.

"O'Brien," he shouted. "Fire! Thirty-fourth and Seventh.

"Sanders! B and E, A and B at Sixth and Eighth!

34

"Carson! Murder one male Caucasian at Central Park Zoo!"

The news did not disturb the men beating on their typewriters. Buffeted by fire and murder, the journalists' equanimity remained intact.

Thadeus Lowry sat at one of the light metal desks in the middle of the room.

"Are you going to write about the taxi driver beating up Santa Claus?" Robby asked.

"Fist fights aren't news," answered Thadeus Lowry, "unless people pay to see them. That's news."

Rapidly, he typed a line halfway down a sheet of paper.

"What is news, sir?"

"News is what sells newspapers. You're news."

"I, sir?"

"Aye, sir. I'll show you. Go find the men's room, wash your face and brush your hair. By the time you get back, I'll have a photographer here."

By the time Robby returned from the men's room, Thadeus Lowry had typed five pages.

"Sit down," he said. "A photographer will be right up."

So Robby again sat on his suitcase.

Thadeus Lowry was banging on his typewriter awfully hard, and awfully fast. Watching him, Robby realized shortly that Thadeus Lowry's desk was creeping forward. The bouncing of the typewriter, when struck, was making his desk move. Apparently unaware he was doing so, Thadeus Lowry kept hitching his chair forward in pursuit of his story and his desk. Robby looked around at where a man was working at a desk behind him. The space around his suitcase was getting narrower. Robby saw he was about to be squeezed between the two desks.

He picked up his suitcase, moved outside the impending accident area, sat down again, and watched. The desks closed on each other faster than Robby thought possible. They bumped against each other. The typing on each desk surface doubled the vibration on the other. The two desks were bouncing up and down together at a great rate.

Thadeus Lowry stopped typing. He studied the quivering surface of his desk.

The other man stopped typing and looked up angrily at Thadeus Lowry.

Thadeus Lowry screamed, "I told you not to put your desk against mine!"

"I have not moved this desk," screamed the other.

"Who did? Someone moved your desk!"

"Thadeus, you moved your desk!"

"I did not move this desk," said Thadeus Lowry with great certainty. "The desk has not moved."

He stood up and proceeded to push his desk away.

"I'm fed up with what you think is your scintillating sense of humor," said Thadeus Lowry. "If you keep distracting me with your childishness, I'll feed your toupee to a goat."

"Goddamn it," the other man said, giving his desk a violent shove to the left. "I don't know what your game is, Lowry, but if you've made me miss deadline, you'll go home without any teeth."

The two gentlemen of the fourth estate resumed reporting the world to the world.

A man with a camera wandered across the city room to Thadeus Lowry's desk.

"Who's this?" he asked, jerking his thumb at Robby. "The new managing editor?"

"He's an Army Air Corps colonel," said Thadeus Lowry. "He's flown sixty-four missions over Europe."

"I've been hearing our pilots are getting younger."

"Photos to the desk for first edition," said Thadeus Lowry. "Airbrush out the background."

"Anything you say, Tad." Crouching, the photographer was focusing his camera on Robby Burnes sitting on his suitcase. "I'll slug it AIR CORPS STILL FINDS WILLING YOUNG MEN."

"Slug it LOWRY-BURNES."

"I wish it were so."

"I'm not really in the Air Corps," Robby said to the photographer.

"I know, kid. You're really a foreign correspondent."

The photographer left and Thadeus Lowry finished writing before his desk caused another incident.

"Now," he said, putting his typewritten sheets in their proper order, "do you have photographs of your parents?"

"Yes, sir. In my wallet."

"Let me see them."

Robby had been wondering if Thadeus Lowry would like to see a picture of his old First World War friend.

Thadeus Lowry gave the photographs only a glance. "Mother . . . father . . ." he said. He clipped them to his folded typewritten sheets and dropped the whole bundle in a wooden box on a corner of the U-shaped desk.

"Let's go home," said Thadeus Lowry, putting on his overcoat.

"The pictures of my parents, sir. Will I get them back, sir?"

"Really, Robby," said Thadeus Lowry. "Journalism does demand its sacrifices, you know."

Passing the colleague whose desk had given Thadeus Lowry trouble, Thadeus Lowry said, "Bastard."

* ● *

Outside the main door of *The New York Star*, the wind and snow assaulted them again.

"We'll have tea before continuing home," Thadeus Lowry said immediately. "You'd like that, wouldn't you?"

Robby remembered that Thadeus Lowry had said his wife drank much and cooked little. "Yes, sir."

The clock in the city room had read six twenty-five.

The snow was above the ankles of his kneesocks.

They crossed the street and entered an establishment remarkably similar to The Three Balls Tavern. The sign outside this establishment read MONKEY'S MEN ONLY.

A man put his glass on the bar and watched enquiringly while Thadeus Lowry ordered a double martini for himself and a Guinness for Robby.

"A short person is following you, Thadeus," the man said.

"Our bundle from Britain," said Thadeus Lowry. "My bit for the war. Fresh from the briny seas. Ours for safekeeping."

The man examined Robby with crossed eyes. "Can you squeeze a story out of him?"

"Already have. With illustrations. Read *The New York Star*."

"I write for it. Do I have to read it?"

"This is Robby Burnes," said Thadeus Lowry. "Mr. Ronald Jasper, our most esteemed police reporter."

"Robby Burnes?" asked Ronald Jasper. "Who could be verse?"

"Well, son." Gin drink firmly in one hand, Thadeus Lowry

handed Robby the glass of stout with his other. "Do you like journalism?"

"You keep nice hours, sir. My father sits at Lords later."

Ronald Jasper addressed the bartender loudly: "I'll have a drink on Thadeus Lowry! He finally got a story to write."

Thadeus Lowry put his elbows on the bar. His shoulders became round. "Ronald," he said, "I badly need a big story."

"You sure as hell do, Thadeus. You haven't had a big story since the Bishop stole the altar plate in 1938."

"A developing story," said Thadeus Lowry. "A big story that would keep the Thadeus Lowry byline on the front page every day."

"You're on such thin ice at the newspaper," Ronald Jasper said, "you must have water on the knee by now."

"I'd be perfectly happy to go out and wait on an iceberg, if only the *Titanic* could be counted on to sink again."

"That's a hard story to update, Thadeus."

"There must be someone left to interview—an obscure cabin boy, whose imagination is yet to go rampant."

"Nice thing about being a police reporter," Ronald Jasper said, testing his drink, "is that it's steady. Evil lurks constantly in the hearts of Man. You poor feature writers have to go find your own news."

"Maybe I could find a nice Nazi spy somewhere in New York who'd give me his story."

"I don't think they list themselves in the yellow pages, Thadeus."

"The war, the war, the goddamned war. *Mort à guerre*. Nothing makes the front page except the war."

"People are tired of the war, Thadeus. They're tired of reading about it, hearing about it, talking about it, thinking about it. They're even tired of escaping from it."

"What we need," said Thadeus Lowry, "is a good, juicy, sensational murder. Something to take the people's mind off the war for a few days."

"Who would read about a single murder, however sensational, with hundreds a day dying in Flander's Field?"

"You're right," said Thadeus Lowry. "Individual murder pales next to universal carnage."

Standing on the brass rail, holding on to the raised edge of the bar with his elbows, Robby was eating from a bowl of peanuts.

"What we need is a heartwarming story," said Thadeus Lowry. "One that takes days to unravel. That involves the people, the reader. Tugs at his heartstrings. Allows him to do something. Allows him to be heroic at home by the fireside."

"A kidnapping," said Ronald Jasper. "What New York needs now is a good kidnapping."

"New York!" exclaimed Thadeus Lowry, brightening instantly. "The whole country needs a good kidnapping, Ronald! The whole world!"

Thadeus Lowry expanded physically to such a degree he knocked Robby off his precarious grip on the bar.

"A sensational kidnapping." Thadeus Lowry stepped so close to Ronald Jasper he stood on Robby Burnes' foot. "That kid actress," said Thadeus Lowry, "Shirley Temple. You don't happen to have the name of Shirley Temple's press agent, do you?"

"I don't think they'd go for it, Thadeus. They don't like that kid taking too much time away from the cameras."

"Maybe not, maybe not," said Thadeus Lowry.

He looked down at Robby Burnes. His protuberant eyes protruded even more. He blinked.

"Please, sir. You're stepping on my foot."

"The little bastard looks green, Thadeus."

"Do you think he might be sick?"

"He must be," said Ronald Jasper. "He looks like Eleanor Roosevelt appearing in public with Franklin."

"God love a goose, Ronald. What do I do?"

"I suggest we have a quick one, Thadeus, then you get him out in the air."

7

Held Up on the Way Home

"Homeward the weary workmen wend their way!"

Despite the six inches of snow soundproofing the abandoned streets and sidewalks of New York, Thadeus Lowry's voice echoed from the stone and brick walls on all sides. Stars were visible above the streetlights. Robby sucked in cold, clear air like long drafts of spring water. Thadeus marched on, snow whitening his cuffs, using his walking stick with a brisk beat.

After as many gulps of air as he could manage, to clear his head, to enable his feet to plow through the snow, Robby ran, the suitcase banging against either the front or the back of his right knee at every step, trying to keep up with the man in whose safe-keeping he was.

"A brisk walk," Thadeus Lowry encouraged, "home to a nice, warm supper."

It was past eight o'clock.

"You do have a home, sir?" Robby asked with great uncertainty.

"In this city," Thadeus Lowry amended himself, "people do not have homes. Allow me to explain. They have apartments. A few rooms for which they pay endlessly, but never come to possess—

pay for the sheer pleasure of running them into filthy, untenable condition before moving out and on."

Robby moved his legs as fast as he could so he wouldn't lose this new instruction, or this new instructor.

"This country is not yet settled," Thadeus Lowry continued, his voice barreling off solid walls on all sides of them. "It's a vast land dotted with impossible, temporary shelters, inhabited by wanderers—travelers from nowhere going nowhere, marking the calendar of their lives by moving days, leaving nothing in their paths but crumpled leases."

"An hotel, sir? Do you live in an hotel? Is that it, then?"

"Not a hotel. Apartment houses have none of the civilities of hotels: no man to greet you at the door; no boys to help you in with your bundles; no warm little bar tucked into a corner of the lobby to make your homecoming convivial—no staff at all, except for a congenital idiot who comes along once a week to dent your wastebaskets against the walls in the pretence that he is emptying them. Hotels, once considered cold shelter for the temporarily homeless, in transient America are the epitome of good living."

"A flat then, sir. Do you live in a flat?"

"Flat is the correct word. We live flat. Oppressed by steam heat. Rooms with walls nearer than we want them. Windows looking out on more walls. We live flat on the level of unembellished boredom. Insipidity as a way of life. Flat, indeed."

"And can you cook at all, sir?"

"By *cook* do you mean opening cans, ladling the contents—which are indiscernible from the contents of all other cans—into a saucepan and then drying out the synthetic garbage over the uncleansing fire of a two-ring electric stove?"

"I mean preparing any food any how, sir."

"By *cook* do you mean to take what the butcher sells you at a vast price as meat but is less meat than you are gold dust—the frankfurter, ground bread packed in a pigskin casing; the hamburger, the eyes and entrails of animals spotted with floor-sweepings; the great American steak, leather tightly stitched with dental floss—by *cook* do you mean to plop these flaps of the American life-style into a frying pan greased with oleomargarine, place over a burner until they shrivel to a size right for filling a tooth cavity?"

"Yes, sir. Anything at all like that, sir."

"No," Thadeus Lowry determined, stabbing his walking stick into the snow. "I would not *cook*."

"But your wife, sir. She *can* cook, can't she? I mean, if there were good reason to?"

"Does my wife share in the illusion common to American women that she provides meals? Yes. Occasionally she makes a contribution to the Great American Dream and provides the appearance of a meal by ripping open packaged, prepared food."

"But will she, sir? Will she cook?"

"No."

At that moment they were crossing the end of an alley. They had crossed several before. Snow-capped rubbish barrels lined each side of the alley entrance.

From this alley stepped a man. He blocked their way. He wore a bulky jacket. His hat almost entirely obscured his eyes and ears.

His hands were in his coat pocket.

Gruffly, he said, "Into the alley, mister, and shuddup. Face the wall and lean your hands against it over your head."

"What is this?" shouted Thadeus Lowry as if sincerely in doubt.

Even Robby had read of Robin Hood and knew the goals of such people who interrupt others on the road.

"It's highway robbery, sir!" Robby dropped his suitcase in the snow and threw his hands into the air. "Stand and deliver!"

"Charlie McCarthy's right, Edgar Bergen," said the short thug. "It's a stick-up."

Thadeus Lowry, his stick at parade rest, remained unmoving. He was looking at the thug with pure incredulity.

"I have no intention of standing for this," he stated, "or of delivering anything whatsoever."

Robby, reaching for the moon, felt his fingers get even colder.

"Into the alley, you big-nosed balloon," said the thug. "I have a gun."

"He has a gun, sir. He says he has a gun."

"This," announced Thadeus Lowry, "is Tootsie's corner!"

The thug jerked his head up and looked into Thadeus Lowry's face.

"Tootsie? You know Tootsie?"

"I am Thadeus Lowry of *The New York Star*," intoned Thadeus Lowry of *The New York Star*. "I know everybody."

"How do you know Tootsie?"

"We met on jury duty," announced Thadeus Lowry, "in 1934. After Tootsie used up his *per diem* and was really down on his luck, couldn't talk to a bookie anywhere, I told him I had observed this corner was available. I believe he has done well, over the years, mugging people on this corner. What, young man, are you doing on it?"

"So you're Thadeus Lowry."

"Of *The New York Star*."

"Nice to meetcha, Thadeus, nice to meetcha." The thug began withdrawing his hand from his jacket pocket, possibly to shake hands with Thadeus Lowry.

Thadeus Lowry swung his cane with remarkable force and accuracy through the air and against the thug's head. A swish and a *thwunk*. The thug's cap went into the snow. He raised his empty hands to his head, but did not touch it.

His knees buckled.

He knelt in the snow.

"I asked you," shouted Thadeus Lowry, leaning over him, "how you have the gall, the audacity to work Tootsie's corner?"

The thug sat on his heels, and then leaned forward. His bare hands groped for hard ground beneath the snow to support himself.

Thadeus Lowry struck him on his back with the walking stick.

"Where's Tootsie? What have you done with him?"

"Stop it, willya, mister?"

Thadeus Lowry caned the man's back again.

"I said I have a gun! You'd better watch out," protested the man doubled over in the snow. "I might use it!"

"Do you really have a gun?"

"Yeah. You think I'm a liar?"

"Where is it?"

"In my pocket."

Sitting on his heels, it took the thug a moment to rummage the gun out of his pocket. With it came a packet of chewing gum, a pencil stub and a house key. He held the gun in the flat of his hand. He looked distastefully at it. He blew the lint off it.

Blood was dripping from his ear.

"Where's Tootsie?" Thadeus Lowry demanded.

"In Florida. At the horse races. He goes every year, this time."

Robby's hands were still up. His eyes were wide at the sight of the handgun.

"I had forgotten that." There was a touch of apology in Thadeus Lowry's voice. "Tootsie's winter vacation at Hialeah."

"You're some Edgar Bergen," said the thug.

"Even if Tootsie's away," questioned Thadeus Lowry, "who says you can take over his corner?"

"He did."

"Who did?"

"Tootsie! Tootsie did."

"Why should I believe that?"

"You afraid I might muscle Tootsie out of his corner?"

"The thought had occurred to me."

"I wouldn't do that."

"How do I know that?"

"Tootsie's my uncle, for Pete's sake. He said I could work his corner while he's south for Christmas playing the horses."

"Are you Minnie's boy?"

"Yeah, yeah."

"How is she?"

"She's fine. I'll tell her you asked."

"Still and all," said Thadeus Lowry, possibly trying to justify his having thrashed Minnie's boy, the thug, "how do I know you'll give Tootsie back his corner when he returns?"

"I'm only home for Christmas. I'm in the Navy, stationed somewhere in the South Pacific, like they say. I'm home on furlough. Uncle Tootsie said I could work his corner while he's away so I can make some Christmas money."

"I see. Tootsie always was very kind. Which of Minnie's boys are you?"

"I'm Richard."

"It's nice to meet you, Richard." Thadeus Lowry tucked his walking stick under his arm and helped Richard up. "Well, well. Minnie's boy. Richard."

"It's nice to meetcha, like I said," said Richard, rubbing the blood off his ear. "I heard my uncle speak of you often."

"Well, well. In the Navy. Serving your country. In the South Pacific. Seen any action?"

"Naw. There are no girls out there. I do better at home in Flatbush."

"I mean, fighting."

"Oh, yeah. That. Every once in a while the Japs fly over and drop bombs on things we just got finished buildin'. Maybe they think they're fightin' us. I dunno. Seems like they're just keepin' us employed, you know?"

Robby said, "Sir? May I put my hands down now?"

"Of course, Robby."

"This is still a robbery, you know," said Richard.

"Richard," said Thadeus Lowry, "I don't like your carrying a gun."

Richard looked at his gun, still flat on his hand.

"Your uncle never carried a gun."

"No?"

"If the police pick you up and you have a gun on you, I wouldn't be able to get you out of trouble."

"I have to carry a gun."

"Why?"

Richard looked around warily. "There are some real weirdos around here."

"I think you had better give me the gun."

"I can't, Mr. Lowry."

"Why not?"

"It's my service revolver. I snuck it home in my duffel bag, so I could work Uncle Tootsie's corner for Christmas, you see. I have to bring it back after Christmas, or I'll be in trouble."

"You can give it to me and pick it up at my apartment before you go back to the South Pacific. After Christmas."

"Yeah. Okay."

Richard gave Thadeus Lowry the gun and Thadeus Lowry gave Richard an address on Park Avenue.

"You should have that ear looked after, Richard."

"You gave me quite a crack on the head."

"I didn't realize you were Minnie's boy, Richard, home on furlough."

"That's all right. Any friend of the family. I appreciate your looking out for my uncle's corner."

"Come for a drink," said Thadeus Lowry.

"I can't. I'm workin'. Only eight more shopping days till Christmas."

"Some other time, then. When you come for the gun. After Christmas. We'll sit and talk. Trade war stories." .

"Okay," said Richard. "That sounds nice. But now I'm robbing you."

"What?"

"I still mean this to be a stick-up."

"You do?"

"I do. Shouldn't I?"

"Tootsie never robs me."

"Listen, Mr. Lowry, I got a crack on the head. You have my gun. We've been talking here fifteen, maybe twenty minutes. I shouldn't rob you?"

"I guess you're right," said Thadeus Lowry. "After all, one should encourage the young in their work. Let me look in my wallet."

"No," said Richard. "Let me look in your wallet."

Thadeus Lowry had his wallet in his hand, but drew it back. "That," he said, "would be an indignity."

"An in-what?"

"An invasion of privacy. I will look in the wallet."

He did so, in the light of the street lamp.

"There are four ones here," he reported. "Will you settle for three?"

"I want all four. This is a robbery. You can keep the wallet."

"But taxi fare," said Thadeus Lowry. "To get this poor, shivering child home."

"Hungry, too," Robby said.

"This poor, shivering, hungry boy home."

Robby picked Richard's cap up off the snow and handed it to him.

Richard said, "The kid needs pants."

"Here's your three dollars," said Thadeus Lowry, holding the bills in his gloved hand. "Don't get me anything too expensive for Christmas."

"I want all four dollars, dammit."

"You do?"

"I do. Shouldn't I?"

Thadeus Lowry beamed at him, and handed him the other dollar.

"Of course, my boy. Here. Tootsie would be proud of you. Never give the sucker an even break. Here's all four dollars."

"Okay." Richard counted the four dollars twice, perhaps to make the sum eight. "Robbin' you's taken a long time, you know."

"Sorry. Now go back to the alley and lurk some more. I'm sure another customer will be along in just a minute."

"Good night," Richard said.

"Good night," said Thadeus Lowry. "Merry Christmas."

• • •

"Mr. Lowry?" Robby called. Two blocks away from where they had been held up, Robby, tripping and slipping, had fallen considerably behind Thadeus Lowry and wanted him to slow down. "Is four dollars a lot to pay for a gun?"

Thadeus Lowry continued his brisk pace, but he did say, "I would have gone higher—if there'd been a need to."

The distance between them grew. Robby heard Thadeus Lowry's voice boom, instructively: "There are lessons to be learned in every business, my boy. Even highway robbery."

8

Care, Feeding and Education Are Discussed

Halfway down the block on a side street they pushed through a glass door into the lobby of Thadeus Lowry's apartment house. There was no man to greet them at the door; no boys to carry the suitcase and, Robby thanked God, no warm little bar tucked into a corner of the lobby to make their homecoming convivial.

While waiting for Robby to catch up, Thadeus Lowry had stood on the front steps of his apartment house and sung sixteen bars of "The Donkey Serenade," loudly.

They went down a long cement corridor with puce cement walls to the elevator, which creaked and swayed as if it were as afraid of torpedoes as H.M.S. *Scaramouche*, but lifted them, over time, to the seventh floor.

"Someone in this place cooks," muttered Robby. "Boiled cabbage."

On the seventh floor they walked down another long corridor to a door marked 7Q. Thadeus Lowry inserted a key and pushed the door open.

"*Chérie*," he called, rather like a lark attaining a treetop. "*Chérie, chérie.*"

48

Through the short, narrow, crimson foyer, in another, more brightly lit room, Robby saw a woman's feet suspended thirty centimeters from the floor. The shoes on the feet were polished red leather, with long heels. At the sound of Thadeus Lowry's voice, the feet landed on the floor, and disappeared from view.

"Lover! Is that you?"

"No, *chérie*, sorry. It's your husband."

In small steps the feet came around the corner and into the foyer. Mrs. Thadeus Lowry was not much taller than Robby, but she was a good deal more red. Her hair was ginger, her sweater rose, her skirt brick, her shoes crimson, and her fingernails and lips currant. Her eyes were bloodshot. The walls of the foyer (the walls throughout the apartment, Robby was to discover) were poppy red. Robby blinked slowly and swayed.

"Ah, *chéri* . . ." she said. She held her martini glass to the side, so it would not spill.

Mr. and Mrs. Thadeus Lowry put their heads together and exchanged fumes.

"Did you have a damaging day?" she asked.

"Brutal. Absolutely brutal." He slipped his walking stick into an umbrella stand like a knight sheathing his sword once inside his own castle walls. "But I filed a wonderful story. Just wonderful."

"You must be exhausted." She nodded. Putting her martini glass down on a hall table, she took his coat and hung it in the hall closet. She gave no appearance of seeing a blue-and-white boy amidst all the red.

"I am, *ma chérie*," he said, handing her his hat. "Simply exhausted."

He stood drooping in the hall while she put his hat on the closet shelf and regained her martini from the Chinese lacquer hall table.

"This is Robby Burnes," noted Thadeus Lowry. "Our bundle from Britain."

Her attention swiveled to Robby. Her eyes grew larger; her face grew larger; her head grew larger; her whole body grew larger. Both hands clutched her martini glass.

Thadeus Lowry said, "Allow me to explain."

"Is he ours?" she asked.

"For the duration."

"The duration of the war?"

"He's the son of a dead duke, it seems. In fact, he must be a duke."

"Are dukes ever that young?"

"Oh, they must be. At some point in their lives."

"Isn't he cute? Look at those knees, Thadeus. Where will he sleep?"

"Too big for a bureau drawer."

"Too small for the bathtub, even with blankets."

"Can't sleep at the foot of our bed. We both have feet."

"And we can't move to a bigger apartment. You remember, Thadeus, I strained my back Christmas shopping."

"Of course, *ma chérie*."

She spoke slowly, loudly and distinctly to Robby. She even had currant lipstick on her teeth. "What do you want, dear?" Her hands concealed the olive Robby had been eyeing in the martini glass. "What can we give you?"

"Marvelous with children, *chérie*," Thadeus Lowry said. "You're marvelous with children."

"Something to eat, ma'am, and a warm tub, and, please, I'm very tired."

" 'A warm tub.' I suppose he means a bath, Thadeus."

"I suppose he does."

Sweat was in Robby's eyes, prickling his scalp, and running down his spinal column. He had never been anywhere as warm as the Lowrys' apartment.

"Please, ma'am, may I have something to eat?"

"Yes, dear, of course. You darling. Go into a nice warm bathtub, and when you come out, I'll have din-din ready for you." She added, "He smells of disinfectant, Thadeus."

"Does he?" Thadeus Lowry sniffed the air. "I've been wondering why I've been nostalgic for the Maine woods all day. Especially seeing I've never been in the Maine woods."

"Right into the tub, darling." Mrs. Lowry pointed ambiguously. "Take your sweet little suitcase. Around to the left."

Robby weaved across the foyer, along the near wall of a red, shimmering, stifling living room, and into the bathroom.

He heard Thadeus Lowry's voice say, "As long as you're having one, I'll join you."

"What did you say his name is?"

"Who?"

"The boy."

"Robby Burnes, with an *E*. Son of the Duke of Pladroman, if I've got it right. Not a very important duke, as dukes go, I suspect."

"He must go to school."

Robby had never lived in the front of a house before, within earshot of grown-ups other than servants. He was uncertain of the decorum of overhearing grown-up conversation. But Thadeus Lowry's domicile had no front or back, no upstairs or downstairs. It had a middle. A very middle. The living room was a divan and two chairs on a rug separated by a coffee table. Steam hissed and snapped from radiators along every wall.

He closed the door to the bathroom and turned the faucets on in the tub and removed the clothes he had been wearing since he had been a very young boy in England. He piled them on the radiator wondering if they would burst into flame.

The only surprise he had in being naked this first time in many, many days, was that his stomach had vanished. It had been a pleasant round object just below his rib cage in which he used to put food. Now he felt for it with his fingertips. Definitely it was gone. Where his stomach had been, Robby's fingers felt a hardness as if touching bone. He had felt that hardness increasing each time he had vomited aboard H.M.S. *Scaramouche*. Water splashing in the tub behind him, Robby jumped up and down, to see himself in the mirror above the wash-basin. Where his stomach had been were horizontal lines of muscle. Robby regretted that: It looked a poor repository for pastry.

Robby lay in the full tub in the company of a bar of soap which floated. It wiggled and wobbled in the waves and went nowhere and reminded him of H.M.S. *Scaramouche*. He thought of the other children aboard ship, and wondered if any of them had been fed yet. And he wondered about the boys at Wolsley School and which meals they were between.

In the living room, Thadeus Lowry was recounting his day. Robby wondered what he could do not to overhear.

"Thus I discovered, *chérie*, it is easier to take over a human life, in these trying times, than to get a small loan from a bank."

"What an amusing thought, Thadeus."

"Then around the corner for a leisurely lunch . . ."

Robby sank beneath the water and counted his toes.

". . . assured him in every way possible," Thadeus Lowry was continuing. "Told him what great friends his father and I were, what a great hero his father was, how he and I had captured a town behind the lines without firing a single shot . . ."

Robby went below the surface of the water and extended his fingers, stretched them as far as they would stretch.

". . . taxi to the office where I spent the rest of the day trying to hammer out a story."

"You're very generous, Thadeus, giving him so much time and attention."

"Must be a big shock to him—coming from war-torn England to the land of milk and honey."

"We mustn't spoil him, Thadeus."

"I think it was a great thrill for him to see the newspaper office. The hustle and bustle. The crackle of the police radio. The clattering of the teletypes."

"Is he especially bright, do you think?"

"Oh, I wouldn't say so. Ordinary sort of kid. Stares blankly at you while you're speaking to him as if he can't quite grasp what it is he's hearing . . ."

Underwater, Robby washed his penis. He was glad that it hadn't gone the way of his stomach.

". . . On the way home we stopped for tea. I was sure he was missing that sort of thing."

"Then he won't want much supper."

"He ate bowls full of crackers."

Robby went below the water facedown and held his breath. He rose to air only when his lungs hurt.

Mrs. Lowry was saying, "How did you ever find time to file a story for the newspaper today?"

"It wasn't easy, *chérie*, it wasn't easy. But, you know, a real professional can work anywhere, any time, under any circumstances."

Robby was dressing in clean clothes, identical to those he had just taken off, from the suitcase. His used clothes, on the radiator, were scorching nicely.

"What's the story about, lover?"

"I think I'll let you be surprised in the morning. Read *The New York Star*. Robby should be very surprised indeed. I've arranged a warm welcome for him, to this land where he's come for safekeeping."

With that much of a clue to reestablish decorum, Robby entered the living room.

"You don't look a bit different," said Mrs. Thadeus Lowry. "Come here and let me smell."

As apparently she was serious about the invitation (her hand was extended limply toward him), Robby drew near.

On the coffee table was a glass of water, with ice in it. On a plate catsup oozed from between two pieces of bread.

"Much better," said Mrs. Lowry, contracting the veins that ran over her nose. "Now sit down and have your supper. Thadeus says you've been eating all day."

"Is that supper, ma'am?"

"I'll get you milk tomorrow, Robby. If my back is better."

In his mind, Robby drank the water and ate the sandwich seventeen times. Sitting on the divan, he drank the water and ate the sandwich once.

"What are we going to do about schooling, Thadeus?"

"He must go to school," said Thadeus.

"But where?"

"The local piss, I suppose."

"The local piss?"

"There must be a P.S. something or other within walking distance. It's the law, isn't it?"

"Quite right. There must be a public school nearby. Well, that's settled. Is tomorrow a school day?"

"Tomorrow is Thursday."

"People go to school on Thursdays, Robby," stated Mrs. Lowry.

"Yes, ma'am."

"It's most important you go to school."

"The trick is," advised Thadeus Lowry, "to leave the apartment in the morning and walk around the blocks in ever widening squares until you find a school."

"Sir?"

Robby's experience on the streets of New York already had caused him to pray that he would never have to enter them alone. If even Santa Claus got it on the streets of New York, who was to protect Robby Burnes? He had seen a highway robber thrashed, then brushed up to rob again.

"But can he find the school by himself, Thadeus?"

"He found America by himself," Thadeus Lowry pointed out.

"Children find schools the way women find hat shops. It's a God-given instinct."

"But what about registering?" Mrs. Lowry rubbed her sore back. "Won't he have to register?"

"What's there to register? He's a schoolchild. Any schoolteacher can see that."

"Yes, of course. You'll like going to school in America, won't you, Robby?"

Robby's been looking forward to going to Wolsley School ever so long now, hasn't he? his mother had asked.

"Oh, yes, ma'am."

The catsup in his stomach yearned to be on the maroon divan.

"We'll set you off with a nice warm breakfast in the morning," proffered Mrs. Lowry. "I'm sure you'll have a lovely adventure—going to school first day."

"S-sir?"

"Yes, Robby. What now?"

"Can I take your gun to school with me?"

"A *gun!*" gasped Mrs. Lowry.

"Good heavens, no," chuckled Thadeus Lowry. "What could happen to you on the streets of New York?"

9

The Streets of New York

After dining at the Lowrys', receiving no other instructions or invitations, Robert James Saint James Burnes Walter Farhall-Pladroman, S.Nob., continued to sit quietly on the divan. He closed his eyes against the maroon, crimson, cardinal, auburn, ginger, currant, rose, brick, poppy and puce and concentrated on keeping his catsup in the narrow tubes which once had led to his stomach.

Thadeus Lowry continued to talk to his wife like a Johnson to his Boswell, only in that minor events were given stature in their telling (it was reported that an envious fellow threw his desk at Thadeus Lowry in the city room of *The New York Star* while Thadeus Lowry was composing a piece of literature for first edition), but not in that their telling enhanced the listener's perception of the significant truths of the day.

Robby's attention to Thadeus Lowry's lying discourse was disturbed by concern for what the radiators were doing to Robby, and what more they might do. Again Robby's body was running with sweat. The air was so heavy to breathe Robby's respiratory system was threatening to go on strike. They were circumvallated by radiators. The steam was so charging in the innards of the radiators, so clangorous in its importuning to be released into the room that fear of imminent death by vaporization was not unreasonable. Yet Thadeus Lowry was not condensed.

One ear went to Thadeus Lowry, the other to the radiators. As the evening went on, Thadeus Lowry came to make less sense, the radiators more: There was a more certain rhythm and accurate responsiveness to what was going on in the pipes than in the human colloquy.

Tintinnabulation vanquished confabulation.

Sleep mastered Robby.

Robby had slept at Wolsley School in a room with five other boys, undisturbed by sniffling, snoring, sudden cries in the night for nannies who could not answer, the traffic of uncertain, sleep-sodden prowls to the water closet and back. He had slept aboard H.M.S. *Sacramouche*, lying on a steel-plate deck, vomit and disinfectant in his nose, undisturbed by sudden shifts in elevation and direction, strategic wallowing, undisturbed by Evacuation Ladies stepping on him in the dark to see if he was all right.

Robby's first night's sleep in New York City was disturbed. Thadeus Lowry was giving witness to his day in a waning voice. The radiators hissed at him. Robby slept. A few meters from his head, just the other side of the living room wall, an argument broke out. A man's voice shouted *"I love you!"* and there was the sound of smashing glass. *"I love you!"* and the sound of crashing furniture. *"I love you!"* and a body thudded against the living room wall. *"My head! You broke my head!"* Seven stories below a woman passed by, singing *Carmen*. A fire department went through the narrow street, its sirens amplifying up the walls. (Somnus said, *Right, Robby—they're just moving hell.*) An anguished human scream came up from the alleys as the first light of day glazed the windows. (*Someone's just discovered he's alive.*) Snorting, trundling snowplows scraped the streets and shovels sang on the sidewalks. Rubbish barrels were tympanized. Buses roared in the morning like lions looking for people to devour. Robby awoke feeling the concerns of the whole world had prowled his sleep.

Yellow pools of weak light surrounded the table lamps. Robby was still on the divan. Thadeus Lowry was still in his chair, chin on his chest. His *chérie* was curled in her chair, ginger hair on garnet chair arm. The radiators had stopped, and the room was cold. Time had stopped. Getting up quietly and moving around the room, Robby felt himself an imposition—animation in an otherwise still picture.

He looked at his supper plate from the night before and at his empty glass of water and at Thadeus Lowry and his *chérie* and gauged the distance between himself and breakfast as equal to the distance between himself and the nearest school. Even if he'd missed Chapel, he might still be in time for breakfast.

In the bathroom, his suitcase remained gaping on the floor. He took his overcoat and cap from the bathroom doorknob where he had left them the night before, and put them on.

And then Robert James Saint James Burnes Walter Farhall-Pladroman, S.Nob., English-speaking, dressed in a blue blazer and red striped tie, cap and coat emblazoned by stags butting oak trees, short pants and kneesocks, yellow hair over his ears, after finding the elevator and descending in it, stepped out onto a New York City street on a winter morn.

The snow was black. Robby would have sworn the snow had come down white. He shook his head.

Robby walked the four blocks around Thadeus Lowry's apartment house and found himself back at his front door. Although some people had looked at him curiously, and others hadn't seen him at all, Robby was relieved: He had gotten around the block without being accosted once. Neither had he found a school.

Continuing to take Thadeus Lowry's navigational advice, Robby went up a street, went left, and navigated an eight block square. It did not bring him back to Thadeus Lowry's door. He went up another street, went right, and navigated a sixteen block square. In nearly three miles of walking, Robby found nothing which looked like a school to him. Nowhere were there iron gates, a gatekeeper's lodge, a long driveway with playing fields on either side leading to a compound of gray-stone, slate-roofed buildings. There were apartment buildings and office buildings, big stores and little stores. There were people hurrying everywhere, heads down to ignore anyone who might accost them. Robby began up another street, remembering Thadeus Lowry's comment that it was the law there be a school in the neighborhood (and that schoolchildren are drawn to school as are ladies to hat shops), when the simple arithmetic of his search overwhelmed him.

His next square, in the search plan, was to have thirty-two

blocks each side. Was New York City big enough? Was he? If he failed to find a school in that square, his next would have sixty-four blocks to a side! Two-hundred-and-fifty-six blocks to a side! Five-hundred-and-twelve blocks to a side!

Robby would miss lunch again.

Therefore, at the corner, he stopped. He looked left, and he looked right. He went in no direction. There were blocks in front of him, blocks behind him, blocks to his left, blocks to his right. Blocks and blocks and blocks and blocks.

Across the street there was a woman who had also stopped. She stood on the curb, squinting at Robby. She wore a brown cloth coat, overshoes, and carried a purse. She was plump.

Robby crossed the street to her. "Please, ma'am, where's the piss?"

"The what?"

"The piss, ma'am. I was told to look for the school which is called a piss. I can't find one."

"The P.S., you darlin' boy." Her hands clutched her purse strap firmly. Through narrowed lids she looked up and down the street. "Yes," she said. "You're lost, aren't you?"

"No, ma'am. I just don't know where I'm going."

Her right hand grabbed Robby's. "I know just where you're goin', you darlin' boy. I'll bring you there."

Greatly relieved, his hand in hers, Robby went down the sidewalk with her. The speed with which the woman moved surprised him. Perhaps she knew that if they didn't hustle he would be late for school. Or perhaps by helping him she was falling behind her own schedule. Attached to her as he was he found that running ten steps, walking five, running ten again was the only way to keep up with her and not have his arm freed from his shoulder.

They came to what appeared to Robby to be wide stairs leading to the basement of New York City.

"Down here, darlin'."

"Is my school underground? No wonder I couldn't find it anywhere I looked."

"That's right, you darlin'. You just come with me."

They went down the steps together. The woman paid money for them both and they went through a turnstile. Robby was astonished to find himself in a train station.

"Oh, ma'am. Do I get to take a train to school?"

"Just this once, darlin'."

With one hand clutching his, the other, with purse dangling from her wrist, pushing his back, the woman shoved Robby aboard a crowded subway train. The door behind them closed, compressing them further. Robby found his face embedded in the rabbit fur of another passenger's coat.

"Glumph!" he said.

The train accelerated quickly to a speed beyond the passengers' ability to adjust. Vertically they squirmed together like eels in a jar. Waist high to most, sometimes Robby's head was twisted upwards. All the tall passengers were pressed so close together they had their faces turned up to the roof for air. Sometimes Robby's head was twisted downwards. The air in neither quarter was desirable. Overshoes, mostly not buckled, took up all but a few inches of floor space. There were two ladies' boots, which did not match, between a pair of man's boots, which did match. One man's boot was way over here; its mate way over there. There was one lady's boot for which Robby could find a match nowhere.

Robby's head was twisted up again. People's arms were raised as if in surrender, clutching at poles and straps. Some ladies' arms appeared to extend from men's armpits. Some men's arms led to ladies' heads.

As they rattled and swayed from stop to stop, the people writhed. More burrowed themselves into the crowd. They turned slow, full circles as people snuggled against them and wriggled around them. All the while their cool, adult, upturned faces studied advertisements above the windows for Alka Seltzer and United States War Bonds. Some tunneled through the crowd to leave the train; others rowed through the crowd with their elbows.

Across the aisle, there was a puddle on the train floor. As the car proceeded and righted itself, the puddle moved to the middle of the floor. The train banked, and the puddle returned to its original bed. The train righted itself again, tipped a little more, and the puddle passed the center of the car. It retreated. At the next inclination of the train, the puddle rushed across the floor and surrounded Robby's shoes. Instantly his feet felt wet.

"Ma'am?" He tugged on her hand. "I'm being stood under by a puddle!"

"This stop's ours." She gave the crushed bones of his hand a further grinding.

"Is my school near here?"

The woman had positioned themselves so that when the door slid open they virtually were catapulted onto the platform. They ascended stairs carpeted with chewing gum.

Robby rose into a world entirely different from any he had ever seen.

Everywhere there were pushcarts. In each pushcart was an oversized sign saying 23¢ or 12¢ or 9¢ or 32¢. Behind most pushcarts stood men with long white aprons over their overcoats, hats pushed back on their heads. Women at the pushcarts wore bulky sweaters and thick shoes and kerchiefs. They were all singing about potatoes a nickel, oranges a dime. More properly dressed people, men and women, snaked among the pushcarts, testing a tomato here, a melon there. They skirted cast-off cardboard boxes and walked on wood shavings and sawdust and excelsior and slush. Robby's guide pulled him by the hand on a circuitous route through the pushcarts. And on the pushcarts were oranges and apples and bananas and melons and potatoes and tomatoes and heads of lettuce and cabbages and sausages and hams and pudent chickens and many foods Robby had never seen before and whose names he did not know.

Behind the pushcarts the woman rushed Robby down an alley piled high on both sides with empty boxes. They entered a building, went through a cold room of hanging beef carcasses and out again onto a side street. They crossed that street and went along the slush on the sidewalk until they came to the building at the top of a T intersection.

She pulled him up the steps, through a door, along a dark corridor to an interior door. There she used a key from her purse.

"Is this my school, ma'am?"

She pushed open the door and gently pushed Robby inside.

He was in what appeared to be a kitchen. There was a sink and a stove and a refrigerator. There were also three cots against the walls.

A man in a plaid shirt sat in a wheelchair at the kitchen table. He looked up from the picture puzzle he was doing. He looked directly at Robby, at the woman behind Robby, then even more directly at Robby.

"Who's this?" he asked, as if provoked.

The woman let go of Robby's hand. She closed the door behind them.

Still in her cloth coat, looking at the man in the wheelchair, her body sagged. Her purse dangling from her wrist, she covered her eyes with her hand.

"Oh, Frankie," she said. "I don't know. Someone important, I think. I recognize him from the morning newspaper."

The man wheeled back from the table, and turned. Full-faced he stared at Robby.

She said: "I think I've kidnapped him!"

10

Kidnapped

"Whaddaya mean, *kidnapped*?" shouted the man in the wheelchair. "What kidnapped?"

"Shush, Frankie. Someone might hear you."

"Someone might hear me! Call the cops! Whaddaya mean, kidnapped?"

"Please, Frankie." The woman who had escorted Robby through the labyrinths of the world now stood quaking by the door. "I don't know what it is I've done."

Frankie banged the heel of his hand against his own forehead as if trying to escape the immediate situation by knocking himself unconscious. He recovered from the blow. "You kidnapped this? This kid?"

"I think I did, darlin'."

He stared at Robby. There was sleep in the corners of the man's huge brown eyes.

"You're *kidnapped*?"

"I was on my way to school, sir, and this nice woman offered to guide me."

"This nice woman kidnapped you? This nice woman, my wife, Marie Savallo, she kidnapped you?"

"Please, sir, she took me on an underground train and through a market where there was a great lot of food, and it was all jolly interesting."

Frankie's big eyes darted to Marie's face. "Did anyone see you come in?"

"We took the back ways, Frankie."

His arms flung out with astonishing speed. He swept the picture puzzle off the kitchen table. Pieces of it flew to the corners of the room.

"You've kidnapped a child? You, Marie? Marie of the never-ending novena? You musta gone nuts!"

"Saints, I don't know what it is I've done, Frankie. It just came over me in a rush, it did. I saw him in the street. He was so cold and hungry lookin'. So beautiful . . . lost." Still in her overcoat, Marie Savallo was fighting tears. "So I took him home with me."

"You want a child—so you kidnap one! Right! Call the men in the white coats to come get Marie Savallo! Booby hatch for her!"

She looked to him truly for an explanation. "What's this I've done, Frankie?"

"You've kidnapped a child, that's what you done! You went out to get a job and you come back with a child you kidnapped! That's what you done!"

"I never did get the job, Frankie."

"Of course you didn't get the job! That's what you went out for! Instead you brought home another mouth to feed!" The flat of his hand made an awful bang on the kitchen table. "And you brought him here! My brother Tony's here, the damned draft-dodger, and you walk in—not with a job—not with a loaf of bread—but with a kidnapped kid!"

Marie Savallo agreed. "Things aren't so good, Frankie."

" 'Things aren't so good,' she says. Kidnappin' a kid will make things good?"

"Shush, darlin', please. People shouldn't hear you shoutin' *kidnap* so loud when there's about to be a child found missin'."

"Have you gone nuts, Marie? Who knows about kidnappin'?"

"They'll never suspect us, darlin'. If only you'll lower your voice."

Frankie lowered his voice. "You want to get me sent to prison, is what you want. You want to get rid of me for life?"

"No, darlin'. Never say such a thing. How could I get on without you?"

"God!" said Frankie Savallo. "A wife who kidnaps children!"

"I couldn't resist him, Frankie."

"I marry a sweet Irish girl and she sets me up to go to prison just like a member of my own family!"

"He's such a darlin' boy, Frankie. Just look at him." She took off Robby's hat. "Lost and cold and half starved he was."

"My uncle says it's always the Irish who get the Italians in trouble. My uncle says the prisons are full of good Italians put there by the holy Irish!"

"Frankie, darlin', this opportunity might be the answer to a prayer, you understand."

"Opportunity! What opportunity! Since when is being sent up for life an opportunity?"

"I tell you, Frankie—he's in the newspaper. This lad's a very important package."

"What paper? Lemme see the paper."

"It's here, darlin'. I wrapped the garbage in it."

While another mouth to feed, which hadn't been fed, watched, Marie Savallo went to the sink's sideboard and dumped garbage out of a newspaper. She spread it out on the kitchen table in front of Frankie. *"The New York Star,"* she said. "See? His picture, through the eggshells. The very same boy, it is."

Frankie Savallo looked back and forth from Robby in the flesh to Robby through the eggshells.

His left hand plowed percolated coffee beans off the newspaper. He read.

Frankie Savallo exclaimed: "He's an orphan, Marie! You kidnapped an orphan!" His fist banged the kitchen table. In truth, Frankie Savallo had the biggest shoulders and chest Robby had ever seen. The man's body was like a triangle with the broad shoulders on top and the shriveled legs in the wheelchair. Robby knew the legs of the kitchen table couldn't absorb too many more blows from the man's fist: "Who's gonna pay ransom for an orphan?"

"Read the paper, Frankie. He's an English duke, or somethin'."

"What's a duke?"

"It's royalty, darlin'. Up there with the King."

"A king?" Frankie looked around at Robby again, his eyes even wider. "You've stolen a king?"

"Like a king, darlin', only not so royal as all that."

"What the hell are you, kid?"

Robby shrugged. "Burnes, sir."

"See, Marie? He says his name's Burnes. There was a kid in school named Burnes. His father did five to ten for aggravated assault."

"I think he's tryin' to say his name, darlin'. If you'd just look, you'd see in the newspaper that one of the names in this magnificent long string of 'em he has is the name Burnes. See that? You know the English, darlin': When one word will do they squander 'em."

"Oh, yeah. Says here, 'The decision was made in England's highest corridors of power.' Where's that at?"

"Must be the Tower of London, Frankie. Oh, some terrible things have gone on in that place!"

"It says 'special ship,' Marie. Look, it says he was sent to America on a 'special ship.' A special ship for this kid!"

"It quotes the Prime Minister, Frankie, Mr. Winston Churchill himself. You've heard him on the radio. Talking about our wee friend over there."

"Look, Marie. Down here by the jelly. It says the King. The King of England!"

Frankie Savallo, his eyes big, turned the wheelchair and came closer to Robby. "You the kid in the newspaper?"

"I don't know, sir. I haven't read the newspaper. But I do know Mr. Thadeus—"

"Of course he is, Frankie. Look at his clothes."

Frankie squinted at the Wolseley School emblem.

"Why is that moose trying to knock over that tree?"

"Moose, sir?"

"Elk, whatever it is. That big goat on your coat."

Marie Savallo was standing beside Robby. "Tailor-made clothes, Frankie. For a child who'll outgrow them before spring."

"What's tailor-made?"

"Everything, Frankie. Take off your overcoat, sonny. You must be warm."

She ignored Robby's overcoat when he tried to hand it to her.

Her fingers unbuttoned his blazer.

"Look at that, Frankie. A tailor-made jacket for a little boy."

Her fingers went between the collar of Robby's shirt and his neck.

"His shirt is hand-sewn, Frankie. And him about to grow like a Jerusalem artichoke."

"I want to know about the moose tryin' to knock over that tree. What does it mean?"

"It means he's very high up, Frankie."

"He's an orphan! Who's gonna pay ransom for an orphan?"

"Well, darlin', someone paid for these clothes. Hand-me-downs they're not."

"Listen, kid." Frankie stuck his finger in Robby's chest. "Are you the kid in the newspaper, or not?"

"I wouldn't know, sir. May I read the newspaper?"

"You can read?"

"Slowly, sir."

"Sure, kid." Frankie wheeled backwards and aside. "Read."

Marie brought a chair upon which Robby knelt as he read, elbows among the coffee grounds. *I think I'll let you be surprised in the morning*, Thadeus Lowry had said. *Read* The New York Star. *Robby should be very surprised indeed.* Robby was very surprised indeed.

At the top of the page was a huge picture of Robby, cap, necktie, blazer, short pants, kneesocks, sitting on his suitcase. There was no background in the picture. Robby appeared to be sitting in space, or on a cloud, or in the land of nowhere. His chin was on his hand, and his elbow on his knee. The expression on his face (which was actually one of curiosity as to how the photographer's big camera worked) looked questioning, pleading, yearning. He looked tired, which he was, and hungry, which he was.

On either side of Robby's picture, in cameo, were the photographs of Robby's parents he had given Thadeus Lowry from his wallet. Their evening wear, and the formal compositions of the portraits made the parents look far removed from the pathetic reality of their son. Too, as their eyes were wide open for their formal sittings, the effect of the arrangements of photographs on the page was that they were considerably concerned, if not startled, at seeing their offspring displayed so prominently within millimeters of their noses.

The photographic layout was held together with the headline:

THE LORD IS AN ORPHAN

Under the photographic display the caption read: *Robert Duke of Pladroman, aged 10, as he arrived in New York from war-torn England yesterday.*

And the story read:

The poor little Duke!

The War ravaging the world is toppling thrones, unsettling the high and the mighty, and making many another distinguished seat uneasy.

Not just the people of every nation are distressed.

The 10-year-old holder of one of England's most awesome titles arrived in New York yesterday, a homeless orphan, a waif, his eyes hollow from his personal brush with current world history.

While other reporters spent the day in pursuit of presidents, dictators and military leaders, your correspondent for *The New York Star* struggled through blistering snow to a cold and windswept East Side dock to discover Robert James St. James Burnes Walter Farhall-Pladroman (Duke of Pladroman), aged 10, lost and lonely, trembling with trepidation at these cold shores of a new land, grievous with grief at the recent loss of his beloved parents, victims of war, a small and discouraged figure sitting astride his only remaining possession in the world, a small, black cardboard suitcase (see picture above).

"Call me Robby," he said, extending the democracy of childhood while extending a cold and uncertain hand to your *New York Star* correspondent.

Lark

Weeks ago, happy as a lark, the 10-year-old boy gamboled on England's green glades, the playing fields of his family's public (private boarding) school, Wolsley School, in England.

Like any other, healthy, high-spirited, 10-year-old boy, he loved to play rugby (football) and cricket (baseball).

The airplanes flying over the school on their flights over the English Channel to deal death blows to the Axis Powers meant no more to him than to any other healthy, happy, 10-year-old boy.

Then came the terrible news that shattered Robby's safe and noble world.

A bomb in the night—a Nazi bomb—emblazoned with the dreaded swastika, directly hit London's famous and fashionable Pladroman House, Mayfair—Robby's home—killing both parents instantly.

Robby's dad, the Duke of Pladroman, a well-decorated hero of World War One, was a distinguished member of the House of Lords (Senate). His mum, the Duchess, was one of London's most noted and loved hostesses, admired for her fragile beauty.

All lost in a single stroke—a school, a home, a family, a way of life.

Haec

"Forsan et haec olim meminisse juvabit," said the poor little Duke, with a shrug of his thin shoulders, which roughly translates from the vulgate as "I can take anything."

His schoolmates and schoolmasters were open in their sympathy for the noble waif. They tried to assure him their love and friendship were steady in the face of his terrible loss.

But the decision was made in England's highest corridors of power that the young Duke must be evacuated to the shores of England's staunchest ally, the United States of America, for safekeeping.

"We are fighting this terrible evil not for ourselves alone," intoned the English Prime Minister (President) Winston Churchill, "but for the next generation, and the next, and the next. We are fighting for the preservation of our good English way of life."

By dark, heavily curtained trains and devious routes, Robby was brought to his ship in the middle of the night.

Special

Dodging bombs, his car, without benefit of any headlights at all, sought out the docks and the special ship, His Majesty's Ship *Scaramouche*.

Fearful days at sea followed his nightmare ashore.

Submarines, with their fearful torpedoes, lurked beneath every wave.

Mid-winter North Atlantic storms were no friends to His Majesty's Ship *Scaramouche*, her captain, crew, and their special human cargo.

Dodging torpedoes, the storm-tossed little vessel limped into New York Harbor yesterday, her stern in the water.

Asked for his first impression of America, the 10-year-old Duke said, "We are all very grateful for what the people of the United States are doing for the besieged people of Britain. His Majesty, the King, has asked me to transmit his thanks."

Correspondent

Having no other course to follow, your correspondent for *The New York Star* had the poor little Duke accompany him to his own home last evening. There he was warmly greeted by the family and friends of your correspondent.

The poor little Duke has come to safe harbor, at last, in the warm bosom of your correspondent's family.

When Robby finished reading, slowly, he looked up, slowly, into the blue eyes of Marie Savallo. Slowly he turned his head and looked into the brown eyes of Frankie Savallo.

11

Worthiness

Picking slowly through Thadeus Lowry's account of Robby's narrow escape from peace, he had not been listening closely to the continuing debate between Frankie and Marie Savallo concerning whether Robby had been worth kidnapping, having already been kidnapped. Frankie Savallo continued to exercise the characteristic of an operatic *basso profundo*: Each new fragment of information which came his way he not only assimilated slowly, he took personally. Every aspect in the affair drew from him thirty-two bars in the lower registers. Counterpoint to the depth of his emotions, Marie Savallo's conversational flights fled from her mouth and flittered around the room like so many glib canaries.

Finally the garbage on the newspaper turned Robby away by the nose. He sat facing the room on the kitchen chair. He did think it splendid of Thadeus Lowry to give him such a resounding phrase to say on behalf of the King. Too, Headmaster would be so pleased at Robby's introducing Latin to America. It might enspirit him.

Marie Savallo had removed her coat and hat and now was sitting, sagging, on the other side of the kitchen table, awaiting the teapot to sound. Frankie sat in profile to them, arms folded across his great chest, as if to defend his heart from any further incursions that day.

Their conversation repeated Marie's contention that she hadn't meant to kidnap Robby, Frankie's insistence she shouldn't have kidnapped Robby, and their joint indecisiveness about what to do with the kidnapped Robby.

Frankie twisted his neck further than Robby thought humanly possible, to face him, and said, "Well?"

"Well, sir?"

"Is what the newspaper says about you the truth?"

"No, sir."

"No?"

"No, sir."

"Then what's true?" Frankie shouted.

"I'm eight, sir."

"What?"

"I'm eight, sir. Not ten. Eight."

"Columbus!"

"He's eight years old," said Marie Savallo. "The little darlin'. Hardly old enough to wash between his own toes, he is."

"Dammit, shuddup, Marie! Are you the poor little Duke or not?"

"My name's Burnes, sir. Robby Burnes, S.Nob."

"You know, Frankie," confided Marie, "even his name's familiar to me. I swear I've heard it somewhere."

"Is it true you know the Prime Minister and the King of England?"

Robby asked, "Sir?"

"What?" Frankie said mildly. Then Frankie said not so mildly: "What?"

"Is the Prime Minister the man who rolls instead of walks and talks as if he were upstairs and he wants you to hear him downstairs?"

"How do I know?" expostulated Frankie. "All I know is the King wears a funny hat with diamonds in it."

"Oh, I know the King all right. He comes to tea. We're both rather keen on the strawberry marmalade and I'm always told not to pig it if His Majesty's there. Mums says he has children at home and has to go out for his marmalade. It's the other one I'm not sure of, the Prime Minister one."

"Christopher Columbus, Marie! He knows the King of England!"

"What did you expect, Frankie? He's a duke. Sure, even the King of England has to have somewhere to go when he goes out."

"Kid—"

"He's a duke, Frankie. You're supposed to call him Duke So-And-So. Duke Robby, I guess, is it?"

"We kidnapped him, didn't we? I'll call him any damned thing I please. What did you call your daddy, kid—your papa?"

"Sir."

"What?"

"I called my father *sir*, sir."

"And what did you call the King?"

"Sir."

"You call everybody sir?" Marie asked.

"Yes, sir."

Frankie looked shrewd. "If the King of England likes strawberry whatever-it-is, what does the Prime Minister of England like?"

"If he's the one I think he is, sir, he likes cigars—great, long ones—and he likes other people to light them for him, sir, as long as they don't interrupt him when he's talking, which means he really doesn't smoke all that much, sir. And brandy at tea time. Nanny says it's a sin, anyone having brandy at tea time, and that's why we'll lose the war for sure."

"We'll lose the war because the Prime Minister of England drinks brandy?" Frankie shook his head.

"At tea time, sir. Nanny says a little brandy at breakfast is all right because I've seen her take it then. Knocks on the door of the heart, she says, and tells it to move along."

"Isn't he a darlin' boy?" The teakettle was whistling. "There's our tea now. Would you like a cup of tea yourself, Frankie?"

"I'll have a brandy. I need an excuse for losin' a war."

"Sure, you know we haven't had anything like that . . ."

She was putting three cups and saucers and spoons on the table. "You'd like tea?" she asked Robby.

"Oh, yes, sir, ma'am."

"I thought you might."

Frankie said, "You just can't ship a kid across the ocean, especially on a special ship! And then just leave him there on the dock! Somebody must be expecting you."

"I was told I have an uncle here, sir, in New York, but I don't."

"The poor darlin'. All on his lonesome."

"Marie." Frankie sighed. He was enjoying dejection. "Let me try to get this through your melon one final time. If the kid don't belong to anyone, who's gonna pay ransom? I ask you!"

"Sure, somebody has to care about the tyke. You should have seen him in the road, Frankie, a wee tired child lookin' as confused as a gentle baker at a butchers' bloody convene."

"Lissen, kid: You got any family? Any family at all?"

"I have a grandaunt in Scotland, sir."

"Fat lot of good that's gonna do us," Frankie said. "From what I hear about the Scottish your grandaunt will send us a rent bill for keeping you. Columbus!" Frankie sighed again and shook his head. "Is your grandaunt rich?"

"Oh, I don't think so, sir. I heard when the war came she had to help her gardeners herself."

"She has gardeners?"

"Sure, Frankie. And we can get the ransom in turnips and squash air-mail from Scotland. Have your tea now, Your Duke-ship." She poured steaming tea into the three chipped cups on the table. "And look what I happen to have." Marie Savallo put an opened jar of grape jelly on the table. And a stack of bread. And a knife. "Dip your knife in that now, lad. And you won't have to wrassle the King for it at all."

"Oh, thank you, ma'am."

"Saints, the child is starved."

"I missed breakfast, ma'am"—which, Robby thought, was as graceful an appraisal of his circumstances as he could muster.

"Look at him eat, Frankie. So delicate he does it there won't be a drop spilled!"

Apologetically, Frankie whispered to Robby, "She can't cook Italian."

"I'm sorry to hear that, sir."

Man-to-man, Frankie continued. "Wait until she gives you what she calls lasagna."

"I'm sure I'll enjoy it, sir."

"You won't recognize it."

"No, sir," Robby admitted. "I wouldn't."

"The way she makes it, it looks like Mulligan stew."

"I'm sure that would be very nice, sir."

"Everything she makes looks like Mulligan stew." Frankie

looked at Marie's back to be sure she wasn't listening. "And it tastes—how does it taste?—it tastes like laundry."

Robby was halfway through the jar of grape jelly.

"Her *agnello dorato*? Mulligan stew with lamb. *Scaloppine di vitello*? Mulligan stew with veal. *Anguilla in gratella*?" Frankie and Robby were giggling behind Marie's back. "Mulligan stew with worms. Everything Mulligan stew."

Marie turned from the stove. "Here we've been jawin' away, Frankie, and no one ever had the decency to ask the child if he had a mouth on him."

Frankie cleared his throat. He became businesslike again. "I want him to answer some sharp questions."

Sympathetically, Marie said, "He missed breakfast, Frankie."

Frankie Savallo pushed his teacup away with his thumb. He lowered his two brown eyes like setting suns and they beamed into Robby's eyes. "Who's going to pay your ransom?"

Knife in the jelly jar, Robby hesitated. "Is that like a restaurant bill, sir?"

Marie sat down at the kitchen table. "Sure, the darlin' boy doesn't know what ransom is, Frankie. I don't think previously he's had much conversation with criminal types."

"I remember something about ransom," Robby said. "From *Robin Hood*."

"Now you've got it, lad," Marie cheered.

"He may be a duke," Frankie said, "but he knows less than a newt."

"And how much should a duke know, Frankie? Tell me that. When you're as important as a duke everybody knows things *for* you."

"Lissen, kid: Who would pay a lot of money to have you back?"

"Back where, sir?"

"Back home."

"But I haven't a home, sir. It went under a bomb."

"There must be somebody who cares about you!"

"I don't think so, sir."

"Think a little, willya? Columbus!"

Fortified by bread and jelly, Robby sat back in his chair, folded his fingers in his lap, and to convince them he was cogitating with great sincerity, squeezed his eyes shut.

And sincerely he did try to think who cared enough about him to pay money to have him back. There were his parents, of course, but they last had been reported seen in two coffins in the same aisle. Nanny had had hundreds of pounds under her bed, *for her old age in Bath*, and Robby doubted not at all Nanny would pay every shilling to have him back, but Nanny in her nightdress, and all her pounds, had been blown up by the bomb and fluttered down into rubble. There was Mrs. Jencks, matron at Wolsley School, but surely she wouldn't pay much to have a boy back when she couldn't tell one boy from another until their noses grew. Robby couldn't think Headmaster would take much out of his own pocket to get a tadpole back when he was surrounded by tadpoles. The family solicitors, Pollack, Carp and Fish, which Thadeus Lowry had mentioned, obviously didn't have any money to spare for a boy, or they would have sent a longer, more explanatory cable. And just the evening before Robby had seen Thadeus Lowry robbed in the street, so Robby knew Thadeus Lowry didn't have any money.

Robby opened his eyes. Frankie was still staring at him, awaiting the answer. "Sorry, sir. I can't think of one person who cares for me. Now may I have some more jam?"

"Of course, you can, darlin'. It's a wonder your pants didn't fall down, with your stomach so empty."

Frankie concluded, "We have to throw him back, Marie."

"Throw him back?"

"He's too little a fish to fry."

"Why, he's not a fish at all. He's a wee homeless boy."

"Homeless! That's what you should have thought of before you kidnapped him! There's no one in the world who'd give up a burp for this boy."

"You mean, throw the little fish back into the sewers of New York? There are sharks out there, Frankie. Bad people." Marie rolled her blue eyes to indicate to Frankie how bad those bad people were. "I couldn't sleep if we did that, Frankie. I have a conscience."

"You have a better idea?"

"Ask your Uncle Guido, Frankie. Now there's a man who knows how to turn a dishonest dollar."

"Uncle Guido won't give me the time of day since I married you. He thinks you're a pipe straight to the police. Only Tony he talks to."

"We'll ask Tony then."

"Tony? Give him some of the profits? It's not bad enough we're feedin' him now?"

"He's your brother, Frankie, and may have a better criminal mind than you. He's never seen the inside of a jail, and yet I know he does not tip-toe through the world in an entirely righteous manner."

"That draft-dodger."

"He's a quiet man, Frankie. A man of peace." Marie leaned forward assertively in her chair. "Frankie, darlin', your Uncle Guido doesn't like you because you're bubble-brained. Next to you, a subway train has more originality in the directions it takes."

"He thinks I'm bubble-brained because I married you! He doesn't *think* it. He *knows* it! You have to be one bubble-brained Italian to eat Mulligan stew all your life!"

"Have you noticed all the grape jelly is gone? And the bread? I've never seen anyone eat a whole jar of grape jelly before."

"The King is a hog," decided Frankie.

"It was very good, Mrs. Savallo. Thank you."

"Shush! Is that Tony now?"

Frankie listened. "If that was Tony, you couldn't hear him."

Marie said, "I didn't hear him." She began to gather the teacups from the table. She said, "I felt him."

Robby turned to the door, just as it began to open.

12

A Man of Peace

Tony Savallo's eyes, steady, direct, were in Robby's as the door opened. His eyes clasped onto the new, unexpected element in the room as if he had seen Robby through the door and had only opened the door to get a better look. Robby had the impression that if there had been a mouse in the corner behind the stove Tony would have seen it, too, instantly, and without moving his eyes.

"Hey, Tony," Frankie said loudly from his wheelchair. "Come meet His Lordship!"

"You'll like some tea, Tony?" Marie was bustling faster than ever. "I'll warm the pot."

Without his appearing to move, the door behind Tony closed. It latched with a barely audible click.

"Come sit down, Tony. Quick, Marie, some tea for Tony."

As Tony came across the room to Robby he took his right hand from the pocket of his windbreaker and kept it at the level of Robby's face. Even when Tony moved he seemed absolutely still. Standing directly before Robby, Tony settled the weight of his body on his right hip. His right pant-leg brushed Robby's knee. Tony cupped Robby's left jawbone in his right hand and turned

Robby's face up fully toward his own. Robby smelled from him the smell of lead pencils. The skin of Tony's face was clear and tight. His eyes were wide-set and black. The immobility of Tony's face appeared to come from its skin having been stretched too tightly over his skull. The long, smooth muscles in his neck were repeated on both sides of his wrist and the back of his hand.

"This is Tony, kid. My brother." Frankie shrugged. "A draft-dodger."

"He's against fighting," amplified Marie. "A man of peace."

"I fall off a roof," Frankie said, "spend the rest of my life in a wheelchair. Tony's got legs, but won't go to war."

Gently, Tony's hand moved up Robby's cheek, opened into fingers and combed through his hair. "War is inefficient," said Tony to Robby. "Don't you agree?"

"It can make a bloody mess, sir."

Tony put his hand back into his pocket and watched Marie putting more tea leaves into the pot.

"Lissen, Tony, sit down."

With his huge arm Frankie swung Marie's chair around, putting it into a more inviting position for Tony.

Even sitting in Marie's chair, Tony still did not seem to be at the table. It was more as if he were on a park bench, looking at everyone across a path.

"See, Tony, it's like this." Frankie was pulled right up to the table, both elbows on the surface. "Marie kidnapped this kid."

Such information, to Tony, was not cause for an aria. It was not even cause for a raised eyebrow.

"Right off the street. He was goin' to school and was lost or somethin'. And he turns out to be this English duke or somethin'. She recognized him from the newspaper. He's in this mornin's paper. Marie, get Tony the paper." Marie hustled from the sinkboard with the crumpled newspaper. "Hey, Marie!" protested Frankie. "The newspaper's still all covered with garbage! Whatsa matter with you?"

She shook the newspaper over the sink. "I didn't know I was going to kidnap a child, especially this child, when I was doin' up the breakfast dishes, darlin'." Quickly she laid the smelly newspaper flat on the kitchen table again in front of Tony. She placed her index finger on Robby's picture. "He ate a whole jar of grape jelly in one sitting, Tony. Would you believe it?"

"See? He's a duke or somethin'. He knows the King. The King of England, Tony."

Tony's eyes flickered acknowledgment of the newspaper laid before him.

"Only, Tony, see? Marie, the dumb broad, when she kidnaps the kid doesn't realize he's an orphan. She has to come home to me to find that out. His parents got killed in the war. Where does it say that? Down here, see? All he's got is an aunt who is a farmer somewhere. It's like that, see? So we've been sittin' here discussin' who's gonna pay his ransom, you got me?"

"Look at his clothes, Tony." Again Marie Savallo tucked her fingers down under Robby's shirt collar as if selling the item through fair examination of detail. "Everything special made for him and hand-sewn like a cardinal at his altar and he's only a wee boy whistlin' in the street."

"But, you see, Tony, we got this big problem: Nobody cares about the kid, see? I mean, that's a big problem for us. An uncle he's supposed to have uptown doesn't exist. The bastard's an orphan, Tony!"

Tony remained like a young lion in sunlight, not blinking.

"And, Tony, you know I can't go to Uncle Guido. You know how it is between us, with Marie and all. He thinks she's an informer or somethin'. And, you know, since I fell off the roof, you know, well, Uncle Guido thinks I got less brains than a mailbox."

Marie put a cup of tea in front of Tony.

He said: "Thank you."

Frankie said, "So what do you think, Tony?"

Marie sat down in the fourth place at table, her hands to her cheeks.

Tony drained his teacup, silently.

"The best idea we got, Tony, is to try hittin' up the King of England." Frankie's laugh at their best idea was a little nervous. "Only you can't just call up the King in England. It's long distance, Tony."

"A fearful long distance," agreed Marie.

"So what do we do, Tony?"

"There must be an embassy," said Marie Savallo. "Of course there is. In Washington, I bet it is. We should call up the Ambassador from England, Frankie." Excited by her own idea, Marie's index fingers made roads through the garbage on the newspaper.

"Tell the Ambassador to tell the King we've kidnapped a little friend of his, a nice little lad in short pants named all those names he'll remember from the competition over the strawberry jam pot, and we want one hundred thousand dollars for his return, and none of his English funny money, by the way."

The Savallo brothers were looking at Marie. Frankie's mouth was open. "A hundred thousand dollars! Have you gone nuts?" Frankie jerked his thumb at Robby. "Who'd pay a hundred thousand dollars for this kid? He's not worth his weight in wood the termites have been at!"

Robby didn't know the value of a hundred thousand dollars, but he did consider one hundred thousand anything rather a lot. On the other hand, at Pladroman House in Mayfair he had seen wood the termites had been at and thought himself more substantial than that. If left to his own appraisal, Robby would assess his worth in neither terms whatsoever.

"I tell you, Marie," Frankie reiterated, "no one would pay one hundred thousand dollars for this kid, duke or no."

"Sure," Marie said quietly, but with great determination, "I wouldn't give the darlin' up for a penny less."

"Tony," Frankie shouted. "Make this woman shut up and tell me what to do, willya?"

Tony got up from the table. He put his hands over his head as far as they would go and clutched them together. He stood on tiptoes and stretched his whole body. He rotated his torso and yawned. He said, "Keep him."

"What?"

It was Frankie who spoke, but husband and wife looked equally shocked and perplexed by the comment.

"It's what you want to do." Tony relaxed from his aspirations and put his hands back in his pockets. "You can't have a kid of your own. Marie wants this kid. She kidnapped him, sure, but not for money. For love." Tony's unmoving eyes included Robby in their scope. "Keep him and love him."

"Tony!" Marie seemed embarrassed and appalled that her criminality should be so impugned before her husband. "It's not true at all."

Tony's eyes locked in hers.

"We're too poor, Tony, anyway," she said. "This is an expensive lad. You didn't see what the boy had for lunch. A whole jar of grape jelly and a plateful of bread. That's all right as an investment, Tony, the fatted calf and all. But, every day, Tony, feedin' him while he's growin'? And would you have me hand-sewin' things for him till I'm old and blind?"

Frankie's eyes, as he stared at Marie, were incredulous. Marie's eyes shifted lowly as if her mind had been violated.

Tony stood nearer one of the cots.

"Tony, before you nap . . ." Marie got up from the table. " . . . I need five dollars for the groceries."

"Sure, Marie." Tony took a bill from his pocket and handed it to her. The number ten was in the corner of the bill Robby saw.

"I'll just get my coat," Marie said. As she moved quickly around the room collecting her coat and hat and purse she kept looking back at Frankie whose incredulous eyes were following her. She seemed to think Frankie was working up to an *aria d'agilita* which would prove too great a strain for her ears. "I'll be back," she said, as she scurried through the door.

"This time bring back the groceries!" Frankie shouted after her. "You bring back a herd of elephants, I'll kill you! Don't bring back a single elephant! Not even one!"

From the cot on which Tony lay came the sound of a chuckle.

Frankie looked at Robby and then at the pieces of his picture puzzle all over the floor. "Columbus," he said to himself. Then he shouted at the closed door again: "You see Mussolini in the street, leave him there! He wouldn't like your Mulligan stew *parmigiana* anyway! Neither would the Roosevelts or the King of France!" In a much lower voice, Frankie said, "Neither do I."

From the cot came no sound at all—not even the sound of breathing.

Frankie muttered, "I wonder what she really went out to do."

13

In Durance

"**C**olumbus!" Frankie Savallo sighed.

Robby was going around the room on one knee picking up the pieces of the picture puzzle. His eyes kept going to one of the unoccupied cots. On one cot Tony Savallo was stretched out, flat on his back, hands folded over his waist. He had not removed his sneakers. Apparently he was asleep—his eyes were closed, his breathing was regular—but there was nothing in his posture which suggested he was relaxed. He looked like a motor which was running in neutral. Working his wheelchair around the room, Frankie scooped the newspaper off the kitchen table, brought it to the sinkboard, and rewrapped the garbage in it. "Columbus!" He sighed again. Robby brought the picture puzzle pieces to the kitchen table in fistfuls. Some of the pieces had been stepped on by Marie.

Finally, Frankie wheeled himself to the table and began studying the puzzle again. Robby stood on one foot, watching him from behind heavy lids. Frankie looked at him. "You must be as tired as a streetwalker in Venice," he said. "Marie pulling you all over the city. Why don't you crawl into that cot there by the stove, and grab some shut-eye?''

Robby was happy to. It had been weeks since he had been in anything resembling a bed. He took off his blazer and shoes, loosened his necktie and got under the blankets.

His pillow was against the white side of the stove. Across the room a torn green shade puffed back and forth in the window draft.

"Got to do something." At the table, Frankie muttered to himself. He had not moved many of the pieces of the puzzle. "What in heck do you say to an ambassador?"

After a few more moments, a few more heavy exhalations on the word *Columbus*, Frankie, with great determination, wheeled himself over to the telephone on a little table by the door. He hesitated, hand on the receiver, then picked it up and dialed O.

"Hello, operator? I want to speak to the King's Ambassador in Washington, D.C. . . . matter of life and death . . .

"Which king? . . . The King of England. What's his name, George the Third. No, George the Third was king when I was in fourth grade. By now it must be George the Fourth or Fifth . . .

"Great Britain? I want the Kingdom of England . . . U.K.? O.K., that must be it. They musta changed their name, modernized it, you know, keep up with the U.S. . . .

"Yeah, I'll wait . . ."

Hand over the mouthpiece Frankie stared solemnly at the floor. "What in hell I say? Hello, Ambassador, this is Frankie Savallo, nice Italian boy, New York. Big kidnapper. My wife she never misses a church but likes a big criminal for a husband . . ." He put his free hand over his eyes. "Ohhhh," he groaned. "They'll put me in jail for a million years. I'll be a little old man in a wheelchair, goin' around askin' everyone if they remember the taste of mozzarella. 'That's Frankie Savallo,' they'll all say. 'Big kidnapper! Kidnapped the Duke of Tootie-Fruitie. His wife got him sent up for life and married his Uncle Guido . . .' "

Suddenly Frankie jerked up in his chair as if called to attention. "Hello? Who's this? I'm calling the Ambassador from England. Are you the Ambassador from England? . . . What am I calling about? I'm calling about a kidnapping, is all. You better let me talk to the Ambassador . . . All right, I'll wait. But make it snappy, this is long distance . . .

"Oh, God, what am I doing? They'd never electrocute a man in a wheelchair. It wouldn't be nice . . .

"Hello? Ambassador? . . . You're not the Ambassador? Where's the Ambassador? . . .

"In *Warm Springs*! Doesn't he know there's a war on? Who are you? . . . Smith-Wilson, head of embassy security. Are you Mr. Smith or Mr. Wilson? What, am I talking to two of you? . . . Oh, one of you with two names. This is . . . never mind who this is. Lissen, we've got a little English boy here, calls himself Robert Burnes, but the newspaper says he's a duke, or somethin', an English duke, sent over here to get out of the way of the bombs, or somethin' . . . Evacuated and sent over here, yes . . . You are English, aren't you? I mean, you don't sound like Mayor La Guardia. So you should care . . . We want some money for this kid, if you take my meaning . . .

"What *for*? So we can give him back! This is an expensive kid. My wife she says he dresses like a cardinal . . . No, I can't afford to keep him. We live in one room, three of us, myself, my wife, my brother the draft-dodger. Whoops, shouldna said that long distance . . . Lissen, you don't understand me. We want money for this kid. He's a friend of the King—your King. They arm-wrestle over the strawberry jam or somethin' . . . Yes, I mean your King. This is an important kid. He doesn't look like much but the newspaper says he's important . . . Burnes, Robert Burnes. He's got lots of other names, too, just like you, but they're in the newspaper across the room with the garbage wrapped in 'em . . ." Frankie sat sideways in the chair and studied Robby in the cot. "Yes, he's got a roof over his head. You think I'm calling from Central Park? . . . Sure we fed him. Who wouldn't feed a starvin' kid? . . . What do you mean, he's all right! He's not all right! We want money for him! Don't you see what I mean? . . . Lissen, buddy, don't tell me there's a war on. Isn't my brother a draft-dodger? . . . Of course you've got funds for such a thing as this. Your King could sell one of his hats, plenty of money . . . I'm not just a good American, I'm better than that—I'm a good Italian-American! . . . We have to do our bit for the war effort! You have to do your bit, too, buddy! . . . Hello? Hello? Mr. Smith? Mr. Wilson? . . . Hello, English embassy? . . . It's my dime! I'm talking to you . . . Guess I'm not talking to you . . ." Frankie hung up the phone.

He sat where he was, by the phone, a moment. "Columbus," he

said. "Phew. What a tight guy. Why should we help out them guys? Won't even pay a little ransom." He wiped the sweat off his face with both hands, sat still another moment, as if exhausted, then turned his wheelchair around. "Least they can't send me to prison for that!"

He wheeled over to the kitchen table and began moving around the pieces of his picture puzzle. "Least I didn't give up a life of mozzarella cheese!"

•   •   •

In his cot, Robby was beginning to think thoughts, hear voices and make choices. *Kidnapped!* He was beginning to understand that he had been taken prisoner, just like an English pilot in Germany or an English soldier in France. The Savallo's one-room apartment did not seem to Robby much like a prison, or a concentration camp. Nevertheless it was durance vile, or it would be durance vile had it not been for the fresh bread, the tea, the jar of grape jelly and the warm cot in which he now snuggled. It was durance.

Robby did not think he was heroic. He did not equate himself with people who could fly airplanes and shoot guns. Nor did he think he was in the hands of enemies, as they spoke nicely of His Majesty, the King. He *was* in a foreign land. Marie and Frankie Savallo had insisted to him he was kidnapped—even going so far as to consult him on how they were to get ransom for him. And they had approached the British government asking for money for Robby at a time when everyone knew the British government was especially hard pressed, financially, keeping all those ships at sea and planes in the air. To that extent they were enemies of His Majesty's Government. Were God and Country awaiting Robby's liberation as breathlessly as They would await the liberation of someone who knew how to fly a plane or shoot a gun? Robby didn't think so.

Having been brought up thus far like every other English boy, on jam and rhetoric, Robby's mind echoed with resounding phrases. *Excelsior! I am not to succumb! I am not to be denied! I am not to suffer the slings and arrows of outrageous fortune! I am to press on relentlessly!* Especially were boys of that era familiar with the wartime code of ethics. Admonitions had been poured into their jugheads through their ears. *It is the duty of every Englishman taken prisoner to escape!*

Robby would escape. He decided that. It was his duty. That much was clear to him. But first he needed sleep, and the cot by the stove was warm and snuggly. Too, he had a curiosity as to whether Marie Savallo's Italian cooking really tasted like laundry. It would be interesting to find that out.

He would escape, all right, but in a proper, gentlemanly, sedate and dignified manner—after he had napped, and after he had dined.

14

With the Aid of the Law

You'd think, in Robby's circum-
stances (plotting an escape from kidnappers) one would be greatly
relieved, upon awakening from a nap, to find a large policeman
standing over one's cot, looking down at one. Through shiny
round glasses the policeman's eyes smiled; the corners of his lips
tucked up into his cheeks in a pleased grin.

Robby had never seen a New York policeman before. The only
other day he had spent in New York it was snowing and only the
muggers had been out. But he had seen many London policemen
and was able to recognize the significance of midnight blue in
bulky material, brass buttons and gold insignia. This policeman's
coat was generous in front, allowing for a bulging stomach, and
furled up on one side, allowing everyone to see the handle of his
handgun. Robby had been in New York City not much more than a
day and already had seen two handguns; in war-torn England, as
he had heard Thadeus Lowry describe his homeland, Robby had
never seen a gun. This policeman's hat was different, too, not
peaked to impale falling objects as is a London policeman's hat,
nor strapped under the chin to prevent its being pinched over a
fence by students who believed pinching policemen's hats the

literary thing to do. This hat lay upon this policeman's head in a much flatter way, as if nailed on to his head some years earlier with the stern injunction never to pry it up.

Seeing a policeman standing over his cot gleaming down at him should have meant to Robby: Here is an arm of society into which a small boy might fling himself with full surety that Right would be done.

However, simultaneously to awakening and finding the policeman over his bed, Robby awoke to other sensations. The first was hunger. Not just your usual what's-for-dinner sort of hunger but a hunger sent up by a stomach which, having been well fed most of its existence, had been deprived of proper food for days adding to weeks, unable to accept what food had been sent to it, because of strategic wallowing, deprived further of proper food during long treks through snow and cold, and then fed bread, jam and tea, which only reminded the stomach that there was proper food in this world, food which could be properly taken and retained. That sort of hunger. The sort of hunger in which the stomach, having been reminded a few hours previously that food did exist, was wild with hope that it would soon be offered more. The stove atop Robby's head was hot. The room was steamy. He smelled a smell, which, although a new smell to him, he recognized instantly as a delicious smell: the smell of things to put in his mouth, savor, chew, swallow, send to his stomach with warmest regards.

He knew, as certainly as God was Episcopal, supper was in the offing.

Therefore Robby was not that sure he was glad to see a policeman standing over his cot. His nasal perception argued with his visual perception. Had Marie and Frankie Savallo been taken up for questioning? *Not now! Not in this crucial hour!* Since having his future indicated to him by the Headmaster of Wolsley School, Robby's education had increased only regarding the elusiveness of food. Clearly, now, he did not want to be rescued from supper!

"Well, Marie," said the policeman, removing his bulk from the airspace over the cot, "when you take to kidnapping, you don't think very big. Sure, even by the pound I don't think you'd get much for him."

Marie Savallo was setting places for four on the table. In his wheelchair, Frankie Savallo was turned away from the room, playing with the dial of a radio.

The policeman investigated the pots and pans on the stove. "What's this, Marie? More of Frankie's Eye-talian food?"

"More of Marie's Irish stew," said Frankie.

"You'll have supper with us?" Marie asked.

"I'll have a wee taste with you, just a smidgeon, understand, before goin' off to headquarters to confirm how hard I've been workin' my shift."

"It's all right, Will'um," Frankie said. "Any brother of Marie's is just like a member of the family."

"Thank you, Frankie," Will'um said as he lowered himself into a seat at table. "I know what that concession means to you."

With hope of being fed before being rescued Robby sat on the edge of the cot and put on his shoes, regretting their lack of polish. He replaced his necktie. Robby was impressed by the civil manner in which this intrusion by the law into criminal matters was taking place. In a Christly manner the policeman was sitting down to break bread with the kidnappers. Difficult social matters hadn't been so smoothly arranged even at Pladroman House. Robby put on his jacket.

Then Robby realized Tony Savallo was gone from the other cot.

Marie's large, blue, wet, soulful eyes looked over at Robby. "Stirrin', are you? You little darlin'. Come up to the table with Frankie and my brother, Will'um, and bring your appetite."

Frankie had turned off the radio and wheeled to the table.

Robby considered it even more socially stressful that a genuine member of the family, Marie's brother, had been sent over to make the arrest. But—Robby was used to people behaving decently under stressful circumstances.

He sat at table himself.

"Lissen, Will'um," Frankie asked eagerly. "Did you read the article in the newspaper?"

"I did, Frankie, I read it chapter and worse. It says 'The Lord Is an Orphan,' which is not news, if I remember my early religious training."

"Yeah. That's the trouble, Will'um. Maybe you can think of somethin'." Frankie sighed into his empty plate. "Has ransom ever been paid for an orphan, Will'um?"

"Not that I remember, Frankie. Adopted orphans, of course, normally attract a better price than natural children, as adoptive parents usually go to greater, less pleasurable extents to have such children . . ." Will'um placed a baleful gaze on Robby. "But this wee slip of a boy might be the sparrow, Frankie, who falls to earth and causes nothing but universal, human indifference."

"Poor wee bird," muttered Marie at the stove. "Booted from the nest without his own wings."

"So you called the English Ambassador, Frankie," led Will'um, rolling on his hams as if to test for places his supper might settle.

"And I'm sure," said Marie, coming from the stove with pans, "the minute he picked up the phone he got all over nervous and burst out in an Italian accent so thick no one had half a chance to understand him."

"Marie, why you say such a crazy thing?" protested Frankie loudly, with a heavy Italian accent.

"Sure, and don't you always, Frankie? The minute you get nervous you sound like the Pope in a cold shower."

Will'um laughed. "And how would my sister know how the Pope sounds in a cold shower?"

Marie said, "I know he takes cold showers."

"You want to hear what I said to the Ambassador or not?"

"Ah, there he goes, Marie: soundin' like a Napoli thrush."

"You guys don't have an accent?" asked Frankie.

"Sure we do, Frankie. We speak English the way it's meant to be spoken—with the authority of the Irish."

"Irish-American is okay, but Italian-American is no good, is that right?"

"Calm down, Frankie, and tell us your story," said Marie, ladling lamb and vegetables covered with melted cheese and tomato sauce on Robby's plate, "in such a way we can understand it."

Robby leaned his head into the steam of the plate and closed his eyes. He wanted to be wrapped entirely in the atmosphere of food.

"Look at the little darlin', sayin' his grace," chortled Marie. "Isn't he a beautiful child, Will'um?"

The contempt in the policeman's eyes cut through the steam of the plates. "He's English," he said, as if contemplating something for which you could pay one dollar and get two dollars in change.

"Well, she can't cook Italian," Frankie muttered. He lifted part of his supper on a fork. "What is this?"

"It's lamb *Parmesan*, Frankie. Like your mother used to make."

"If my mother ever served my father such a thing," announced Frankie loudly, "I would never have been born!"

"Is it really that good?" Will'um said. "I must try some."

"Italian cooking," protested Frankie. "Marie boils meat and potatoes, pours tomato and cheese over it, calls it Italian cooking!"

Now that his host, Frankie, had picked up a fork, to attack his food but not eat it, Robby picked up his own fork. And Robby ate.

Marie sat in her place. "Now, Frankie, you were saying . . . ?"

"I called the Ambassador. Down in Washington, D.C. Long distance on the phone. They call England the United Kingdom now. Bet you didn't know that, Will'um."

"Sure," said Will'um. "They've been callin' the auld place the United Kingdom ever since it began splittin' up. It's like us chasin' all the Indians out of the middle of the country and then callin' the place Indiana. There's no truth in names, Frank. Take your own, as a case in point."

"You stay calm, too, Will'um," directed Marie. "Don't we want to hear about the one hundred thousand dollars?"

"I'd like to hear about that," Will'um said dubiously.

Robby was not too amazed that Will'um ate with his hat on. Indeed it did look as if it had been nailed to his head. Besides, Robby's parents had had a frequent guest at Pladroman House, Rabbi Michael, who always ate with his hat on. Rabbi Michael had a melodic voice and always said he only came to Pladroman House for the eclairs. Robby was amazed, however, that Will'um ate while still wearing his handgun. Through dinner, while savoring, chewing, swallowing, Robby sneaked looks at Will'um's handgun.

Frankie said, "I goes: Ambassador, this is the biggest gangster in New York!"

Will'um asked, "You gave him your name, Frankie?"

Frankie blushed. "You think I'm stupid?"

Will'um glanced at the wheelchair and the telephone by the front door. "But you did call from here?"

"We keep that telephone in case anything happens to Frankie when I'm not here," Marie said. "Dreadful expense it is, too."

"It's a wonder the police aren't at the door this minute," said the man in the policeman's uniform, under a policeman's hat, wearing a policeman's badge and gun, eating his dinner at the Savallos' table. "If you hear a noise, Frankie, quick slip into me handcuffs—or we'll both be in trouble!"

"I goes: Ambassador, you tell George the King we got a little friend of his who likes strawberry jam—Duke . . . I still forget his name . . . and if he doesn't cough up a lot of money he'll never see his friend again."

"How much money, Frankie?" Marie asked. "How much money did you demand?"

Frankie blushed. "A hundred thousand dollars."

Sitting back on his chair, beefy hand on Robby's shoulder, Will'um asked, "Did you actually threaten to kill the child, Frankie?"

Red-faced, Frankie looked apologetically at Robby, who continued to eat his dinner. "Of course I did."

"That's the important thing, Frankie." Will'um shook Robby's shoulder affectionately. "You've really got to threaten to slaughter the tyke. Make it graphic, in the tellin'. You've got to say if they don't pay up, first you'll slice off his ears, then chop off his fingers, his toes, one by one, then chop off his hands, his feet, pluck out his eyes. And if they don't pay up at all you'll sever his head from his body and send it to them in a parcel." Will'um patted the back of Robby's neck. "That's the way to do it, Frankie."

Robby ate quicker.

"Very instructive, Will'um," said Marie Savallo. "That's why I went out and found Will'um in the street, Frankie, and had him home to supper. He has so much more experience in the law than we have."

"Is that about what you said to the Ambassador, Frankie?" Will'um asked.

Frankie swallowed. "Sure. I didn't play around none. He knew I meant business. I told him we want money for the kid."

"And what was the Ambassador's name, Frankie?" asked Will'um.

"I don't know," Frankie said. "How many ambassadors from England are there?"

"Only the one."

"He was the Ambassador, all right," insisted Frankie. "He talked like he had a mouthful of marbles."

"Proof enough," said Will'um.

"And what did the Ambassador say?" asked Marie. "What arrangement did you make to get the one hundred thousand dollars?"

Frankie looked at the center of the table, swallowed, looked at the floor each side of him, swallowed again. Lamely, he said, "I told him I'd call him back in a day or two."

Marie stared at her husband, at her brother, and at her husband again.

Will'um said, "I don't believe a word of it."

"Believe it!" Frankie shouted. "End of the month I'll give you my telephone bill! Long distance to Washington!"

"Well . . ." said Will'um.

"You're a cop! Believe in the evidence! Even my brother, Tony, knows that! Even in his sleep, Tony says, 'No evidence. There's no evidence'! "

"Shush, Frankie!" Marie gasped. "You're not supposed to mention *your* brother to *my* brother! Tony's a draft-dodger, mind you, and Will'um here is in the law!"

Suddenly, Frankie's face went white. He sat forward and put his elbows on the table. His eyes sought out, searched Will'um's.

"Honest to God, Will'um, we haven't seen Tony in months." Frankie was speaking rapidly. "Last we heard from him he was in Colorado, Texas—"

"Sure, Frankie." Will'um waved Frankie's mouth closed with his hand. "And he works for your Uncle Guido and hasn't been seen since this mornin' on Second Avenue."

"Tony?" Frankie looked pleased. "You say Tony's in town? Hey, Tony! Maybe he'll stop by, see us, Marie!"

"Honest, Will'um," added Marie. "We never see Tony."

"Speaking of evidence . . ." Will'um cleared his throat. "I observe that there are three beds in this room. Who's the third one for? The maid?"

Frankie and Marie looked at each other.

"That's for the kid," Frankie said, nodding toward Robby.

"But the bed was here last week," Will'um said. "And the kid wasn't."

"Well," laughed Frankie. "We were hopin' you'd stay overnight, Will'um."

"The bed's been there a long time," said Will'um.

"For a long time we been hopin' you'd stay overnight," insisted Frankie.

"And that's all I'll hear about evidence from you, Frank Savallo." Will'um pushed his plate away with his thumb.

Fluttering, Marie stood up. She grabbed Robby's plate. "You'd like some more, wouldn't you, darlin'?"

"I would, ma'am. I missed tea."

"Sure, and doesn't he eat like an Eye-talian, though?" mused Will'um. "Now you see it; now you don't. Food on his plate comes and goes just like that will-o-the-wisp brother of yours, Frankie."

"And without spillin' a drop, Will'um," Marie said from the stove. "Did you notice?"

"He eats like a cop," said Frankie, softly. "The kind who clean out a grocery store without stoppin' at the cash register."

Marie put a filled plate in front of Robby. And Robby ate.

Sitting down at her place at table, Marie asked, "Do you have any ideas, Will'um?"

"What does he know?" scoffed Frankie. "He's a flatfoot! A cop! Your brother!"

"Indeed I do have an idea," said Will'um. "One I think that would work and get you your one hundred thousand dollars. For your old age, Marie."

"Do you, now?"

"I do. Mind you, it's only my sister's old age I'm thinkin' of, seein' Frankie here doesn't work much since fallin' off that roof while doin' a job for his Uncle Guido. A moonlit night it was, too. Tell me, Frankie, did the moonlight get in your eyes?"

"Will'um, be kind," admonished his sister. "A terrible thing. Spendin' your life in a wheelchair just because a shingle gave way." Will'um pinned her with a caustic look. "Of course," she admitted, "the shingle was five stories up on a dark night."

Sitting back in his chair, legs crossed, arms folded across his chest, Will'um waited for the silence indicating complete attention. "It occurs to me," said Will'um, rolling the only R he had to roll, " 'The Lord Is an Orphan' and all that . . . well, it occurs to me that that article in the newspaper we all enjoyed readin' so much . . . well, you might say it was tinged with the brush of sentimentality. Wouldn't you say it was a wee bit sentimental, Marie?"

"I wept when I read it, Will'um."

"I'm sure," rolled Will'um, "many another woman at her kitchen sink readin' this morning's *Star* felt the same as you did, and wanted to rush out into the streets of New York and clasp the wee, homeless boy to her bosom."

"You think so, Will'um?"

"You're not an unusual gel, Marie, except you married a man who thought he had the wings of an angel right up to the moment he found himself in midflight."

"Go on, Will'um, and stop teasin' my husband."

"Now, who was this man at the *Star* who wrote this piece?"

Marie dashed to the sink counter.

"Thadeus Lowry, the name is."

She brought the smelly newspaper back to the table.

Will'um bent his head to confirm the byline. "Ah, yes. Thadeus Lowry. I think somethin' can be worked out, Marie, considerin' the power of the press, and this man's excitin' literary ability."

Will'um stood up and adjusted the flap of his coat over his holster.

"I don't know what you're thinkin', Will'um," said Marie.

"If I told you," said Will'um, "Frankie here might insist on helpin' me, and we'd never come to know if the plan might have worked on its own merits."

"He's not thinkin' anythin'," scoffed Frankie. "He's eaten, and now he's leavin' so he won't have to help wash the dishes."

"You're good to help us, Will'um," Marie said. "What with your career and all."

"Blood is thicker than water," said Will'um. "Thicker than whiskey, too, although I don't know how I'd ever find that out, havin' supper at your table."

15

The Power of the Press

"**M**y God, Frankie! Look what I've got!" Next morning Marie Savallo stood in the door of the apartment, hat and coat on, eyes big with alarm. Her purse dangled from one forearm. Together, her arms clutched a newspaper to her bosom.

"You go out for a job and kidnap a kid!" shouted Frankie from his wheelchair by the window. "Today you go out to get a job and come back right away with a newspaper!"

Such was the conversation which awakened Robby Burnes next morning. The night before, having eaten more than he ever had in his life, his head lolled, his eyelids had lowered while he was still at the table thinking about getting up and making good his intention to escape. He had felt strong arms putting him into the cot; warm fingers undressing him.

"Look at this, will you?"

Marie put the newspaper on the kitchen table. Frankie wheeled over to it. Instantly his lips began to move as he read.

Robby jumped naked out of bed and looked for his clothes. Between the other side of the stove and the apartment's back wall, cater-corner from wall to wall, ran a short clothes line. Hanging

96

from the line, looking as dejected as only wet laundry hung inside to dry can, were his shirt, his underwear, his stockings. Now, Robby saw, he was a prisoner of wet. His shorts and his blazer were over the back of a kitchen chair. He put those on.

On one leg Robby stood behind Frankie's wheelchair and looked at the newspaper.

E X T R A

ORPHANED DUKE KIDNAPPED

By Thadeus Lowry

The same photograph of Robby sitting on his suitcase was on the front page. The caption read: *Save the life of this child!*

A sub-headline read: STAR COLLECTS THE RANSOM. YOU, TOO, CAN GIVE.

In the silence of Frankie's and Marie's reading, Robby also read:

> Little Robby Burnes, the 10-year-old Duke of Pladroman, who arrived on these shores a scant two days ago, has been kidnapped.
>
> *The New York Star* has set up a special fund—The Robby Burnes Ransom Fund—in hopes of fulfilling the ransom demands of those holding the child in captivity.
>
> The Lord is an orphan.
>
> After the special bylined report by this correspondent appearing in yesterday's *New York Star*, regaling the harrowing and horrendous adventures which have befallen the 10-year-old scion of one of England's most noble families in escaping war-torn England, more misfortune has befallen the blond, blue-eyed, 10-year-old-boy who yesterday captured the hearts of all New York.
>
> And all New York—every New Yorker, every reader of *The New York Star*, every American—you, dear reader—are asked to contribute to the poor little Duke's return to safekeeping.

Ransom

> The kidnappers telephoned your *New York Star* correspondent last night and demanded ransom of $100,000 to be raised by public subscription and paid at once—or else.

The voice on the other end of the telephone wire was cold and menacing—surely that of a man who has lived a degenerate, degraded life far outside the law. There was no doubt on the part of your *New York Star* correspondent that the caller would stop at nothing to attain his ends, however foul these ends are.

Immediately, *The New York Star* presses were stopped. The front page was ordered remade.

What matters the tides of battles, the oratory of heads of states, when the specter hovers over the city of a little lost boy, cowering in some cold corner, starved and beaten, a knife at his throat?

Fate

Is this American?

Can not even one small boy find peace and security, warmth and love, for one day on these shores that have hosted millions of the poor and needy of other lands, without being confronted by fear and violence, his life imperiled anew?

What are those abroad who send their children to us for safekeeping during these dire days to think?

"I can take anything," the 10-year-old boy had said the day before, in speaking of his recent past, both parents having been murdered by a Nazi bomb, his school friends lost, a harrowing escape across the cold, storm-tossed North Atlantic dodging torpedoes.

The 10-year-old boy did not know what fate, what new horrors awaited him on these shores he had approached so trustingly.

Spirit

Yesterday morning, Robby Burnes (as the 10-year-old Duke of Pladroman democratically calls himself), up from a bed soft but new to him, comforted by the family of your *New York Star* correspondent, who had guaranteed his safekeeping in the United States to the government of Great Britain, full of specially ordered kippered herring, muffins and weak tea—his favorite breakfast—set off for his first day of school in the new land.

As he started bravely down the street, he turned back and

waved gaily, full of confidence, at the loving, proud couple in the door seeing him off.

The night before, over a special family celebration dinner of roast duck and sausage and plum pudding with his loving guardians, he insisted that next day he would seek out the school himself, settle himself in, and make his own way, in the true American spirit.

But little Robby Burnes never reached the local public school.

Mum

No word was heard of him until the cold, menacing voice of the kidnapper telephoned your correspondent at *The New York Star* last night.

One hundred thousand dollars in exchange for the freedom—almost certainly, the very life—of a 10-year-old orphan.

The publisher and editorial staff of *The New York Star* reached the decision without hesitation to set up a special fund for the return of Robby Burnes. Our prestige abroad, as a responsible people full of heart, is at stake.

Would you have the free world think of America as a place where a child, sent for safekeeping, disappears within 24 hours?

Robby's mum, the late Duchess of Pladroman, was known as one of England's most charitable ladies. She would rush to benefit any worthy cause, especially any cause concerning the welfare and safety of children.

Consider what your own freedom is worth. Of more importance to you, we are sure, consider what the safety and freedom of your own child is worth.

Send whatever you can afford—a dollar, five dollars or more—to The Robby Burnes Ransom Fund, care of this correspondent, *The New York Star*, to help regain the freedom, save the life of this child!

" 'A little lost boy, cowering in some cold corner, starved and beaten, a knife at his throat'!" expostulated Marie Savallo. "My God, Frankie, this is terrible. I'll go find Will'um at once."

• • •

No matter how many times Robby tested his clothes during the day, they remained wet. He did not fancy making his escape into a New York winter without stockings, shirt or underwear. Although aware of his duty as an Englishman, Robby was also aware that he ought not to turn out improperly attired.

At the kitchen table he helped Frankie Savallo with the picture puzzle, which was not at all easy. As the picture developed, Robby discovered it was of the Sahara Desert, which has no landmarks. Fitting pictures of sand which were as big as the top of his finger to other pictures of sand, with neither color nor shape to distinguish piece from piece, soon became one of the more arduous tasks of his life.

Midafternoon, Marie appeared in the door again. This time her arms were stuffed with newspapers.

"Oh, Frankie!" she wailed. "I couldn't find Will'um at all!"

Robby helped her spread the newspapers on the kitchen table. Under the newspapers pieces of the puzzle separated.

HAVE YOU SEEN ROBBY BURNES? shrieked *The New York Star*. There, on the front page, was the same picture of Robby, disembodied. Only his head remained, staring at the reader with such pathos that even Robby himself felt a tinge of sympathy.

E X C L U S I V E

$10,000 TOWARDS $100,000 RAISED
STAR PUBLISHER DONATES $5,000

BY THADEUS LOWRY

Someone has seen Robby Burnes—of that New York Police are certain.

A 10-year-old boy cannot disappear off the streets of New York in broad daylight without someone seeing him.

Have you seen Robby Burnes?

Already, after the report by this correspondent in this morning's *Star*, $10,000 has been pledged to The Robby Burnes Ransom Fund.

The first $5,000 was donated by the publisher of *The New York Star*.

By decision of the publisher of *The New York Star*, after consultation with New York City Police and the Federal

Bureau of Investigation, this amount—$10,000—will be given to anyone coming forward with information leading to the rescue of Robby Burnes and the arrest and conviction of his kidnappers.

Uniform

A ransom of $100,000, to be raised from the public, the readers of *The New York Star*, has been demanded by the kidnappers for the safe return of Robby Burnes.

Certainly those involved in his kidnapping—those who know where Robby Burnes is—have seen him.

Distinctive in appearance, the 10-year-old Robert Duke of Pladroman, who arrived, an orphan, after harrowing adventures from war-torn Europe Wednesday, when last seen was still wearing his English school uniform—a blue cap, blue overcoat, blue kneesocks, blue shorts and jacket, white shirt and striped tie.

Emblazoned on both his cap and jacket pocket is the Wolsley School emblem—a stag sharpening his antlers against an oak tree . . .

The report then went on to recap Thadeus Lowry's Thursday morning story of Robby's arrival and Friday morning's story of his kidnapping, plus instructions to the reader how to subscribe to the Robby Burnes Ransom Fund.

All the other Friday afternoon newspapers which Marie Savallo had brought home clutched to her breast in a jumble reported the juiciest elements of the story which had appeared that morning in "another New York newspaper." At least two of the newspapers announced they were cooperating with "another New York newspaper" to help raise the ransom. Contributions could be sent directly to them.

Robby was reported as ten years old in all the newspapers, which pleased him but made him doubt the accuracy of journalism.

"They've got ten thousand dollars already, Frankie," Marie said, "between breakfast and lunch!"

"And look what they're doin' with it!" shouted Frankie. "The first money they've got they're out lookin' for us with it! They've put bloodhounds on us!"

"A fearful lot of money," said Marie with awe. "Ten thousand dollars. Perhaps we should accept it as a reward, Frankie?"

"Read what it says, Marie! You need a conviction to get a reward! That means somebody has to become a convict. Who are you gonna convict? Frankie Savallo?"

"No, no, darlin'. I wouldn't think of it."

Frankie had wheeled to the windows overlooking the alley at the back of the apartment. He pulled down the green shades. "Lissen, Marie. You sure nobody saw you with the kid?"

"I can't be sure, darlin', but I was circumspect in me comin'. But wasn't it yourself who shouted 'Kidnap!' for all the world to hear the first hour we were at home?"

"I never said a word out loud, Marie. I swear to God!"

" 'Swear to God!' You swore so the whole street could hear you, let alone saints Mary and Margaret takin' their well-earned rest."

"You've done a terrible thing, Marie!" Frankie shook his head violently. "Terrible!"

"I may have done, at that," admitted Marie. "But, Frankie, how are we goin' to get the ransom, if it all keeps goin' to reward money?"

The Savallos remained quietly at home that evening. Frankie played with the radio dial. Each time a news broadcast began he changed the dial to a station offering a comedy or music program. Wordlessly Marie cleaned the one-room apartment as might a woman expecting a great many guests, a wedding or a funeral—or as might a woman expecting to leave the apartment for a prolonged period of time.

During the evening there came a knock on the door. "*Hoosh, Frankie!*" hushed Marie. Frankie snapped the radio off. Marie stood still, listening. The knock was repeated. Marie put her index finger to her lips. Shortly they heard steps retreat down the corridor. Only after a restless fifteen minutes did Frankie click on the radio again.

Trying not to be noticed, Robby tested his clothes hanging on the line time and again. He decided that whatever Marie had done in washing them had made them permanently wet. After a supper of potatoes and bread in warm milk—"Eat up," Frankie said grimly to Robby. "At least she can't say it's Italian"—Robby crawled into the cot to keep warm and, while his clothes tried their best to dry, fell asleep.

• • •

EXCLUSIVE

Robby's picture stared out from all of the Saturday newspapers, except *The New York Times*, and they all repeated, with imaginative variations of their own, except *The New York Times*, the legend of Robby Burnes as first written by Thadeus Lowry.

Marie's slinking in and out of the one-room apartment, her coat collar up, her eyes sliding left and right, buying all the editions of all the New York newspapers, clutching to her breast all these pictures of Robby looking pathetic might have indicated her uncommon interest in the crime to a casual observer. Such a casual observer, if pragmatic, might then have called the cops. But, as Robby had already discovered, people in this large city were not apt to be casual observers. For the most part, he had reasoned, they were too wary of being observed themselves.

Again *The New York Star* led the press and ran the EXCLUSIVE banner line.

NEW THREAT TO ROBBY'S LIFE
$27,242 Raised So Far
Your Help Needed
Police Perplexed

By Thadeus Lowry

Again last night your correspondent for *The New York Star* was confronted by the icy, menacing voice of the kidnapper of 10-year-old Robby Burnes.

He called, he said, regarding a report by this correspondent in last night's *Star*. Your correspondent reported in last night's *Star* that the first $10,000 raised for the release of Robby Burnes would be used as a reward for anyone coming forward with information leading to the discovery and return of Robby Burnes and the arrest and conviction of his kidnappers.

The first $5,000 was donated to The Robby Burnes Ransom Fund by the publisher of *The New York Star*.

The cold, metallic voice said that if any of the ransom money were used as a reward, or even as an offer of a reward for information leading to the capture and conviction of the kidnappers, "the kid won't live to say his prayers on Sunday."

Efforts to trace the telephone call were frustrated by electronic failure. Telephone executives said the trace only led back to a police station monitoring the call.

The publisher of *The New York Star*, in conjunction with the New York Police, instantly withdrew the offer of a reward.

Good Job

New York City Police are perplexed by the disappearance of the 10-year-old Duke of Pladroman.

"This is a real professional job," said Police Captain Walter Reagan, in charge of the case. "These kidnappers knew what they were doing."

Repeating "it was a real clean job," Captain Reagan speculated yesterday that an extensive, well-trained gang of professional criminals had this kidnapping planned long before previously thought possible.

Conjecture is that while Robby Burnes was waving goodbye to his loving guardians Thursday morning on his way to school, a net had already been prepared by this unknown professional gang of kidnappers.

"It was neat work," said Captain Reagan. "I take my hat off to them."

Riveter

So far, $27,242 has been raised toward the $100,000 ransom demanded for little Robby Burnes.

Not enough, if the life of Robby Burnes is to be saved!

Kind people have been giving their hard-earned money unstintingly to The Robby Burnes Ransom Fund.

The children at Manhattan Public School 169 (the school to which Robby Burnes was going Thursday when he was kidnapped) Friday donated $47.

"It's really our War Bond money," said Clarissa Allbright, a student caught in the schoolyard after school. "Principal said for once we can give without interest."

St. Theresa's Parish, in the Bronx, is having a special Holy Name Bingo Evening tonight. Profits will go to The Robby Burnes Ransom Fund.

Bingo organizer Guido Savallo said, "It's the least we can do. Kidnapping a kid's a terrible thing. I mean, stealin's one thing, but stealin' a kid . . . you know? I mean, you can tell whoever'd do a thing like that don't have no family of his own, you know what I mean?"

"I want to donate $1 to The Fund to get the little Duke back," said Mrs. Morris Blumgarten, 82, of Brooklyn. "How would I feel if my husband didn't come home from work one night?"

Thomas (Tootsie) Auchinchlos, just back from a vacation in Florida, donated $116. "That's okay," said the Manhattan street-worker. "I won it on the ponies anyway."

One donation, of $20, was signed, simply, "Rosey the Riveter."

A bowling club in Huntington, workers in a Newark paint factory, an infantry troop at Fort Dix about to go overseas, perhaps never to return—all have given to The Robby Burnes Ransom Fund.

What about you?

"Uncle Guido!" Frankie Savallo screamed as if he could communicate with his uncle directly through the newspaper. "Whaddaya mean? Whaddaya mean 'Kidnappin' a kid's a terrible thing'? Always criticizin' me! Read this, Marie! It's Uncle Guido, runnin' the bingo up in the Bronx. Right here he says, 'You can tell whoever'd do a thing like that don't have no family . . . ' My own Uncle Guido said that! Right here in the newspaper! About me!"

"Hoosh, Frankie. It's all right."

"Here, I fall off a roof for him in the middle of the night, spend the rest of my life in a wheelchair, and here in the newspaper he says I ain't got no family! My own Uncle Guido!"

"Frankie, you know he's just sayin' that for the Holy Name," Marie soothed. "None of that bingo money will see anythin' but the darkness of his own pocket. Now you know that, don't you, darlin'?"

"Yeah, but Marie—insultin' me here in the newspaper. My own Uncle Guido! What does he mean I don't have no family of my own? I got my Uncle Guido, don't I? Whatsa matter with him?"

"Console yourself, Frankie. Here's this policeman sayin' it's a nice professional job and he takes his hat off to us."

" 'Nice professional job'! Even the cops say it's a 'nice professional job.' And my own Uncle Guido says it's notta nice!"

"Calm yourself, Frankie. Your Uncle Guido would be jealous, if he knew."

The New York Times, on page thirty-six, also reported the kidnapping of Robby. Or reported its having been reported.

Boy Reported Kidnapped

It has been reported by *The New York Star* that Robert James Saint James Burnes Walter Farhall-Pladroman, S.Nob., son of the late William Duke of Pladroman, was kidnapped in New York City Thursday.

A ransom of $100,000 is demanded by the kidnappers to be raised by public subscription. The boy arrived in New York Wednesday aboard an evacuation ship from England. He is eight years old.

"Hunh!" said Frankie at this last report of a report. "Fat lot of good *The New York Times* does us!"

"But it's right!" chirped Robby. "It says I'm eight years old!"

And the Saturday evening edition of *The New York Star* reported that the Robby Burnes Ransom Fund was up to forty-two thousand dollars.

"Look at that!" exclaimed Frankie. "Forty-two thousand dollars!"

And he looked at Robby with a new appreciation.

"That's all well and good," questioned Marie in a soft voice, "but how do we get the money?"

Frankie thought about that quietly.

"Do you think you might swallow your pride, Frankie darlin'," Marie asked gently, "and ask your Uncle Guido how we collect all this perfectly marvelous ransom people have put up for us?"

"My Uncle Guido!" scoffed Frankie. "He's not my uncle anymore! He says I don't have a family!"

"Anyway, Frankie . . ." Marie studied her fingers fanned out on the kitchen table. "Precious little of the ransom we'd see if your Uncle Guido collected it for us."

"My Uncle Guido—" Frankie began his expostulatory aria. And he sang and he sang and he sang. He sang high on the scale, and low on the scale. He recited, he declaimed, he reflected. Uncle Guido had never given him much encouragement, he remembered. Uncle Guido had stolen a bicycle for Tony—not Frankie. Uncle Guido bought off the police the time Tony stole the mail truck; he never did such a thing for Frankie. Uncle Guido gave Tony a job smashing the windows of stores which were late paying protection to Uncle Guido; Frankie had to work putting eggs in boxes in a huge, cold warehouse. Uncle Guido gave Tony a new mohair suit; he sent Frankie up onto an icy roof five stories high. Now Tony came and went as he wanted, and Frankie was in a wheelchair. All because of Uncle Guido! Frankie was inconsolable. Frankie was heartbroken that Uncle Guido should criticize him that way in the public press. "Uncle Guido! Columbus!"

Supper was potatoes and french toast. Frankie wailed all through it. Robby took supper as an excuse to dress in his now dry stockings, underwear, shirt and tie.

After supper, while Frankie continued to expostulate in his chair, Marie undressed him, and bathed him with a sponge. Robby watched from the cot. Like most domestic routines, this scene was enacted without either participant speaking directly of it. Frankie could not undress himself without great difficulty, could not fetch water from the kitchen sink, could not wash himself thoroughly. Therefore Marie did it. And when Marie lifted Frankie bodily from the chair, a look in Frankie's eyes communicated with Robby more completely than could any five-act opera. Frankie's powerful arms were around Marie's neck. Although they were helping him to pull himself up, they were pulling himself up against her strength. Robby saw Frankie's eyes over Marie's bent shoulder. *You shouldn't be here, kid*, Frankie's eyes said to Robby. *No way you should be here.*

So, later, after the radio was off and Marie had helped Frankie lift himself from the wheelchair into his cot and Frankie's eyes had signalled the same message to Robby, *You shouldn't be here*, and the lights were off and Marie was snuzzling in her separate cot and the problem of how they could collect the ransom had not been solved, Robby solved the problem by removing it: Quietly he turned back the blankets of his cot, stepped into his shoes, knotted the strings, tiptoed to his overcoat and cap on a chair, picked them up, tiptoed to the door, and opened it.

"Robby?" Frankie whispered from his cot.

Robby stood still in the open door.

"Good luck, kid. Thanks for helpin' me with the picture puzzle."

Robby closed the door behind him quietly, and tiptoed down the corridor.

16

Philology

Robby escaped.

However, the question presented itself almost immediately upon his arrival on the dark stoop outside the Savallos' tenement that, although escaping is All Well and Good, clearly the Right Thing to Do, to where does one escape in America when one is escaping? From what Robby could see, America was all over the United States. And thus far in America Robby had been left shivering on a dock for eight hours, force-marched through a snowstorm, plied with liquor, starved, robbed of his parents' pictures, marched some more, mugged, starved some more, insulted, sent off on a fool's mission (to find a school in a land where there obviously aren't any), kidnapped, nearly suffocated in an underground train, and finally fed while the adults at table casually talked of his eventual dismemberment. He had escaped . . . but from what? Jam, lamb and eventual dismemberment. He was to press on relentlessly . . . but to where?

Subsequently, Robby was to decide that rhetoric is not unlike marmalade: It's exciting enough to take into one's system, but after a slightly sticky sensation turning vapid in one's innards, one is left with little substance other than having had a sweet illusion.

Before him America lay dark and still. He was on the top of a stoop at the top of a T-intersection. The road before him seemed to go nowhere but along itself; it was lightless and changeless. The street that ran from his left to his right was identical in its rightness and leftness; neither side had any characteristic which made him decide in its favor. Robby had already learned that walking blocks and blocks and blocks in New York was no guarantee of getting anywhere, even when one had an idea of where one wanted to get. Both streets before him were broken with potholes and curbs which had not withstood the weight of time. What little light there was reflected icily from the streets' black surfaces. Black snow formed ranges between sidewalks and streets. The hundred or more windows he saw in the brick buildings around him were blind with drawn shades. Smashed vegetable crates and excelsior from Saturday's market hours littered the sidewalks and streets.

To that point in his life Robby had not had great experience in making choices. He had never had to decide before where he was going, because he had always been told. He was going to breakfast, to chapel, to class, to luncheon, to nap, to sports, to tea, to commons, to bed. He was going 'round with Tom the driver to the garage to get petrol for the Rolls; he was going to the zoo; he was going to the Thesigers' for tea. There had always been some place to go; the future was downstream and to get there all one had to do was flow along nicely. Standing on the stoop, Robby even wondered if he might not sneak back into the Savallos' kitchen apartment and whisper-ask Frankie, now that Robby had escaped, where was he supposed to go—but, no, Robby remembered that Frankie seldom went out these days. The last place Frankie had gone had been five stories up to an icy roof on a dark night, from which he had descended involuntarily and speedily.

When escaping from a kidnap situation, Robby expected a logical place to go would be to the police. But the police, in the figure of Will'um, had known of Robby's plight and done nothing to encourage his freedom except advise the kidnappers, share their dinner with them, and recommend dismemberment. Robby had heard his father say that police control crime, but it was an education to Robby to discover how precisely, directly and deliberately police control crime. Subsequently, Robby would phrase the reality of crime as a perfect syllogism. Crime exists; police exist: *ergo* crime and police coexist.

Frankie had already appealed to His Majesty's Ambassador to
the United States and even if Frankie hadn't expressed himself
clearly regarding the captivity of Robby Burnes, whoever answered
the embassy's phones clearly expressed complete indifference. Perhaps there would be more concern if the embassy knew that Robby
was no longer sheltered nor fed, but Robby had understood one
fact regarding the British embassy above all others: It was *a long
distance.* Supposedly the school to which he had been assigned
was within the neighborhood of the Lowrys' flat, and he had never
gotten there. *A long distance* in America, Robby already understood, was prohibitive.

Robby wondered where the Evacuation Ladies might be found
on a late Saturday evening. At least they knew his name. They had
called it enough. They knew Burnes, Robert as coming between
Adowitz, Abraham and Collins, Peter. Robby envisioned the Evacuation Ladies' Saturday evening as sitting around a warm parlor in
cardigans practicing their roll-calling. Besides having no idea how
to contact the Evacuation Ladies, Robby's pride came to the fore.
On Wednesday Robby had been a problem which the Evacuation
Ladies had solved to their own satisfaction. Problems solved on
Wednesdays should not reappear on Saturday evenings. It would
disappoint them. Possibly make them think they'd shirked their
work.

And Thadeus Lowry. Shivering on the stoop Robby thought
long and hard about Thadeus Lowry. Contacting Thadeus Lowry
would be easy. All he need do was ask anybody—if there happened to be anybody around. Everyone knew Thadeus Lowry of
The New York Star, had said Thadeus Lowry of *The New York Star.*
Thadeus Lowry might be glad to see him. Thadeus Lowry had
done several days' work now, Wednesday, Thursday, Friday, and,
Robby presumed, Saturday, and might be glad to return to one of
the clubs where he was a regular and discuss again the time in
1938 when the Bishop stole the altar plate. Doubtlessly all this
work would have been damaging to Thadeus Lowry, in his *chérie's*
terms, brutal, in his own, absolutely exhausting. However, Robby
was shrewd enough to realize Thadeus Lowry might not be glad to
see him. He and Ronald Jasper had discussed that Thadeus Lowry
had not had a good story since the Bishop stole the altar plate in
1938 and that Thadeus Lowry stood on such thin ice regarding his
continued employment at the newspaper that he was getting water

on the knee. It was clear to Robby that Thadeus Lowry had a good story now. The Thadeus Lowry byline had been on the front page of *The New York Star* three days running. Even *The New York Times* had reported the news that Thadeus Lowry had a story. The goal of one hundred thousand dollars raised from the public via Thadeus Lowry's prose had been set. Robby tried to envision the expression on the face of Thadeus Lowry if Robby—when less than half the money had been raised—skipped gaily into the city room of *The New York Star* chirruping some playful ditty as "Never fear, Uncle dear, I'm here" between editions. The expression on Thadeus Lowry's face might be similar to that on the face of Frankie Savallo on that dark night just after leaving a roof five stories above the ground and discovering he couldn't fly.

Besides, reasoned Robby, Thadeus Lowry and his wife had a disdain for food which Robby did not share. In the short time Robby had spent with Thadeus Lowry, Robby had discovered that being well-fed was an illusion to which Thadeus Lowry clung most fervidly and uselessly. He dreamed meals, luncheons, teas, dinners and breakfasts before they happened and after they had never happened. He even reported savory meals in the newspaper, dinner of roast duck, sausage and plum pudding, breakfast of kippered herring, muffins and weak tea which no one had ever savored. Robby knew he had had chowder biscuits, bread, water and catsup.

Robby thus came to make his first mature decision in the most mature way. His criterion was that element upon which all worthy decisions are made, the fulcrum upon which everyone decides where he will *go* next, what he will *do* next, upon which all life plans and employment projections are settled, upon which nations are constructed and collapsed, governments are elected and ejected, revolutions are raised and subsided, wars started and stopped. Robby decided on behalf of his stomach. He was going to *go* where there was food; he was going to *do* whatever was necessary to eat. So decide we all.

Robby considered where he had seen food since arriving in this land of milk and honey. Why, to make the legend good: *right in front of him!* In bringing him to her home, Marie Savallo had marched Robby through an open-air market full of oranges and apples and bananas and melons and potatoes and tomatoes and heads of lettuce and cabbages and sausages and hams and pudent chickens and food Robby had never even seen before. And the market was right in front of him! At most, down half a block and through that building full of animal carcasses now closed. In the dark it did not look it, it did not seem possible that this landscape was the fringe of an area peopled with aproned men and women all trying to empty their pushcarts full of food. Having a memory of the past, Robby knew a hope for the future.

He decided to stay right where he was. He decided to *go* nowhere.

Yet it would be a long night, and a cold one. Standing on the Savallos' stoop he already knew it to be a long night and a cold one. He needed shelter. An enclosed place, off the snow and out of the wind. A place where he had some hope of snuggling into warmth.

The landscape didn't offer much. At first he didn't think it offered anything at all. The stoops were solid, the cellar-ways fenced, the sidewalks and streets snowbound and slick. There was a small paneled truck parked at the curb in front of him.

He went down to the van, tried the handle of the back door, and, to his surprise, it opened. With his hands he rummaged around inside. On the floor of the van were burlap sacks of potatoes. He had shelter, food, and a place to snuggle himself into warmth.

He had reasoned, sought, and found.

Robby climbed into the back of the paneled truck, pulled the door closed behind him, snuggled among the sacks of potatoes and, having recapitulated ontogeny, fell asleep.

• • •

Robby felt and heard a door slam.

Then he heard and felt an engine start.

The motor was making the paneled truck vibrate.

Robby's shelter began to move down the street, away, he feared, from his source of food.

Tossing off the potato sacks, Robby crawled forward and pressed his nose against the glass separating him from the cab. There were no streetlights. Cars and trucks in the wartime streets had hooded headlights. He had only a three-quarter view of the head of the man driving the van.

Yet Robby knew it was Tony Savallo.

He sank back against the potato sacks under the little window. *Good old Tony Savallo. Loving Tony Savallo. He placed the clear, tight skin of his hand against my cheek and tousled my hair. Masculine Tony Savallo. Smelled of lead pencils, as a man should smell of something. Kind and gentle Tony Savallo, a man of peace. Wouldn't go to war; rather help his uncle run bingo for the church. Calm and still Tony Savallo. Said little but "thank you." Slept with the dignity of a kingly sarcophagus at Westminster. Wise, understanding Tony Savallo. Understood more than greed in Marie's kidnapping me, perceived her loneliness and compassion and love. Good old Tony Savallo!*

The van slowed, stopped.

Robby got up again, knelt on the potato sacks, pressed his nose and cheeks against the small, thick window. Behind the driver's wheel, Tony was looking through his open window. He was watching a man walking along the sidewalk. Robby could see the man as a walking silhouette against an empty lot covered with fairly white snow. Tony was pointing something through the window, at the man.

There was a colossal bang.

On the sidewalk the man's back curved. His arms rose above his head. His hat fell off.

There was another colossal bang.

The man staggered sideways on a colt's legs, then crumpled. He sank beneath the knee-high wall of snow.

Robby inhaled, deeply, quickly. His scream rose in volume and pitch. It scraped his throat and vibrated his nose. *Tony shot a man!* Robby screamed even louder and higher on the exhale. *Tony murdered somebody!*

Tony Savallo's eyes, showing vast white areas around the steady brown pupils, appeared in the window. His face had an expression. It was first the expression of horror, then of rage. His face disappeared.

Robby screamed again. The van jerked into gear. Robby fell back onto the potato sacks. The van moved quickly, took corner after corner at high speed, its rear wheels slipping. Robby was rolled left, then right, then left again.

Finally rolling over, Robby spread his knees and his hands wide, got his balance, and worked his way up to the window again. Tony's right hand worked the shift lever and swung the wheel. His left hand steadied the wheel despite its still having a gun in it.

Robby saw the van beginning to pull up at a curb of a narrow street. He darted for the back door.

As soon as the truck stopped, Robby opened the door and jumped out. He slipped on the ice and sprawled on the ground. He saw Tony Savallo's feet land on the ground.

Quickly, Robby scurried under the van.

He watched Tony's feet step up into the back of the van. He heard Tony kicking and tossing potato sacks around.

Tony's sneakers appeared on the street, behind the van. For a moment they did not move. Then lightly, silently, quickly they moved onto the curb, over a low mound of snow. As Tony moved into the alley, Robby could see, from under the truck, that Tony carried the gun in his right hand.

"Whup, whup," said Robby. Lying under the truck at first his legs made a running motion but got him nowhere. "Whup!" Robby ordered. His body organized itself and Robby dragged himself out from under the truck. He became upright. He ran across the street and began to run down the alley opposite from the one taken by Tony.

Robby ran down the middle of the block, across a street and into the next alley. Even though he assured himself no one, not even Tony Savallo, would spot a small, dark figure pumping down a narrow dark alley, Robby ran as fast as he could. Then he remembered the backs of his knees were white and probably as easy to spot as a bunny's tail in short grass. Then he reasoned that Tony Savallo, being more than twice his size, doubtlessly could run more than twice as fast. Then he recalled from Frankie's comments, Marie's comments, his own observations, that one didn't *hear* Tony Savallo, one *felt his presence*. Robby felt the presence of Tony Savallo. Then Robby turned his head.

Tony Savallo, gun in hand, appearing to lope easily like a young cheetah out for a preprandial turn in the bush—his face expressionless, the brown of his eyes steady in skies of white—was right behind him.

Robby ran faster than any classmate or games master would ever think possible. However, while running, Robby realized this effort to outrun Tony Savallo down dark, slippery alleys held little future for him.

He took the closest turning, into a yard where a car was up on blocks. Without slowing even slightly, he headed toward a fence

which was at least three times his own height. He had no conviction that he could jump the fence. If he had had opportunity to
study the matter more at that point in his life, Robby would have
known a human being cannot jump a fence three times his own
height, without aid. Being ignorant of such conclusions, Robby
jumped. However carefully scientists figure all contingent elements
into their measurements and equations, sometimes they are ignorant, too, of the human element, which, in this instance, was sheer
terror.

"Whup, whup!"

Robby saw the top of the fence pass beneath him and then the
ground rush up to greet him. He landed on his feet, knees slightly
bent, on cobbled stone.

Crouching, Robby panted and looked around some householder's backyard. In the moonlight he could see that the house
along one entire side of the square backyard was brick. There were
no lights on. The basement door, down a step or two, had an iron
grille over it. In the yard were a few odd boxes, small, round
objects which may have been discarded flower pots, and rubbish
barrels with lids on them.

In a moment Tony Savallo would clamber over the fence Robby
had so astonishingly vaulted.

As noiselessly as possible, with the aid of packed snow, Robby
climbed into a rubbish barrel. He squirmed down, and reset the lid
on top. Like a mole, trying not to rock the barrel much, he burrowed down into the rubbish. He tossed some old newspapers,
cartons, and bottles over his back, shoulders and head. Scrunched
thusly, Robby tried to recall some Resounding Rhetoric, from
Church or State, encouraging someone Hiding Under Garbage, but
nothing came to mind.

He heard nothing.

Until he heard, in almost the exact tone Frankie had used in
whispering good-bye to him, "Robby? Hey, Duke?"

Tony Savallo's voice, just outside Robby's rubbish barrel, was
calm and gentle.

Robby tried not to breathe. Considering the stink of the air he
had to breathe it was comparatively easy for him to breathe little.

"Hey, Duke!"

Something in the rubbish barrel (other than Robby) moved. To
keep it quiet, Robby clamped his hand over it. From its contours

(although he had never held one before) he guessed (rightly) his coinhabitant of the rubbish barrel was a mouse. Its heartbeat was frantic in Robby's hand.

The air improved. Tony had removed the lid of the rubbish barrel.

"Hey, Duke? You're here somewhere. I know that. I'll hurt you less if you give up now, kid."

Robby, deciding he didn't want to be hurt at all, remained silent.

The lid to the rubbish barrel was replaced. It was not on tight. Robby could feel a draft of air.

"Duke?" Tony's voice, intermittently questioning the air, faded. "Robby?"

Not being able to hear Tony, Robby never was sure when Tony left the yard. After a while, Robby felt less of Tony's presence and made himself more comfortable in the rubbish barrel. Still keeping some rubbish over him, Robby sat on the bottom layer of newspapers and leaned his back against the barrel's curved side.

He brought the mouse to his lap and played with it. He walked it from hand to hand. He tried to hand-feed it some of the commissary from the barrel: eggshells, coffee grounds, cigarette ashes. He could not tell in the dark if the mouse was actually eating the menu, or just investigating each piece offered.

In time, the mouse's heartbeat slowed, as did Robby's.

• • •

In the first light of day Robby knelt in the rubbish barrel. He lifted the lid in its center, and, using the rim of the barrel as a turret, had a good look around.

Tony Savallo was nowhere in the yard. Closely Robby scrutinized the top rails of the three sides of fencing. On one board stood a drooped, bedraggled blue jay, looking as if it had spent the evening with Thadeus Lowry. The bird assured Robby no one else was around. There was no door in any of the three fences.

Robby leaned the lid of the rubbish barrel against the barrel's side and stood up. He put the mouse in his overcoat pocket. He arranged the pocket's flap so the mouse would have air to breathe. Then he climbed out of the barrel and replaced the lid.

Intellectually, Robby knew that only hours before he had leaped over that fence in a single bound. Now looking at it in the light of day he swallowed hard. If he had done such a thing once, he must be able to do it twice, but he didn't think so. Backing up across the yard, he contemplated what a running start might do for him and decided not much. Perhaps nighttime terror had taken him over the fence once, but daytime reason would smash him against the fence as certain as the King was English. There were too few boxes to pile up against the fence so he could climb over. He considered a combination of boxes and rubbish barrels might build him a stairway over the fence. The narrow brick house was silent. Dragging a rubbish barrel over the cobblestones would be noisy.

He went down the two steps, put his hand through the grille, turned the handle of the basement door and pushed. It swung open. The basement was pitch black. He pushed the grille and it, too, swung open. Robby stepped into the basement, closed the grille, and closed the door behind him. Then he couldn't find the handle of the door again, to open it, to let in light.

Across the basement from him was a live, red and yellow, glowing thing. Robby stared back at it. It grew neither more nor less threatening. Then, suddenly, it did flare, grew bigger, redder. There was a wheeze and a dreadful clanking. The noise crossed the basement to him until it was directly overhead. Heat descended upon him. The increased light from the furnace permitted Robby to see its staunch squatness, its ungainly, octopus arms extending, twisting and turning throughout the basement and into the ceiling.

It also permitted him to find the cellar stairs.

On tiptoe he crept up the cellar stairs to the door at the top. Very slowly he turned the doorknob and pushed the door open a few centimeters. He put his face close to the door and peered through the slit between door and door frame.

A woman, entirely naked, stood in the kitchen with a coffeepot in her hand. Startled, she did not turn her head. Only her eyes darted to Robby, then swelled. She threw the coffeepot and hit the cellar door.

Then she screamed.

Robby pushed open the door and ran into the kitchen. He was looking for a door which would let him out of the kitchen. However he was stopped in his tracks, distracted, fascinated by the dance the woman proceeded to do. She began jumping up and down, one leg at a time, as if pedaling a bicycle. Her hands darted from her breasts to her crotch and back again in a great flurry as if she were sending a very urgent message by semaphore.

Her eyes remained round and staring.

"Morning, sir, ma'am."

She released one arm from its futile duty long enough to reach to the sink board, pick up a bottle of milk and hurl it at him. It smashed against the wall just over his shoulder, providing plain evidence that her aim was improving. Still doing her silly dance, she moved forward to the stove and grabbed a frying pan by its handle.

Robby pushed backwards through a swing door, turned around and found himself in the main corridor of the house.

A man in a bathrobe, his hand on the bannister, was rushing down the stairs. "Where are my glasses?" he shouted. "What's happening?"

The front door was directly in front of Robby. He ran for it, yanked it open, and scurried through it.

The man, his arms outstretched to grab Robby, dashed into the edge of the open door. "Damn!" he yelled, putting his hand to his face.

The naked lady, still wielding the frying pan, stood on the other side of the man in the front hall.

Robby reached in and pulled the door closed with a slam.

"Damn, damn!" Robby heard through the door.

"A boy!" the woman hollered. "He came up out of our basement! A thief!"

Standing on the front stoop of their house, Robby looked left. And he looked right. And he looked directly across the street.

And directly across the street, leaning against a lamp post, in his green windbreaker, arms folded across his chest, stood Tony Savallo.

The door behind Robby began to open.

17

Taking Stock

"Thief! You little thief!"

Robby jumped off the steps and began running along the sidewalk to his right. Behind him, standing on the steps of his house in his bathrobe stood the householder slandering Robby in a loud voice. Across the street, not far behind him, trotting easily, was Tony Savallo.

"Whup, whup," Robby encouraged himself.

Sunday-dressed people were gathered around a newspaper kiosk on the corner. Some were examining their front pages; others were chatting with each other. There were tall stacks of newspapers awaiting quarters. Leaning against the stacks, hanging from a telephone pole, propped against a No Parking sign, were large posters touched up in color—too much color, red! white! and blue!—of Robby looking cold, lost, hungry, forlorn, sitting on his suitcase. The poster line read:

HAVE YOU SEEN ROBBY?

Robby's blodgy face was on the front of every newspaper he saw. Dashing through the crowd he would have liked to have stopped and given the casual strollers on a nice Sunday morning greater opportunity to *see Robby* but as Tony Savallo was only a few steps behind him Robby decided it was preferable to keep himself a blurred streak. Breathless, the most he managed to utter on his quick passage through the group was "Whup!, whup!" which he knew to be an expression inadequate to his situation. Out of the corner of his eye he did catch the headline of *The New York Star*.

$63,000 RAISED FOR ROBBY

"Whup, whup!" Robby cried out plaintively to no effect, as he darted through the forest of knees. "Whup!"

Halfway down the block, across the street, there was a church. Its bells were tolling. Its doors were open. People were climbing the steps to it. In the street in front of the church were many, many black limousines.

Recollecting from his narrow reading, mostly of *Robin Hood*, that churches universally were regarded as places of sanctuary, Robby quickly decided to attend services. Nearly being hit by a large LaSalle, Robby ran across the street and up the church steps. He received a few sour looks from the parishioners for his shoving them around the knee joints in his hurry, but a few benign looks as well from grown-ups always glad to see the young hasten to suffer unto God.

An ornate, carved sign in the vestibule identified this as the CHURCH OF JESUS CHRIST MATERIALIST. A brass plaque below it notified people that the current pastor was the Reverend John Maple.

Looking back through silk stockings and striped trousers Robby saw a pair of sneakered feet making its way through the mob at the top of the stairs. Apparently Tony Savallo was not going to hold as sacred the sanctity of the church. Clearly he had not read *Robin Hood*.

Robby entered the auditorium of the church, avoided the clogged main aisle, turned to his right, then left, and went down the right aisle. The church was nearly full. He took a seat in a pew just forward of a thick pillar. Two old ladies, one who had a great many chins and the other none at all, made more work of making room for him than was necessary. Their smiles were grimly righteous.

Catching his breath, Robby looked around him. It was a huge

church. In place of an altar was a long table with twelve chairs around it. The pulpit was high. In front of the podium at its top was an iron grille, but not of the sort he had seen in English churches. This grille was more like the grilles he had seen tellers sit behind when he had visited English banks.

The bars were thin and vertical; under them was a rectangular open space as if for passing things through. The woodwork of the pulpit had a symbol repeated on it a dizzying number of times. The symbol was a vertical "S" with two vertical lines through it.

Robby recalled that it was Sunday and that a cold, metallic voice had notified Thadeus Lowry that Robby might not live to say his prayers on Sunday. Robby found a shred of cabbage in his hair and dropped it on the floor. The women beside him were beginning to point their noses at him. Robby decided to pray.

He went forward onto the kneeler, folded his hands, and closed his eyes.

Oh, Lord! Giver of life, please don't take away mine while I'm still using it, he began.

The woman beside him, out loud and with some apparent distress, said, "Oh, Lord!"

Why bring me through this vale of sorrow and tears to this crazy place where ill-wishers lurk around every corner? For the paths of righteousness in this new land, unless tread upon carefully, surely lead straight to hell.

Someone else, possibly the man in front of Robby, was heard to say, "Oh, Lord!" Robby also heard a distinct sniffing from the ladies beside him.

Why not bring a scourge of locusts upon the houses and down the necks of all those ill-wishers who are trying to dismember me, in particular one Tony Savallo, who I'm beginning to suspect is behind me again?

Not meaning to question Your infinite wisdom, Sir, but how come I'm a hundred-thousand-dollar Duke made to lie down with mice in a rubbish barrel?

. . . Of course, in Your infinite wisdom and mercy I did discover I can run like hell . . .

The sound of sniffing was growing in a widening pool around Robby. Peeking through his clasped fingers, Robby saw a great many faces were turned toward him, and there was distress upon each face.

Oh, Lord, forgive me, your most unworthy servant, for coming into Your house of worship smelling like a garbage pail. Peeking again through his fingers, Robby saw the ladies beside him had moved as far away from him as possible—which wasn't far. *Perhaps it is Your Divine way of making these ladies beside me exercise the tolerance inherent in Your Divine Teachings.*

The Sniffing Was loud.

Oh, Lord, not a sparrow falls from a tree without Your gracious Eye upon it.

I was never sure what Your Grace, in His infinite wisdom and mercy, ever actually did about the sparrow once it clunked to the ground, but I promise to read that passage again, if I live.

Oh, Lord! Don't forget your tadpole!

Robby felt a sharp pain in his ribs. It was caused by the index finger of the lady of many chins sitting beside him. For a bad moment, Robby thought the ladies beside him, flunking Christian tolerance, were expelling him from the pew, having determined he enjoyed nothing akin to the odor of sanctity, and thus were sending him to his certain death. No, the organ was exhaling at a high volume and it was the need of the ladies that Robby stand with the rest of the congregation and raise his voice in song. Perhaps they thought they could be saved by having the air in their immediate vicinity vigorously stirred. They jammed an opened hymn book into his hands. "Silence Is Golden" was on the left page; "The Silver Tongue" on the right.

Robby did not know which song they were singing, so, with Divine Gusto, he sang one verse of one song and one verse of the other, alternating lines for the third chorus. This technique had always worked so well at Wolsley School that he had been permanently excused from choir practice.

The mouse in his coat pocket, doubtlessly invigorated by the joyful noise, scurried chirruping among the lint. Robby stroked the wee beastie with his thumb.

As the hymn was wearing down—especially around Robby, where people were looking at him again, as apparently his noise was not making them joyful—Pastor Maple climbed into the pulpit so slowly one would think his every step weighted by centuries of consideration. His robe was a peculiar shade of green. Stitched into the robe were faces and pictures Robby couldn't recognize, and the Arabic numbers 5, 10, 20, 50, 100, 1,000.

"Amen!" Robby always gave his best to every amen to make up for earlier transgressions with both words and music.

The congregation rustled onto their seats, coughing and blowing their noses pre-emptively.

Pastor Maple blessed the congregation by describing the letter S in the air with his hand, then slashing two vertical lines through it.

"*E Pluribus Unum,*" he announced.

The congregation hushed for the lesson.

"Take stock!

" 'Hearken: Behold there went out a sower to sow.

" 'And it came to pass, as he sowed, some fell by the wayside, and fowls of the air came and devoured it up.

" 'And some fell on stony ground, where it had not much earth, and immediately it sprang up, because it had no depth of earth; but when the sun was up, it was scorched; and because it had no root, it withered away.

" 'And some fell among thorns, and the thorns grew up, and choked it, and it yielded no fruit.

" 'And other fell on good ground, and did yield fruit that sprang up and increased; and brought forth, some thirty, and some sixty, and some a hundred.

" 'And he said unto them, He that hath ears to hear, let him hear . . .'

". . . My fellow sowers—are we all reapers?

"Or do we cast our seed upon less than fertile ground and thus cause the gnashing of Divine teeth?

"Are we careful in our sowing?

"Take stock! I say unto you: Take stock!

" 'Is a candle brought to be put under a bushel, or under a bed? And not to be set on a candlestick?'

"Is your seed capital to be hidden away in the dark vaults of banks or in long-term bonds, yielding little interest?

" 'For there is nothing hid,' saith the Lord, 'which shall not be manifested; neither was anything kept secret, but that it should come abroad.'

" 'If any man have ears to hear, let him hear.'

"How many times have you cast your seed upon rocks and thorns?

"How many times have you taken your precious capital and

tossed it carelessly into some investment without first thoroughly examining the prospectus?

"One sower carelessly cast his seed into a business whose growth potential had already peaked, and thus lost his capital gains!

"He sowed other seed among over-the-counter stock, and lost his dividends!

"He cast other of his seed among blue-chips preferred and profited neither by capital gains nor high dividends!

" 'If any man have ears to hear, let him hear.'

"But he also cast his seed upon fertile ground: he investigated some companies in depth—he researched their profit margins, knew their price/earnings ratio; he inspected their real estate, visited their factories; he met with their executive staffs, enquired of their home lives, and he judged them. Thus he accurately gauged their potential growth. And on this ground he cast his seed.

"And from these seeds, he brought forth some thirty, and some sixty, and some one hundred percent returns!

"Take stock!

"And the Lord saith, 'It is like a grain of mustard seed, which, when it is sown in the earth, is less than all the seeds that be in the earth.

" 'But when it is sown it groweth up, and becometh greater than all herbs, and shooteth out great branches; so that the fowls of the air may lodge under the shadow of it.'

"Take stock!

" 'Take heed what ye hear. With what measure ye mete, it shall be measured to you.

" 'And unto you that hear shall more be given!'

"The Lord saith, 'For he that hath, to him shall be given; and he that hath not, from him shall be taken even that which he hath!' "

Even though Robby had been intensely interested in this lesson, finding in it Good News indeed, and liked the way Pastor Maple spoke (he kept the cadence of his speech by jiggling coins in his pocket) Robby became aware of an increasing sensation of prickly heat at the back of his neck. Able to stand it no longer, Robby took a quick look behind him. There, only two pews away, sat Tony Savallo in his green windbreaker, expressionlessly listening to the sermon. The pillar of the church had not protected Robby at all! He was within clear view of Tony. Witnessing the mysterious ways of Tony Savallo made Robby very warm.

" 'For the earth bringeth forth fruit of herself; first the blade, then the ear, after that the full corn of the ear!' "

The lady with many chins beside Robby sat listening in rapture to the instructive Pastor Maple. Even with her face raised toward the pulpit she had more than her share of chins.

Robby took the mouse out of his pocket, reached over, and put it in the lady's lap.

" 'Know ye not this parable? And how then will ye know all parables?' "

Robby had not long to wait for a reaction. The lady, however enraptured by the words of Pastor Maple, ultimately became curious regarding what had been put in her lap and was moving about there. She looked down, then drew herself up to such an extent that for a moment she had but a single chin. "Aaaaaark!" she said loudly, and predictably, "a mouse!"

She brushed it off her lap in an un-Christian manner. She cast it upon the back of the pew in front of her.

The mouse bounced off the pew back and landed, momentarily stunned, on the kneeler. The woman's feet were beating on the floor beneath the kneeler. In a flash the mouse was off the kneeler and scurrying around among neighboring feet with such energy that shortly a large number of people were taking up the cry, "Aaaaaark! A mouse!"

People were scrambling without divine dignity. Some tripped over each other trying to get out of their pews. Others blocked the way by standing on the kneelers. Others—more tensile in joint—jumped up to stand on the seats.

Robby, popping from floor to pew seat to kneeler back to pew seat again, went against the general trend of his pew-mates and came out in the middle aisle—half a church away from Tony Savallo.

"Whup, whup."

Robby headed for the pulpit. Pastor Maple was peering through his grille, craning and straining to see what had so upset his congregation. What was the new panic? At the front of the auditorium, Robby crouched low, turned left and left again and scampered back down the aisle farthest from where he prayerfully

hoped Tony Savallo was being stampeded to death by Christians
thrown to a mouse.

• • •

In the church vestibule was a freckly boy Robby's age.

"Quick!" Robby demanded. "What newspaper do your parents
read?"

The boy turned his head toward the central door to the auditorium. "What's going on in there?"

"I said, what newspaper do your parents read?"

Archly, the boy said, "*The New York Times*, of course, and *The
Wall Street Journal*."

Robby didn't know how he had fared in *The Wall Street Journal*,
but he did know *The New York Times* considered him an item for
page thirty-six—and without photograph.

"Thank God," Robby said. "You're taking me to your house for
lunch."

"Why should I do that?" the boy squeaked.

From the auditorium came the noise of bangs and bumps and
shouts and shrieks. Someone even said "Jesus Christ!" prayerfully.

"Because I want lunch!" Robby exclaimed.

Something in the boy's eyes indicated to Robby that he considered Robby fallow ground upon which to cast even a single cara-
way seed.

Robby hissed into his freckles, "If you don't take me to your
house for lunch I'll ram this"— He put his fist between the boy's
face and his own—"so far down your throat, takin' your teeth with
it, you'll get a chance to chew your breakfast twice!"

Such was the threat offered Robby at Wolsley School by an older
boy who wanted the compass Robby's family chauffeur had given
him. Robby had found the threat entirely effective. Now he hoped
the freckle-faced boy was similarly intimidated.

He was.

"Okay," he said. "You stink."

"What's your name?"

"Roger vanWankle," the boy admitted, "the Third. You really
stink."

"Okay, Roger. You tell your parents you know me from school, and that you invited me to your house for lunch. Or your last meal will be your own teeth."

"Okay, okay. But, you know, you really stink."

He tried to pick the smell out of his nose.

The vestibule was beginning to fill with red-faced, perturbed people.

"Tell your parents my name's Robby. Uh—Robby Burnes."

"They'll never believe it."

"Good."

"I won't have to tell 'em you stink."

"Come on, Roger. Let's wait for your parents in the car."

Robby took the boy by the elbow and headed for the front door of the church.

"Kids in my school," protested Roger vanWankle the Third, "don't stink."

18

The Odor of Sanctity

"**H**ow come you smell of garbage?" Roger vanWankle enquired reasonably after he and Robby had attained the backseat of the vanWankle Cadillac.

"I spent last night in a garbage barrel," Robby admitted.

Roger said, "Oh," as if spending the night in a garbage barrel is the way anyone might be expected to spend an odd night or two of his life. "Are you running from the police or something?" he asked, as if that, too, were within his purview of normal existential experience.

Robby reviewed his philological exercise of the night before: Thadeus Lowry, Will'um, Tony Savallo. That morning Robby had run through a surrealistic forest of his own photograph hanging from people's hands, staring up at him from the street, even hanging from lamp posts. He said mildly, "I feel pressed."

"You don't look pressed," said Roger, casting a critical glance over Robby's clothes.

The chauffeur opened the door again and Mr. and Mrs. vW stepped in.

"Why, Roger," said Mrs. vW, looking at Robby.

"This is Robby Burnes, Mummy," Roger recited through clenched teeth. "A kid from school. I invited him home for lunch."

"How perfectly delightful," said Mrs. vW, not sounding convinced. "But, Roger, darling, you know you should warn Cook before you invite anybody to lunch."

"I know," was barely audible through teeth clasped so tightly Robby doubted Roger would ever be able to get them separated again.

Mr. vW sat in a corner of the car and gathered his overcoat over his paunch. He had given Robby the merest glance, obviously consigning him quickly to that category of animate life to be seen little and not heard at all.

Mrs. vW scanned Robby's tailoring and smiled warmly.

"I know you boys like the winter air." Mrs. vW began to crank up the windows. "But we must think of Mummy's coiffure."

"I really like the winter air, Mummy," urged Roger, obviously thinking more of his mother's nose than her hair.

The long Cadillac embarked from the curb.

Through the rear window Robby saw Tony Savallo writing something on the cuff of his windbreaker.

"Really, Pastor Maple is such an inspiration," proposed Mrs. vW. "Such a pity his service was interrupted by a Communist conspiracy."

In his corner of the car, Mr. vW snorted.

"It was a Communist conspiracy, wasn't it, Ralph?" asked Mrs. vW of her husband. "Letting all those rats free during his sermon?"

"Of course it was," stated Mr. vW with no uncertainty at all. "Who else would do a thing like that? Can't let decent, law-abiding Americans have a moment's peace even in their churches Sunday mornings."

"Still," philosophied Mrs. vW, "I found the forces of good and evil, dear Pastor Maple and the Communists' rats, battling it out for the hearts and the minds of the congregation even more inspiring. I do hope you boys took a lesson from it."

"Yes, ma'am," said Roger, faithfully.

Robby said nothing. It was his opinion that Pastor Maple's entire *logos* had been routed by a mouse.

"Unfortunately our favorite Congressman, Representative Jerry Bradshaw, took a lesson from it," said Mr. vW bitterly. "It inspired Bradshaw to nick me for ten thousand dollars in the church aisle."

"Ralph! Whatever for?" Mrs. vW's nose rose in surprise. It sniffed and rose higher in repugnance.

"He's got to block a bill in Congress for me. He's made it a pretty expensive bill, I'll tell you."

"What bill?" Mrs. vW was twisting in her seat, looking out all sides of the car.

"A bill that stipulates that all blankets made for the United States military—Army, Navy, and Marines—must be manufactured in the United States of America."

"Seems reasonable," commented Mrs. vW, clearly distracted.

"Darling! You're not thinking! The vanWankle blanket which we sell on contract to the United States military—the Army, Navy, and Marines—is manufactured at the vanWankle Mills in Canada!"

"So they are," noted Mrs. vW.

"Such a bill would put our blanket operations out of business!"

"I would think so, yes."

"It would mean we would be producing a half a million blankets a year without a market!"

"A chilling thought," she said.

"We would have to shut down the Canadian mills," said Mr. vW. "Or retool them to begin making commercial, competitive blankets. Good God!"

"There must be lots of cold Canadians."

"They have their own blankets," Mr. vW said with dismay.

"Does something smell?" enquired Mrs. vW.

"Everything smells," offered Robby. "Roses smell nice, but noses smell better."

"Anton," Mrs. vW addressed the chauffeur. "Speed up. There must be a garbage truck somewhere in the area—although, for the life of me, I don't see it."

"Yes, ma'am."

"New York doesn't collect garbage on Sunday," said Mr. vW. "Or on any other day of the week."

"They don't collect garbage on Sunday?"

"I'm sure they don't collect garbage on Sunday."

"But, Ralph, I distinctly smell garbage. Don't you smell garbage?"

"I think I smell New York," said Mr. vW.

"I don't see a garbage truck anywhere," she repeated, looking through the car windows north, east, south and west.

"That's why you smell garbage," said Mr. vW. "Because you never see a garbage truck."

Mrs. vW relaxed against the Cadillac's leather seat and petted her mink.

"Ralph, that seems terribly unreasonable—introducing a bill in Congress the sole purpose of which is to put our blanket company out of business. Who would think of such a thing?"

"Pecuchet."

"Who's Pecuchet?"

"Pecuchet makes blankets in Cleveland."

"Oh, I see. He stands to make a lot of money if this bill is passed?"

"He does indeed. Which is why he got the bill introduced to Congress, through his friendly congressman."

"I'm so awful at practical business matters," said Mrs. vW.

"Pecuchet has given his representative to Congress a fortune." Mr. vW's nose had begun to twitch. "Anton, drive a little faster, will you?"

"Yes, sir."

The car was oozing up a lovely wide boulevard with a green mall. Robby was hoping to spot a pile of garbage somewhere.

"The smell is getting worse, Ralph."

"We'll be home soon."

"That's what I mean. Do you think Park Avenue has seen its better days?"

"If the smell of New York has gotten to Park Avenue, my dear, there's no place in the world left to go."

"Could the smell be in the car? Anton, is there something rotting in the car?"

"No, ma'am."

"Perhaps you left some groceries in the trunk."

"No, ma'am."

"Anton," Mr. vW charged: "Something smells."

"The car looks clean enough," said Mrs. vW.

"Anton," Mr. vW stated: "The car isn't clean enough."

"It can't be the car, Ralph. We didn't smell it going down to church service."

"Anton," Mr. vW questioned suspiciously: "Did you let something smelly into the car while we were at church service?"

"No, sir."

From his corner Roger's blue eyes glared at Robby. Roger's head was tipped. The palm of his hand covered both his nose and his teeth.

Mr. vW said: "Anton, did you watch the car every minute we were gone?"

"Yes, sir."

"I bet you did. I'll bet a Communist threw a pile of garbage or something in this car while we were at church service."

"Oh, Ralph!" Mrs. vW examined the area around her feet with distress. "Do you really think so?"

"Just the sort of thing those damned anarchists would do—put a pile of garbage in the car of decent people while they're at church. Anything to upset the fabric of society!"

"A pile of garbage!" echoed Mrs. vW to Roger and Robby, her eyes brimming with the distress of the insulted.

"I'll bet they planted it under one of the seats." Mr. vW bent down over his paunch and examined the floor between his feet.

"Oh, Ralph," protested Mrs. vW, looking increasingly uneasy. "They couldn't have!"

"Well, you don't see any garbage trucks around, do you?" said his head from between his thighs.

"No one would be so mean."

"That's what they do," said the red-faced but erect Mr. vW, resettling his hat upon his head. "Instead of working for a living, driving garbage trucks around, picking up garbage, they plant garbage in the cars of decent people while they're at church!"

Mr. vW was settling into this conviction nicely. He looked to his family for support.

Roger knew his father was wrong, but said nothing. Mrs. vW already had said no one, not even Communists, could be that mean. Robby nodded with full assurance at Mr. vW and said, "I'm sure you're right, sir."

Robby didn't know what Communists were, but he had heard his father speak ill of them. If evil-doing could be attributed generally to Communists, Robby didn't mind his odor specifically being laid at their door as well—especially so close to lunch.

"Do hurry up, Anton!" ordered Mr. vW, his fingers pinching his nose.

19

Tempest in a Bathtub

When the limousine arrived at the apartment house a uniformed, epauleted, mustachioed, white-gloved doorman stepped out from under the canopy and opened the door. And from out of the car rushed three members of the vanWankle family, pale, breathless, and quivering from a lack of oxygen. Robby Burnes left the car with the equanimity of a person who knew some problems were inescapable.

"Give this car a cleaning!" Mr. vW shouted over the roof of the car to Anton, who had quickly escaped through his own door. "We'll not have the Communists thinking they can sabotage the car of decent people on a Sunday morning!"

A man dressed in formal clothes opened the apartment house's lobby door for them. Another piloted them up in the elevator.

"Ralph," said Mrs. vW, twitching her nose in the elevator with renewed alarm. "The smell! It's here, too!"

First Mr. vW gave the elevator man a suspicious look. Then he sighed. "The Communists are everywhere."

In the vestibule of the vanWankles' apartment was a statue twenty feet high of a naked lady. In her Venus mount was a clock. In time, Robby noticed it was twenty minutes to one.

"You boys go play in your room, Roger," said Mrs.vW as the butler helped her off with her coat. "Lunch at one-thirty. I'll tell Cook we have a guest."

The butler turned to take Robby's coat. The butler's eyes popped. The butler blanched. The butler stared.

Robby handed the butler his coat and gave the butler the smile Robby had long since learned to give servants, in which smile is acknowledged complicity in the universal conspiracy of servants and children against masters and mistresses, fathers and mothers, all adults and other guests. Only by so acknowledging and cultivating such a traditional conspiracy do children survive in well-run households.

The butler said nothing.

Robby followed Roger down a vast, tall and wide corridor to Roger's room.

Roger closed the door, about-faced on his heel, and pointed a finger at Robby. Two fingers of his other hand pinched his own nose.

"You're not coming to lunch smelling like a garbage truck," he said forcefully albeit nasally. "My father will fire all the servants as Communists and I've just got this bunch broken in!"

"I know, I know," conceded Robby. "How do I get my shoes polished?"

"Your shoes have nothing to do with it!" Roger insisted. "You stink! You've gotta have a bath!"

"I had a bath Wednesday."

"This is Sunday!" exclaimed Roger.

"At school we only get tubs once a week," said Robby, thinking he was scoring a good defensive point.

"Well, you don't go to my school," said Roger. He escaped through one of two matching doors.

Robby heard a bath being drawn. He had spent the night in a rubbish barrel. The real problem was not in his person; it was in his clothes. Robby's bathing wouldn't make his clothes smell a bit better. They, too, had spent the night in a rubbish barrel.

Roger's room was comparable to Robby's, at Pladroman House, except the furniture was newer and not at all broken. Robby's grandfather, when a boy, had punched up Robby's bed so unmercifully that ever after the occupant was inclined to tip out its left side. The grandfather had lived to sire an heir and numerous nasty rumors. The armchair by the fireplace in Robby's room had been sprung by Robby's father's nurse, who, tradition had it below stairs, was fat enough to be often spoken of as a possible stand-in for the Inns at Lincoln Court. Robby's own father, it was reported, had kicked a leg out from under the desk in the room upon receiving news he had flunked an examination in Greek. Ever after, that corner of the desk had been propped up by Volumes D through R of the *Encyclopaedia Britannica*. Looking around the room, Robby thought either Roger's ancestors had been far more careful with their furniture, or Roger hadn't any ancestors at all, which struck Robby as a funny thought.

Roger came through one door and the butler through the other simultaneously.

"Yes, Cabot?" said Roger.

Cabot said, "I thought your . . . guest . . . a friend from school, is he? . . . might be bathing before luncheon, and thought I might see what can be done about his clothes."

Robby smiled conspiratorially at the butler.

"There isn't time," said Roger. "What his clothes need is a match."

"We English perhaps know a bit more about brushing up . . ." The butler winked at Robby, and picked Robby's clothes up off the floor. "I'll just take these along and see what can be done with them."

The butler exited with Robby's clothes draped over his arm. He carried Robby's shoes between thumb and forefinger.

Roger sat on the closed toilet while Robby sat in the tub.

"So why did you spend last night in a garbage barrel?" asked Roger.

Robby said, "Because I was stuck in a backyard with fences all around it."

"Then how did you ever get out?"

"Oh, it was all right once the sun came up and I could see."

"What were you doing stuck in a backyard?"

"I got chased there. You see, I saw this man, Tony Savallo, shoot another man. Murder him. And Tony Savallo was chasing me. He wants to murder me, too. So I jumped over this high fence into a backyard, and then I couldn't get out."

"Tell me another," said Roger.

"It's true! I swear on a Bible! Last night I saw a murder."

"Yeah, sure," said Roger. "Tell it to the Marines."

Robby shrugged. Even in his short life, Robby had had this experience with truth before. The last thing people are wont to believe, sometimes, is the truth. Once Robby had told his nanny his mitten had been eaten by a guardsman's horse, when his mitten had been eaten by a guardsman's horse. Robby had been denied tea, not for having lost a mitten, but for lying.

Roger said, "It's okay you're coming to stink up my house instead of going home to face the music, but aren't your parents worried about you?"

Adhering strictly to the truth, Robby said, "They're not in New York this weekend."

In his heart Robby was saddened that his truth had not been believed. He had been thinking he might appeal to the vanWankle seniors during luncheon, tell them his whole terrible story, hope they would lay it all out as a Communist conspiracy and grant him their sympathy and aid. From Roger's reaction Robby knew now such a plan was hopeless. If a boy his own age wouldn't believe the story, Robby could not expect adults to believe. After all boys believe in many things—exercise, honesty and friendship, to name three—to which adults give lip-service but seldom practice. Seldom does one adult get up from the playing field and honestly admit his own error to save his friend a penalty. Even to his own ears, now having said it, Robby's story seemed more a nightmare than a true history. Children sometimes believe in nightmares, but adults, never.

"Are you a member of the Church of Jesus Christ Materialist?" Roger asked.

Again Robby shrugged. If truth did not serve him, he might as well lie. "Life-long."

"Then why weren't you at Sunday School? Why have I never seen you before?"

"We're new to this parish," said Robby. "I'm enrolling next week."

"In midyear?"

"Right after Christmas. Look for me."

"You'll never catch up. It's terribly hard."

"Is it?"

"I'm having to take private tutorials Wednesday afternoons. With Pastor Maple."

"Oh," Robby said, again observing American soap did not sink.

"I'm having trouble reading the stock tables," Roger continued. "The print's awfully small, you know, and when you have to read the par value, the year's high and low, as well as the asking and the bid prices, it gets damned confusing. And," he said significantly, "you have to add zeroes to the number of stocks traded every day, to arrive at the volume."

"Oh," Robby said. "I see."

"But, as Pastor Maple says, practical Christianity is worth it." Roger sighed. "And we're learning to read annual reports. I've read the car companies so far, airlines and the oils."

"Didn't Jesus throw the money-changers out of the temple?" asked Robby.

"Yeah," said Roger. "Pastor Maple says he doesn't want donations made to his church in change, either. He wants it in bills."

"Guess I'll need tutoring," said Robby.

"You're lucky. You'll probably get Tuesday afternoons with Pastor Maple. That's earlier in the financial week. Less to remember."

"Good."

"The thing that worries me," said Roger, picking a fingernail, "is my soul."

"Your soul?"

"Yeah. Whether I'm good enough, you know, as a person, to receive the Word of the Lord directly from Pastor Maple."

"Sure you are," Robby said. "Didn't you refuse me lunch until I threatened to shove your teeth down your throat?"

"That reminds me," said Roger. "How are you going to make it up to me? I mean, lunch. How are you going to pay me back?"

"That's easy," said Robby, thinking quickly. "Before I leave I'll give you a piece of advice."

"A stock tip?"

"A piece of advice."

Chin on hands, Roger thought. "Pastor Maple says good advice is very valuable. Is your advice good?"

"Is lunch?" Robby was beginning to get the hang of a life by trade.

Roger considered the proposition and apparently decided to suspend negotiation, at least until he saw what lunch was.

"But I keep having these impulses," he said. "Like, you know, I see a beggar on the street and, you know, it actually crosses my mind to give him a dime."

"Have you confessed this to Pastor Maple?" Robby asked solemnly.

"Yes," said Roger. "He says I must harden my heart against those who vouchsafe nothing."

"There, then," said Robby, meaning to console.

Robby ducked his head below the surface of the warm, soapy water. When he came up he found himself in a freezing downpour.

"We have a shower for that!" Roger shouted. He stood over Robby, his hands on a different set of knobs. The water was turning scalding.

"I'll fix the knobs!" Robby gasped. Instantly, he grasped the idea of a shower. He had never seen one before. Instantly he also concluded, finally, absolutely, irrevocably, after the collection of much evidence, that everything—absolutely everything about Americans, even their bath-taking—was violent. Only Americans, he decided in a flash, can turn a nice, warm leisurely bath into bad weather.

"If you wanted a shower, why didn't you say so?"

"Right," Robby said, fighting with the knobs while standing under the torrential spray. By the time he got the knobs set properly to provide a spray somewhat nearer his skin temperature, Roger had left the bathroom. "You'll be a bloomin' bishop!" shouted Robby, turning the squall off.

From the bedroom Roger said, solemnly, "Thank you."

Cabot was standing in the bedroom with clothes for Robby. The blazer and short trousers and tie and cap and overcoat were Robby's, beautifully brushed and pressed and smelling as if they had just come in from a walk in a greenhouse. The shoes were Robby's, looking as if they had never trod the earth. But the shirt and the underclothes and the kneesocks weren't Robby's at all. They were identical to Robby's but they were new.

Cabot winked at Robby.

He took the towel from Robby's shoulders and gave him a vigorous rubdown. Finishing, he said, "There you are, Your Grace."

It did not surprise Robby too much that Cabot recognized him. From Robby's experience with servants he knew they were apt to read more entertaining newspapers than were the householders.

His father's newspapers were unrelievedly gray. The servants' newspapers had brightly colored comics, on Sundays, and big headlines about "LOVE NESTS." His father and mother never had anything to talk about except Churchill and Roosevelt and Hitler and Mussolini and Parliament and the Congress and the War. The servants were really up on the news of the world, and their conversation was much more interesting.

While Cabot was dressing him and Roger was fiddling around his desk Robby considered trying out the truth on Cabot. Whenever he'd had a problem servants had solved it. But what could a butler do? Sundays were busy days for butlers. There were always people in and out for tea and drinks and dinner, and Saturdays always tarnish at least one set of silverware. It isn't fair always to be running to servants with problems. Robby's father had told him so the night he spent three hours looking for his favorite pipe. *It's not a servant's job to locate missing pipes!* he had expostulated over and over again during the hunt. (Robby finally found the pipe in the left pocket of his father's smoking jacket.) Servants have their own work to do.

Cabot handed Robby the gold sovereign. "I believe your father gave this to you, Your Grace?"

Robby smiled. "Yes."

"I found it in your trousers. I think you'd better keep it, Your Grace." He slipped the sovereign into the handkerchief pocket of the blazer. "People in this household will relieve you of it as proof of their generosity."

While helping Robby on with the blazer the butler whispered in Robby's ear, "Is there anything I can do for you, Your Grace?"

Robby considered again. *It's not a servant's job to locate a missing. . . anything!* "Yes, please," he said. "Could you give me doubles for lunch?"

20

A Congressional Bill

Robby sat with the vanWankle family at lunch.

Roger, freshly inspired by Pastor Maple, ate greedily. The senior vanWankles, wanting nothing to go to waist, cast yearning glances at the food on their plates, and talked. Robby, having spent the previous night in a rubbish barrel and having other good reasons not to want food to go to waste, ate silently and heartily.

"My, how you boys eat!" trilled Mrs. vW. "I don't know where you put it all. Do you know where they put it all, Ralph?"

Ralph looked from boy to plate, to plate and to boy. "No matter how much money you give the government"—he shook his head sadly—"you don't know where it goes, either." He tasted his mock turtle soup, replaced his spoon, and concluded: "The government isn't a grown-up."

"Where do you live, Robby?" asked Mrs. vW.

"Mayfair, ma'am."

"Oh, that's nice. I think Clara Bow used to live at the Mayfair."

Even at his age Robby had learned that totally inadequate answers usually are grasped as entirely satisfactory—in polite conversation.

Robby was saying as little as possible.

He had a better use for his mouth, at the moment. He had discovered in the few days he had resided in this land of milk and honey that full-blown meals were as infrequent as tea shops in the North Atlantic. When one came across a proper meal one was wise to triple up on it, to make up for yesterday, do right by today, and conserve for tomorrow.

Cabot was most obliging. Like any well-trained butler he knew how to sidle food onto a plate (or off a plate—whichever was required, to avoid embarrassment) prestidigitatiously. As the main course was soufflé, sausage and mustard pickle—each of which food is distinct in color and shape and therefore easily measure-able—Cabot's genius shone.

Across the table from Robby, however, Roger noticed the frequency with which Robby was being served. Roger was not about to vouchsafe nothing. Each time Robby was served, Roger signalled Cabot, with his eyes or a wave of his hand, that he, too, would be served again. Cabot ignored half of Roger's signals, but could not ignore Roger's more blatant wavings with both hands. Roger, however, had been eating regularly and well. Competing with someone who had ceased to think of meals as a rightful and regular occurrence proved hard on Roger. During the courses of luncheon Roger's face broke into a sweat, his skin reddened, his cheeks puffed, his eyes protruded. His fingers yanked at his shirt collar as if his neck had grown noticeably between one-thirty and two. Clearly Roger was miserable in this eating competition, but he stuck to it with great fortitude.

Too, Robby spoke the minimum at luncheon because he did not want questions raised by what the vanWankles might think of as his accent. Robby knew he did not have an accent, but he had discovered so far in America that not only did everyone have an accent—everyone had an accent individual from that of every other American. Thadeus Lowry (Robby was to describe later) spoke Rhetorical-American. Words marched out of his mouth with huge strides as if the end of any sentence were The In Place for a word to be. His wife, his *chérie*, spoke a soft and sibilant Martini-American. Her words were pronounced deliberately through a spray which never reached beyond her gums. Marie Savallo spoke Devout-American. Every word lilted from her mouth reverentially as if aimed at only the ears of resting saints—even when that word might be *kidnap, ransom* or *murder*. Frankie Savallo spoke Exuberant-American. Words scrambled from his mouth in a great, loud hurry as if the right to speak freely were a new right, and one apt to be curtailed any moment. Pastor Maple spoke Pulpit, which Robby later would define as a universal language comprising two parts Divinity, one part Wonder, three parts Exhortation, three parts Pomposity, and five parts Collection Plate Indicative. Listening to them at luncheon Robby heard from the vanWankles an accent he would describe later as Business-American. Words sashayed from the vanWankles mouths with their eyelids fluttering and their hips wiggling, so eager to be heard without being loud, so eager to convince without argument, that the listener might forget, or never realize at all, that the principle behind seduction is not entirely generous.

Robby remained as silent as possible throughout luncheon because he suspected that that which the vanWankles might think of as an accent on his part would cause questions for which totally inadequate answers would not be grasped as entirely satisfactory. Talk might turn uncivil. The vanWankles might discover they were feeding a homeless English boy at their table and quickly reason there was no profit in doing that. They were sowing their mustard pickle upon a destitute foreigner. Such a discovery on their part would imperil his having dessert.

"That emblem you're wearing," Mr. vW said to Robby, referring to the Wolsley School crest. "That bull is shaking all the leaves out of that tree, right?"

"Yes, sir."

"And shaking down fruit and nuts, too, I'll bet," he said with a good degree of spiritual satisfaction.

"Yes, sir."

"Doubtlessly," Mr. vW said respectfully, "that bull will make a pile."

"Doubtlessly, sir."

"I find all this very disturbing," said Mrs. vW, properly introducing the main topic with the main course. "Representative Bradshaw actually came up to you in the main aisle of the church, as we were leaving, and said he wanted you to give him ten thousand dollars cash."

"He did," confirmed Mr. vW.

"To block passage of a bill forbidding us to sell blankets manufactured in Canada to the American military."

"Right."

She said, "It does seem corrupt of him. I mean, to want so much."

"You have to understand the figures," said her husband, counting his sausages off the platter. "Pecuchet paid his congressional representative in Ohio ten thousand dollars to introduce the bill into Congress. He paid Jerry Bradshaw, our representative, five thousand dollars not to oppose the bill."

"But why did Pecuchet do that? Why did he pay Jerry anything?"

"He knows I've been an active supporter of Jerry for years. Well, in fact, that Jerry's in my pocket. He had to pay off Jerry not to oppose the bill."

"It all seems wrong, somehow."

"Actually, I'm very grateful to Jerry for coming to me. He could have just pocketed the five thousand dollars and kept quiet. I wouldn't have known there was such a bill in Congress until it was too late to do anything about it."

"So telling you that he's accepted a five-thousand-dollar bribe from Pecuchet earns him another ten-thousand-dollar bribe from you?" Mrs. vW was frowning at her soufflé.

Her husband shivered. "Don't use the word *bribe*! *Bribe* is entirely the wrong word for it." Mr. vW seemed entirely sure on that point. However, there was a long moment before he offered a word in substitute for *bribe*. "Political contribution," he said. "These guys have to run for office every two years, you know. That takes money."

"A political contribution for something in return . . ." Mrs. vW hesitated on the brink of spoiling luncheon, or a marriage, or both.

Mr. vW shook his knife at her. "A representative can't pay for a political campaign out of his own pocket every two years. He has to have the help of his friends. And if he can't help his friends be prosperous, then his friends can't help him!"

"Sounds perfectly reasonable, when you say it that way," Mrs. vW admitted.

"It's the American system," Mr. vW chortled. "How else could it work?"

"But, Ralph. Our representative to Congress, Jerry Bradshaw, is getting a total of fifteen thousand dollars, the net result of which is nothing at all—a bill introduced to Congress and not passed."

"Would you rather see the bill passed?"

"Of course not."

"Ten thousand dollars is cheap at the price. Pecuchet has spent fifteen thousand, and he gets nothing at all. See? Our representative is better than his representative."

"I'm so glad," she said.

"One of our most precious rights as Americans," Mr. vW lectured his son, Roger, whose eyes were beginning to bulge with an unwanted intake of food, "is our right to pursue happiness. Which, in a system of free enterprise, can mean only one thing—our right to make a buck." Roger's freckles were running together in digestive strain. "Does this mean that simply because a man becomes a public servant he must give up his right to pursue happiness, his right to be enterprising, his right to make a buck?" Sweat rolled from Roger's upper lip into his mouth. "It does not. When we vote a man into office, we are conferring upon him influence. And influence, like every other commodity—be it gold, silver, reputation, goodwill—has its value. Influence is the equity a politician develops during his career. Like any other equity, it can be sold, converted into cash, precisely as the politician sees fit." Mr. vW turned his attention back to his wife, having lectured her, obliquely. "That's all Jerry is doing."

Mrs. vW was impressed. Her eye shadow was stretched to the point of revealing pores. "Why, darling!" she sputtered. "That's beautiful! Never in my life have I heard the political system explained so . . . so . . . so poignantly."

Mr. vW shrugged modestly. "Those dudes who wrote the Constitution knew what they were doing, all right. They all had families to support." He laughed. "None of them ended up in the poorhouse!"

"I certainly hope you boys have been edified by what you just heard," Mrs. vW said.

Roger swallowed reluctantly. "Yes, Mummy."

Robby said, "Yes, ma'am."

"How are you going to make this contribution to Jerry?" Mrs. vW asked her husband. "Is there a hurry about it?"

Mr. vW looked at his watch. "He's leaving for Washington on

the four o'clock train. He'll be standing outside the cocktail lounge in the Hotel Clemens at three-thirty."

"Ralph, you're not going yourself?"

"No," he drawled. "I never have yet. But it is Sunday. All my lawyers are at home with their families. I have the money in the safe, of course. I keep myself prepared for weekend emergencies like this."

"You can't go yourself. Someone might see you."

"Yeah." He scratched the back of his neck. "Someone might see me slip an envelope to a congressman in a hotel lobby the week before a bill important to my business comes up before Congress . . ."

"Not everyone understands the political system as well as you do."

"It would be just the time some nosy person would be passing by, recognize the two of us, put two and two together . . . Why," he said, "it would mean another bribe!"

"You can't send Cabot," she said. "I have the Ladies' Committee from the Church coming to tea, to discuss those buildings the Church owns in Harlem. You know how the residents there keep demanding light bulbs in the hallways, if you'd believe it, when they really ought not to go out at night!"

"I need a courier," admitted Mr. vW. "I'd sorely miss the opportunity to say hello to the Ladies' Committee. They do such good work."

"Maybe," speculated Mrs. vW, wriggling her eyebrows at Robby in such a way Robby wasn't supposed to notice, "we can think of someone who would be happy to run a little errand for us."

"Maybe so," agreed Mr. vW, immediately brightened by a solution which would permit him to say hello to the Ladies' Committee instead of his congressional representative.

"Robby, darling." Mrs. vW laid her forearm on the table in a supplicating manner. "Would you mind terribly doing us a little favor?"

"No, ma'am." Dessert hadn't appeared yet.

"We'll send you back to the Hotel Mayfair in the car with Anton if you'll stop off at the Hotel Clemens on the way and give an envelope to a man standing at the door of the cocktail lounge in the lobby. Will you do that for us?"

"Of course, ma'am." Robby knew that nothing was for nothing in the vanWankle household. He had attended their church.

Dessert was chocolate ice cream and vanilla wafers. Roger barely survived it.

• • •

The clock in the alabaster lady's Venus mount was striking three when Cabot helped Robby into his freshly brushed coat in the vestibule of the vanWankles' apartment.

Mr. vW had given Robby a sealed envelope and repeated his instructions again in the greatest detail. Robby was to be sure the man to whom he gave the envelope answered to the name *Bradshaw*.

Robby had left the senior vW's lurking in the living room.

Of the vanWankles, only Roger stood in the vestibule to say good-bye. And he did not stand well. His necktie was down, his shirt collar unbuttoned. His face was flushed from food. His legs bent just enough to indicate they no longer wanted to carry around such a big lunch.

"See you in church," Robby said to him.

"Wait a minute," Roger said. "You owe me something."

"Of course," Robby said. "What?"

"You promised to give me a stock tip."

"Not a stock tip," said Robby. "A piece of advice."

"Okay," Roger said impatiently. "A piece of advice. What is it?"

Robby looked up at Cabot, and then stepped nearer to Roger and whispered in Roger's ear, "Steer clear of becoming a duke."

Roger drew back. *"What?!"*

" 'Bye. Thanks, Cabot!"

Anton awaited Robby on the curb with the back door of the Cadillac limousine open. Robby crossed the sidewalk with dignity and got into the car.

Despite his seeing, halfway down the block, apparently studying the architecture on Park Avenue, Tony Savallo.

21
Pushing and Shoving

Oozing down Park Avenue in the back of the vanWankle limousine, Robby knew the slight peace of the moment and the heavy trepidation of the future. It had been only three meters from the door of the apartment house to the car and during that trudge Robby had been escorted, somewhat shielded, by the huge doorman. Tony Savallo could have shot Robby in the instant Robby crossed the sidewalk only if he had had his gun drawn and half-aimed while dawdling on the sidewalk admiring the architecture. Toying with a handgun while apparently engaged in esthetic pursuit would establish an irony anyone, such as a doorman or a chauffeur, might observe and question. Thus reasonably unprepared, Tony Savallo missed his chance to shoot Robby Burnes through the head outside the vanWankles' apartment house. Anton closed the back door on Robby the instant Robby scurried into the backseat.

Through the windows, as the limousine went in a U-turn around the mall to head downtown, Robby saw Tony Savallo getting into a taxi. Anton had his instructions, first to the Hotel Clemens to wait for Robby while he gave ten thousand dollars to a member of the House of Representatives, then to take Robby to the Hotel Mayfair, where Robby didn't live, but someone named Clara Bow might have, once. All the way down the avenue and through a cross street the silhouette of Tony Savallo's head remained steady in the backseat of the taxi behind them.

Robby didn't wait for Anton. He leapt out of the car as soon as it drew up to the curb in front of the Hotel Clemens. He brushed by the hotel doorman, who was dressed in the uniform of a riverboat captain. He threw himself at a door shaped like a vertical paddlewheel and flooded through it. He jumped up three or four stairs.

At the top of the stairs standing near the wall stood a man in a Chesterfield coat. A Boston bag was on the floor at his feet. Near him was a door decorated with the outlines of champagne glasses and beer tankards. The sign over the door said THE BRIDGE. With glassy eyes the man was watching the revolving door as if it were a roulette wheel about to turn up his fortune.

Hand clutching the envelope in his pocket, Robby approached the man. "Please, sir?"

The man's eyes barely flickered from the entrance to the hotel. "Go along now, sonny. Your mother's looking for you."

"Please, sir, are you Mr. Bradshaw?"

"Yes, yes, but I can't do autographs now. I have a train to catch."

"Mr. vanWankle sent me, sir."

"vanWankle?" Bradshaw's glazed eyes popped fully surprised in Robby's face. "vanWankle sends children to do his dirty work now, does he?"

"Dirty work, sir?"

"Dirty enough. Either I take ten thousand dollars from him or he gives thirty thousand dollars to the scoundrel campaigning against me next election. Don't you call that dirty?"

"I don't know, sir."

"Well, I do. It's not the Congress of the United States that's corrupt, young man. It's the citizens of the United States. Won't let a politician do his job properly. Always threatening him this way and that."

"He said to say something about blankets, sir," Robby said, looking anxiously at the hotel entrance as the revolving door kept dispensing people toward the steps. "He said to say something about keeping you warm at night."

"Blankets!" huffed Bradshaw. "What do I care about blankets? Tell me that!"

Robby considered the question seriously. "We all like blankets, sir."

"What I care about are my constituents! The honest ones!" The Congressman belched. "The hard-working, God-fearing honest people of this district who elected me to represent them in Congress!"

"Yes, sir. I'm sure, sir."

"In order to serve the good people I have to put up with the pushing and shoving of the vanWankles and the Pecuchets of this land! Do you understand that?" Bradshaw looked over Robby's head, as if addressing more of an audience than a small boy. "Does anyone understand that?"

"I'm sure someone understands that, sir."

"Threats!" Bradshaw squeezed his eyes closed, wrinkled his nose and shook his head. "Some calls 'em bribes. I calls 'em threats!"

"Sir? I'm in somewhat of a hurry myself—"

"Either I play ball with those what got the money or I get thrown out of the ball park, retired for lack of funds, never again able to stand up at bat for issues important to me, vital to my constituents!"

"But you sleep warm at night, sir?"

"Bah!" Bradshaw swayed. "Blankets!"

"Yes, sir, blankets." Robby held the envelope out to Bradshaw but the man's eyes remained closed. The fingers of his right hand pressed the spot between his eyebrows as if to force individuation of the thoughts which swirled within. "Sir!"

In the revolving door Tony Savallo was behind a woman in a mammoth fur coat.

"Sir!"

"Blankets," moaned the people's representative to Congress. "Oh, my God—blankets!"

"Sir!" Robby tried to place the envelope in the pocket of Bradshaw's overcoat, but the pocket was too full. "Whup!" screamed Robby as Tony Savallo got through the crowd to the bottom of the stairs.

Stuffing the envelope back into his own pocket, Robby ran through the crowded hotel lobby. "Whup!"

From behind him he heard the bellow of an enraged man. Robby looked back as he ran. Bradshaw had picked up his Boston bag and was staggering with it into the crowd of the hotel lobby. Tony Savallo had passed Bradshaw and was much nearer Robby.

"Scamp!" the people's representative was bellowing in a well-practiced aggrieved voice. "Come back here! You have something of mine!"

·   ●   ·

Hotels, at least those in the august class of the Hotel Clemens, by presenting thick carpets and thick drapes, heavy chairs and divans awkwardly placed, all decorated in amoebic patterns, attempt to impose standards of subdued behavior upon their guests, which imposition permits the hotel to present its guests with larger bills. One is not expected to be raucous in front of an oversized landscape of the Cathedral of St. John the Divine, or to perceive purple and yellow divans as common hurdles to be vaulted.

On that Sunday afternoon with Tony Savallo a few steps behind him, trying to yank something out of the pocket of his windbreaker as he ran, Robby abandoned dignity and presented the management of the Hotel Clemens with behavior shocking to any decor. When he looked back at the bellowing Bradshaw Robby bumped an end table, sending the lamp on it to crash on the rug. Two divans were back to back, holding two different sets of people who were holding two different sets of conversations under their hats. Robby jumped on one divan, over the backs of both, and down the other, bouncing the people on both divans and elevating their polite murmurs to angry shouts. He gave not a glance at the large painting of the Cathedral of St. John the Divine. Passing the hotel desk he knocked over several upright suitcases, scattered three overnight cases, and caused one agitated lady to knock her own hat off.

The dining room had only a few late lunchers in it. Forgetting for the moment the negotiations he'd had to endure, the concessions he'd had to make to secure his own lunch, Robby went under the table of two late lunchers, a man and a woman dawdling bored over their coffee as if waiting for a fashion magazine photographer to come by looking for just the right illustration for an article entitled "Weekend Fun in the City." Their table still had a long tablecloth. The bored couple became active immediately and began to kick at him with four feet. Her fashionable slipper got Robby on a cheekbone; his pliant black got Robby between two ribs. Deciding that under their table was not a good place to hide shortly after the feet began to kick, Robby scurried out and became upright again. He spotted a swing door to the kitchen and headed for it. A waiter carrying a tray on one hand came through the swing door. Gracefully he stood aside and held the door open for Robby, and said, "Yes, sir."

Halfway through the bright, white kitchen a salad cauldron on wheels was in Robby's path. It was not much of an obstacle for him. Hoping to make it more of an obstacle for Tony Savallo, Robby spun the cauldron around him with some energy. He then ran backwards. A cook, using a knife as long as his forearm, looked on with disinterest. Tony grabbed the cauldron by its rim and pushed it ahead of him as he ran. Robby turned again and made it through a door to a storeroom. He heard the rim of the cauldron clank against both sides of the door frame.

Robby tripped over one box in the dark storeroom, followed his nose to fresh air and found himself on a loading dock.

The alley was wide enough for two trucks to pass. After jumping off the loading dock Robby, who was beginning to think with the instinct of the hunted, realized that he had less cover than a quail four meters over a shooting blind. Signs every few feet read LOADING PLATFORM. Across the alley the signs read RAILROAD LOADING PLATFORM. Robby crossed the alley at a trot. Getting onto the railroad loading platform required another great leap, but, as he had been practicing leaping in terror and therefore had some confidence in himself, Robby picked up his running pace to make the leap. He increased the pace even more when he heard a gunshot. At precisely the right instant a second gunshot caused all his muscles to leap and he found himself with both feet on the platform.

Through a wide door Robby found himself in a huge room. Many signs read LOST AND FOUND AREA. Many, many trunks, suitcases and wooden crates, stamped, stickered, stenciled, with labels dripping off them, all suggesting they shouldn't have been lost in the first place, were stacked on top of each other under thick layers of dust.

Hands on his knees, Robby grabbed breath. In the alley Tony Savallo had shot at him twice. Tony was getting careless. Tony was getting impatient. Tony was getting desperate.

Robby worked through Lost and Found and pushed through a door to the main concourse of the railroad station.

• • •

Railroad stations are entirely different from hotels lobbies, Roby immediately realized. Whereas he had attracted great attention (which had done him no good) running through the hotel lobby, he attracted no attention whatsoever running through a railroad station. Of course railroad stations do not set up hurdles to subdue people. The main piece of art in that railroad station, Robby couldn't help noticing, was a huge, bright work of a young woman sitting in a most uncomfortable-looking position in a red bathing suit on a beach smoking a cigarette. Beneath her people looked and acted more excited than subdued. They hurried and jostled each other and yelled directions at each other. Those standing in groups, waiting with each other, saying hello, saying good-bye, spoke loudly, laughed openly, and did not hide their tears. Most of the men in the concourse were in military uniforms. One man, in fact, identical to any man in the Hotel Clemens who had shouted angrily at Robby for running, in the railroad station ran right into Robby, bowled him over and never stopped to observe any manners whatsoever.

Robby got up and looked in all directions through the crowd. For the moment he could spot Tony Savallo's green windbreaker nowhere. Which meant that for the moment, standing in the middle of the railroad station, Robby didn't know in which direction to run. He did not know in which directions Tony Savallo wasn't.

Robby went up to a group of men he recognized as naval officers. They wore blue uniforms with brass accoutrements, white hats with black visors. One or two of them glanced at Robby, but the conversation on the game at the Point continued. Robby did not like to interrupt naval officers, especially when it seemed they were discussing tactics. 'Round the left end was being debated with a slash through the middle. Robby trusted resolution of this question would end the war that much sooner, and thus remained silent as long as possible.

When he began to feel Tony Savallo's presence again, he plucked at the sleeve of the officer nearest him.

"Please, sir," he said.

"No shoe shines," said one of the officers.

In fact their shoes shone enough to make a good valet blush.

"He's not a shoe-shine kid," said another. "Look at his clothes. What's that insignia he's wearing?"

"You lost, kid?"

"Please, sir, I'm being chased by a murderer who kept me in a rubbish barrel all night."

"What? Where you from, kid?"

"England, sir. My name's Robby Burnes and just everybody's looking for me—except everybody who sees me, except nobody sees me, you see, sir, except Tony Savallo, who keeps chasing me because I saw him shoot a man dead in the streets, sir, and I know who he is, you see, sir—"

"He's English," said one.

"If he were any more English he couldn't talk at all," said another.

"Calm down, kid," said a third. "Tell us what's the matter?"

"He's been chasing me all night, sir, all day—"

"I didn't know an ox was powerful enough to uproot a big tree like that," said the officer, still studying the Wolsley School emblem.

"Who's been chasing you?"

"Tony Savallo, sir."

"I don't think you can train an ox like that."

"Ton-he Sa-va-lo. What does Sa-va-lo mean?"

"It was all right, sir, I had nowhere to go, and I understood that, all right. I made the best of it, honestly I did, but I've begun to upset people, sir, a naked lady in her kitchen this morning, she threw milk at me; I upset a whole churchful of people, I did, I put a mouse in a lady's lap; all the people at the Hotel Clemens, they yelled at me, and kicked at me, and I'm beginning to think less of myself for all that, I am. Honest, sir, I never raised trouble before, I haven't!"

"You put a mouse in the lap of a naked lady?"

"What naked lady? Where, where?" asked another officer.

"What's he talking about?"

"That kid's suffering from bad dreams."

"Only things are getting serious now, sir. Tony Savallo shot at me twice just now in the alley. He shot at me. Twice."

"Where's your momma, boy?"

"She's dead, sir. She died in the bomb. Thadeus Lowry took my picture of her."

"Is somebody shooting pictures?"

"Wouldn't you say, sir, things are getting serious?"

"Listen, son, I'll take you to Lost and Found."

"Oh, no, sir, not there. I've been there."

"You've been to Lost and Found?"

"It's all covered with dust, sir."

"What I think we have here, gentlemen," said the eldest officer, "is an escapee from Lost and Found."

"Yes, sir," said an officer.

"Bring him back, will you, Tom? Someone at the information desk should be able to help you."

"Yes, sir."

"Oh, no, sir, not that room! That room's no good at all, sir!"

The officer called Tom put his hand on Robby's shoulder. "It's all right, son."

When the officer moved his arm, Robby saw the green of Tony Savallo's jacket. Then he saw Tony Savallo.

"Oh, no, sir!" Robby ducked his shoulder from beneath the officer's hand.

Both Tony Savallo's hands were in his jacket pockets, but Tony was moving steadily toward Robby.

Robby ducked again as the officer was reaching for him, turned and ran.

"Oh, whup, whup, whup!"

Across the station Robby saw a gate closing on Track 19. He ran straighter for it than any bee ever made for a honeycomb. He skirted a man in a brown uniform so narrowly he left the man pirouetting in midconcourse. The momentum of the heavy pushed gate was such that the trainman pushing it tried to stop it as he saw Robby approaching at high speed but could not. Robby danced sideways through the narrow aperture.

Even on sneakered feet Tony Savallo skidded into the diamond-grilled gate.

From the other side of the gate Robby saw Tony's arm pull back and curve to reach into his jacket pocket.

"Whup!"

Robby ran down the station platform. The train was moving

with him. Shortly the train was moving faster than he was. Train steps drew abreast of Robby. Remembering how Thadeus Lowry got into taxicabs, Robby ran a few steps sideways with the train and sat on its steps. He pulled his feet up.

He looked back along the train.

Still on the other side of the blurring gate was a patch of green.

• • •

"Ticket?"

"Oh, yes, sir!"

When Robby had caught his breath he found himself a seat in a coach car. He was near the front of the car. The old conductor came through the door, enquired of Robby, then proceeded on, punching tickets held out to him.

He turned back to Robby. "Ticket?"

"Yes, sir!" Robby answered agreeably.

The conductor continued down the aisle and did not turn back to Robby again.

The man in the seat next to Robby was in a sailor's uniform, smelled of beer, and was comfortably asleep. His ticket was in the holder in the seat in front of them and had been punched by the conductor.

Robby expected a nice, long train ride. He put his hands in his pockets and slumped in his seat. In his pocket he discovered he still had the envelope containing ten thousand dollars. *Scamp! Come back here! You have something of mine!* Robby had tried to give it to him. The politician had not stopped talking enough to listen. *Thief! You little thief!* had yelled the householder that morning from his front door, his naked, surprised wife behind him. Robby considered that he had been yelled at quite a lot for a Sunday.

He expected the train would carry him to some other place altogether, a place utterly without Tony Savallo. The trains he had taken from London had carried him long distances, to Edinburgh, once to Leeds, often to Wolmwold. The people in these places had never been the same people as those he'd left in London. Except for the people who travelled with him, different places had different sets of people in them altogether.

Robby was right in that he did have a nice train ride, and it did bring him to someplace altogether different. He was right about nothing else.

Very shortly the train stopped. He sat up straight. Another platform had appeared beside the train.

A sign over the platform read 125TH STREET.

No one in Robby's coach made a move to get off so Robby reasoned that wherever they were all going (including him) they hadn't gotten there yet. He settled back in his seat.

More people got on the train.

The train did not move for a longer time than it had taken the train to get there. It was dark out. Dim lights shone on the station platform. No one aboard seemed disturbed by the half-hour delay. Robby remembered the Lost and Found room at the main railroad station and understood that it took a lot of time for a railroad to lose that much luggage and freight. Beside him the sailor snored on every third inhale.

Finally there was a renewed banging of doors and cold drafts swept through the coach.

Through the train window Robby saw Tony Savallo's head appear in a stairwell. It rose at a reliable pace and below Tony Savallo's head, incredibly enough, was Tony Savallo's whole body. His right hand was in his jacket pocket.

Robby was so amazed, so incredulous, so doubting of his own eyes that he leaned over the sailor's inert body and stared through the window overlong.

Tony's face registered that he saw Robby. The train began to move. Tony headed for the steps at the rear of Robby's coach.

Robby bolted out of his seat, through the door at the front of the coach, and jumped down the steps to the platform. He caught his balance and stood still. If he crossed the platform he would be visible from the train windows. He stood as close to the train as possible as it pulled itself past him. He remained where he was, making the most of the blind spot until the train was 'way up the track.

Only then did he cross the platform and saunter down the long, iron stairs which Tony Savallo had climbed.

22

In the Lap of America

"**H**ey, boy. You lost?"

"No, sir."

"Whatcha doin'?"

"Nothing, sir."

The skinny young man crouched in front of Robby, his dark face looking at him through the dark. The whites of his eyes stood out like moons on a perfect night. "You need he'p?"

"Hep, sir?"

"You need he'p?"

"No, sir. I don't think so."

Robby didn't know what hep was, but he had been taught properly not to accept things he didn't know. So far, since coming down the stairs from the railroad station, standing on the sidewalk, he had been offered a drink from a brown bottle by a smelly, staggery old man who didn't speak at all understandably, and Robby had not accepted the drink. Now this young man had come along and noticed him and offered him hep.

"You sure you don't need he'p?" The young man looked at him as if he doubted him.

Robby looked back at him, not sure.

"You don' look to me as if you belong here, at all."

"Sir?"

"You belong downtown."

"Yes, sir."

"You goin' downtown?"

"Yes, sir. I guess so."

"You must be waitin' on someone, that it?"

Robby looked at his shoes. He wasn't *on* someone. He raised his eyes to the face of the man, who had stood up.

"All right, boy. You make up your mind you need he'p I'll be over there in that drugstore. You hear? I work behind the counter there."

"Yes, sir."

Robby watched the young man cross the street, walk to the corner and go into the drugstore. *Hep must be something you get in a drugstore.*

"Hey, Lilly! Hey, Lilly!" Across the street five boys, somewhat older than Robby, had stopped on the sidewalk. They were calling in his direction. "Hey, Lilly! Hey, Lilly! Hey, Lilly!"

Robby looked around himself in the dark. There was no one else to whom they could be calling.

"Lillypad!"

"Whatcha doin', Lillypad?"

Robby backed into the area under the stairs leading to the railroad station. He felt there was no light on him.

"You come over here, Lillypad, we'll cut your stem off!"

All the boys must have found that funny because they all laughed. They continued along the sidewalk. Three of the five had their hands in the back pockets of their trousers. One of the other two rolled over a rubbish barrel, spilling its contents into the street. That, too, must have been funny because they all laughed.

At the far corner one of them shouted, "Comin' to getcha, Lillypad. Cut yo' stem off!"

They turned the corner, and were gone.

It began to snow. There was little light in the street. In the windows in the brick buildings across from Robby there were only a few slits of light. There were no lights in the window of the drugstore at the corner. The sign saying STRON'S DRUGS was big and painted black against white so Robby could read it in the little light there was. When the drugstore door opened, as people went in and came out, a shaft of yellow light fell on the sidewalk. There were few cars going by and the headlights of all those were half-lidded to prevent their being seen from the air. It was in the headlights of a car that Robby first noticed it was snowing.

There had been several people walking the streets along the two sidewalks. There had been a few young men in uniform with girls; a few young men in uniform without girls, together; a few young men in uniform, alone. There had been the smelly, staggery old man with the brown bottle. There had been two women, each alone, both hurrying. One had worn a nurse's uniform and cape. There had been the young man in the reindeer sweater who offered Robby hep and asked if Robby were waitin' on someone. There were the boys who called Robby Lillypad.

Until Robby stepped into the shadow of the stairs everyone on the street seemed to notice him, look at him, *see* him, even those who had not spoken to him. For the most part, if their looks expressed anything they expressed mild curiosity. The woman who was not in a nurse's uniform looked as if she might speak, perhaps wanted to, but decided against it. In his days and nights so far on the streets of New York, America, Robby felt few had seen him until he came to this dark place. He had run right through a crowd of people looking at his picture in the Sunday newspapers, but none had seen him. He had sat stinking in a crowded church, and many had looked at him certainly; none had seen him. He had upset everyone in the lower floor of the Hotel Clemens (except the waiter who held the door open for him), and everyone had yelled at him, two had kicked him, but no none had seen him. Of course Marie Savallo had seen him and one thing had led to another. The vanWankles' butler, Cabot, had seen him and done his best for him. Robby marveled that in a world of people ordered by their newspapers to look for him so few had seen him.

Robby felt snowflakes on his cheeks. He looked up. The iron steps to the railroad station were latticed. Some snowflakes came right through them.

Of course Robby had seen black people before. There had always been some black people on the streets of London, and he had seen many black people on the streets of New York. Black diplomats and their wives had come to tea and dinner at Pladroman House. Robby had loved the long, graceful robes the men wore. His family had a special friend who was an English black man, who had married the Cullinan woman. They had stayed at the country house at Wolmwold a whole winter while the man wrote a book which everyone said was quite good and which was published in England and France. Robby had never been in a place before where all the people were black.

He supposed that was why people on this street were seeing him. They were all black, and he wasn't.

Or they all read newspapers, really read them, and no one else did.

It was snowing hard. Robby looked across the street to the drugstore and wondered again what hep was. The time might be coming when he wanted some of whatever it was.

On the opposite sidewalk a man hurried along clutching his coat collar to his throat.

Robby did not know what he was thinking. The aftertaste of marmalade was gone, even the stickiness; he was out of Resounding Rhetoric. There come times when one thinks nothing, and this was Robby's first. Resolve, Fortitude, Duty were made of the same alphabet as Fear, Cold, Hunger. He had followed Reason, he had followed Instinct, and he had no idea Where He Was. Literally and figuratively, Robby was freezing where he stood.

• • •

He had stamped down the snow in the patch where he stood but outside that patch the snow had accumulated to just over the soles of his shoes.

Then around the corner near the drugstore came the most marvelous, the shortest and the least tall parade he had ever seen. Flags flying, bands playing, horses prancing and pipes singing could not have struck Robby as half so marvelous.

First around the corner came a large, heavy woman who waddled like a duck. Cradled in each arm was a large, brown grocery bag, necessarily held out against her ample bosom as if even foodstuff, the growing things of this earth, potatoes and carrots and onions, whatever was in the grocery bags, needed to press against her vitality to improve, to take sustenance from her. As the bags were obviously heavy and the sidewalk was slippery her head bobbed between the bags with every step. Her feet were not webbed but even from where Robby was standing he could see they were large and flat. Despite their large size there was something extra about them that made them appear to flap. He was to see that she walked in the snow in red cloth bedroom slippers which were so variously torn it was a wonder she kept them on. The ripped sections of the slippers flapped as she walked.

Behind her came a giggle of little kids in two loose lines like ducklings. They jumped up and down and bowed to make snowballs and waddled backwards and detoured and returned and yelled and laughed and caught snowflakes on their tongues and held hands and stuck snow down each other's backs and punched and tickled. One doing a cartwheel slipped in the snow and landed hard on the sidewalk and yelled "Ow!" and even that did not impede the merry line. They punched and tickled. Last in line soberly walked a girl wearing glasses, reading an open book the bottom part of which was propped against her hip bones.

Robby's previous efforts to find a school not having been very successful, this new method presented itself to him. *Here*, he decided, *is a school going somewhere to happen.*

He crossed the road to them and ambled along beside them, joined their formlessness, and the various ducklings looked at him, and saw him of course, and in less than a moment Robby felt the friendly *splat* of a light snowball against his forehead and he said, "I say!" and he said, "Right!" and bent over to make his own snowball and was attacked from the rear, snow was tucked into his shirt collar and melted and slid all the way down his spine which gave Robby's snowball a worthy target, which it missed.

The children were dressed more in country wear, Robby thought, than city, and more in summerwear than winter. Their shoes were plimsoll sneakers, little good in the snow. Their trousers and skirts were light cotton, little good in the cold. And their pullover sweaters, those who had them, and windbreakers were too big and too small depending on who was wearing them.

The line turned a corner, frisking, and another. Then it turned up a long flight of cracked stairs leading to a tall, crumbling brown building.

Robby stopped on the bottom step.

At the top, still holding her bags, the woman held the door open with her rear while the ducklings passed into the building.

The woman squinted down the steps at Robby. "What you doin', bo' weevil, out this late all by yourself? You want to get snatched up by them what makes dog food?"

"No, ma'am."

It was then Robby saw her red, torn cloth slippers. They were very wet.

"You been followin' me?"

"Yes, ma'am."

"Lordy Lord, you do make 'em."

The last in line, the girl who persisted in reading her book in the dark, stumbled through the doorway.

"You get yourself home, little bo' weevil," the woman said. "You don't belong 'round here."

She stepped farther into the vestibule of the house, letting the door go. The door swung shut.

A snowflake landed on Robby's nose.

He turned around. He sat on the step. He was warmer from having played with the children. He began to think again.

Frozen tundra. His nanny had read to him about both deepest jungle and frozen tundra and it was a good thing she had, as Headmaster had known about neither place. People in frozen tundra built houses of snow and lived in them although how they could had always been a puzzle to Robby as he couldn't figure out how they ever lit their fireplaces without turning their houses into bathwater. His shoe scuffed the snow on the lowest step. It seemed a poor building material but he could understand people in the frozen tundra building their houses of snow if that was all they had. It was all he had. Never again would he climb into the back of a truck thinking he had found shelter for the night. The once he'd done so the truck had moved and brought him to a place to see what he had not wanted to see. All the buildings he saw had doors on them and all the doors were closed. Surely this was not enough snow to commence construction. He looked at the sky. There seemed to be plenty of snow falling, more than enough, by the looks of it.

He reasoned that all he had to do was wait until there was enough snow and then build himself a house. Snow would keep the snow out. He wouldn't worry about how to heat his snow house until after he had built it.

The door behind Robby opened.

A duckling stood in the doorway on one bare foot.

"Mrs. Clearwater said if you're such a dumb boll weevil you don't know where you belong you'd better come in out of the night."

"Oh," said Robby. "Right."

• • •

The building appeared to be nothing more than caked dust.

Robby followed the duckling up two flights of broken wooden stairs, down a short corridor and through an open door into a bright room.

A large, single, shaded light bulb hung from a cord in the center of the room. The walls were a bright yellow. In the room was a large brown rocking chair, with a curved back, curved arms, and a curved seat. In one corner was a sink with its pipes exposed; next to it was a brown wooden table with a hotplate, boxes of cereal, two bottles of milk, a few bowls, spoons, glasses. Next to the table a blue curtain hung in a narrow doorway. In the other far corner was a tall, neat stack of folded green blankets.

Otherwise on the floor—almost everywhere on the floor—were mattresses. Thin, gray, black-striped mattresses.

And on the mattresses, in various states of undress, was the full giggle of children. One girl, her back leaning against the stack of mattresses, read. In the nearest corner two boys wrestled. Four sat cross-legged playing cards. One boy lay propped on an elbow singing a song with the words "Don't trouble me, Harry/You've seen better days." Each looked up at Robby when he entered, even the reading girl, even the wrestling boys, and each saw him.

The boy who led Robby up the stairs went to the wrestling match and jumped on it.

Mrs. Clearwater was at the brown table mixing cereal and milk in a huge bowl. She, too, was barefooted.

"Lordy Lord, bo' weevil, don't you know where you belong?" she asked.

"No, ma'am."

Robby took off his wet shoes and crossed the mattresses to her.

"You ain't got no home?"

"No, ma'am."

"No mama, no papa, no one to take care of you?"

"Not right now, ma'am."

"What happen to your folks, bo' weevil? They up and leave you, or you up and left them?"

"They got killed in the war, ma'am."

Robby watched her crumb bread into the mix.

"There ain't no war 'round here."

"I'm not from around here, ma'am. I'm from England."

" 'Cross the Land o' Goshen?" Mrs. Clearwater smiled at herself.

"Across the ocean, yes, ma'am."

"How'd you get here? Bo' weevils can't swim that far, usually."

"A terrible ship, ma'am. Called the Scarey-Much."

"Hunh! A ship called the Scarey-Much brought you to my door. I never heard such a story." With strong forearms and a thin tool she opened a tin can of peaches. She glanced at him sideways. "How come you're dressed that way?"

Robby looked down at his clothes.

"You been in a play?" She dumped the peaches into the mixing bowl. "Hunh! Overcoat and short pants. What folks dressed you that way?"

"Yes, ma'am. They were white."

Slowly she stirred the mixture in the bowl. "You got a shirt, jacket and coat coverin' up your elbows but your knees are stickin' out as if each one had an eyeball and the job of seein' where you're goin'."

"Yes, ma'am."

"Your knees are almost as blue as your eyes. Don't think they're supposed to be, though." In the bowl things were turning into a thick, yellowish paté. "That picture on your hat and on your coat. Doesn't seem a good enough picture to have sewn all over you. Why's that cow got her horns stuck in that tree?"

"It belongs to the school."

"What does, the cow?"

"No, ma'am. The cow doesn't have a school. I mean, the school doesn't have a cow."

"You sure talk funny, too. What folks taught you to speak that way?"

"Yes, ma'am. They were white."

"Never saw a worse-dressed bo' weevil than you. Whoever sends you out in this weather in those clothes is punishin' you, bo' weevil. Take off your coat, 'slong as your shoes are off." Robby took off his coat and cap and dropped them on a mattress. Mrs.

Clearwater glanced at him again. "Lordy Lord there's another cow with her horns stuck in a tree. Must mean somethin' important where you come from. Likely your people aren't partial to cows. Or trees." She kept breaking up the mixture in the bowl with the edge of her spoon, and stirring again. "I know I haven't got a pair of pants for you. Maybe tomorrow in the Baptist poor box I'll find some. Franklin had a pair of pants, but Arthur's wearin' 'em, and I don't think he's done wearin' 'em yet, are you, Arthur?"

"Done wearin' Franklin's pants?" answered one of the wrestlers, the one momentarily on top. "This boy ain't never goin' to need to wear pants again! Ow!"

"Bo' weevils," said Mrs. Clearwater. "They're everywhere! Aren't they just?"

"Yes, sir, ma'am."

"Seein' your folks gave you so little, at least did they spring a name on you?"

"Oh, yes, ma'am. I got lots of those."

"Try a few on me."

"Robert James Saint James Burnes Farhall, I mean, Walter Farhall-Pladroman, ma'am."

"Phew-ie! Did I hear James twice in that string?"

"No, ma'am. James once and Saint James once."

"Like that cow all over your clothes. Once your folks decide on somethin', they sure do stick to it. What does anybody want with all those names?"

"My father once said they had to load me up with names to satisfy the families."

"Well, I hope they're satisfied. Bo' weevil, they set you out with near a dozen names and cold knees. I'd rather have one good name and a pair of pants, if I were you."

"I saw you out in the snow in slippers, ma'am."

"I got snowshoes. Somewhere. But an old woman's feet aren't impo'tant. No one's supposed to be responsible for an old lady, see?"

"No."

"Well, you are a nice boy. Did I hear Robert start that string of names you rattled off to me?"

"Robert James Saint James—"

"Robert will do just fine. More than fine. You ain't slept in a while, either, have you, bo' weevil?"

"I spent last night in a rubbish barrel."

" 'Course you did. You ain't the first, you ain't the last, and you ain't the only." She indicated the world with her spoon. "There are bo' weevils out there right now, in this snowy night, hunkerin' down in rubbish barrels. Hunh! Think of a world that can afford wars and can't feed the children. Hunh! Don't you never spend no night in no rubbish barrel while I'm alive, Robert. You hear me?"

"I certainly won't, ma'am."

"Say what?"

"I'll never spend no night in no rubbish barrel while you're alive, ma'am."

"You know what else I think, Robert?"

"What, ma'am?"

"I think it's been too long since I had a huggin'."

Robby looked at the bigness of her.

"Can't go too long without a huggin'," Mrs. Clearwater said. "Makes me worry." She put down her spoon and took Robby's hand. "You come he'p me out."

At the rocking chair, Robby hesitated.

"Now don' you worry 'bout the other bo' weevils," Mrs. Clearwater said. "I've about taken all the huggin's from them they can stand for just now."

Both her arms were out and when Robby climbed into her lap they folded around him. He drew his knees up onto her. Through his right ear he could hear her heart beat. The skin of his face could feel her breath.

The chair began to rock, slightly.

Robby said, "It's snowin', ma'am."

"I hear you, bo' weevil."

"I was going to build a snow house."

"And I know you would have built a fine snow house, Robert. Just fine."

"You see, I was sent to America . . ."

"You're here, li'l bo' weevil. I'm America. Lordy Lord, I got black blood in me, and white blood, and yellow blood, and red-Indian blood, all in me. You're in the lap of America, bo' weevil. You go ahead and cry. I'm America; there ain't no mo': I'm just an ol' cow with my horns stuck in a tree."

23

The Charitable Lady

"**H**unh! Look at that snow." In the morning Mrs. Clearwater stood, hands on her hips, looking out the window. "The charitable lady will never get here."

Breakfast was a more orderly procedure than supper had been. Blankets were folded and stacked in a corner of the room. Teeth were brushed at the sink with four toothbrushes. At the brown table Mrs. Clearwater put together another cereal mix. Heddy braided Ugly Mary's hair while Ugly Mary continued reading her book. Traffic to and fro the toilet alcove, behind the brown curtain, moved efficiently. The children pulled on their clothes and tied their laces. The bigger children helped the smaller children.

During supper the night before the games had continued. The card game changed players several times. Ugly Mary, cereal bowl in her lap, continued reading. Robby and Franklin and Arthur and Wellmet raced cockroaches along a narrow strip of floor, a raceway they made by separating two mattresses. After many races it was not established which cockroach was the fastest. Starting them over again and again and cheering them down a whole mattress-length wore the cockroaches out though, made them dizzy and stagger and try to escape under the mattresses. One cockroach clearly had more stamina than the others.

"Time to get the blankets, Franklin." Mrs. Clearwater had cleaned the bowls and glasses. "Hunh! We got nine mattresses and blankets and thirteen humans. Lordy Lord, if you're goin' to send me more children, please send me more mattresses and blankets with 'em!"

With the sole of a sneaker Franklin exterminated all the cockroaches except the one which had shown the most stamina. That one he told Arthur to put in a jar for safekeeping.

Then Franklin and Wellmet dealt out the blankets.

Ugly Mary finally put down her book. She looked at Robby and blinked. Her eyes shone with an extra vitality, an extra understanding. Robby knew that in touching her smooth, clear skin he would feel her vibrancy.

"That Mary," Mrs. Clearwater said to herself. "She has all the life there is or ever was or will be, all in that brain of hers. Hunh! Hasn't she, though?"

When they were all in their underwear Robby got a blanket and followed Ugly Mary to a mattress and they laid down together under it. All the while Ugly Mary's eyes were laughing. Under the blanket she punched Robby once, in the stomach, and giggled.

"Now you bo' weevils get under your blankets and pretend you're asleep, and soon you will be," said Mrs. Clearwater.

Under the blanket Ugly Mary smelled like the binding of a book.

Mrs. Clearwater turned off the overhead light. Robby fell asleep.

During the night, Robby felt something moving among them, and woke up. In a robe, Mrs. Clearwater stepped lightly among the bodies, stooping over again and again, tucking a blanket up to a chin, collecting an arm here, a leg there to replace it under the blanket.

She covered Ugly Mary's panties with the blanket.

"You awake, bo' weevil? You go to sleep, hear?"

"Yes, sir, ma'am."

"Your skin sure do show in the dark, bo' weevil."

"Yes, ma'am."

She covered Robby's legs, which he felt were cold.

Mrs. Clearwater continued through the room, stepping and stooping, like a gardener tending her flower bed.

Robby watched her settle down then, on her own mattress on

the floor, a great mountain seen from any perspective, seen now over a considerable range of hillocks, only some of whose names Robby knew.

In the dark Robby put his hand on Ugly Mary's arm, then on her shoulder. Then he put his cheek on her shoulder. The weight of his head did not wake her. He felt the magic of her vitality. He breathed in the smell from her. He fell asleep again.

"Robert will come to help me clean the church today," Mrs. Clearwater said during the busy breakfast. "Maybe we'll stop and register him at the school on the way home."

Some (Randolph, Franklin, Arthur and Wellmet) were insisting there was no school that day, because of the snow. They shouldn't even bother going down to the school to check, they said. Instead they should all go out and play in the snow before the plows came. Others (Heddy, Toby and Ugly Mary) disagreed strongly and said they should hurry up and leave for school earlier than usual, as the snow would slow them down. Mrs. Clearwater said, "You hurry up to school, and no playing in the snow on your way. You want to sit in wet skins all day?"

Through the window Robby watched them in the street. Some were hurrying to the school, not to be late. Others were playing in the snow schoolwards, to sit in wet skins all day.

Mrs. Clearwater was on her hands and knees looking in a corner cupboard. "Where are my snowshoes?"

Watching her, Robby was sure no snowshoes could fit in such a small cupboard. He knew no snowshoes which would fit Mrs. Clearwater could fit in such a small cupboard. He doubted snowshoes which would fit Mrs. Clearwater would need looking-for at all.

"Here they are!"

Out of the closet she pulled a pair of floppy overshoes so holey, cracked and torn, Robby knew them incapable of either keeping snow out or her feet in. As galoshes they were as illusory as a Thadeus Lowry meal.

Mrs. Clearwater sat in the rocking chair to pull on her boots.

Watching her, Robby said, "You genuinely like children, ma'am?"

"Well, I love 'em," she said. "Why you ask?"

"A man I know once said if I ever meet an adult who genuinely likes children I should let him know and he'll build a statue to that person."

"Hunh!" said Mrs. Clearwater. "People do love to turn each other into stone statues. It's one more way of ignorin' the flesh and the blood of us."

There was a thump and a bump and a stamping from downstairs and a giggle all the way up the stairs.

Randolph was the first to burst into the room. "No school! I told you so! I told you no white teacher could make it through that snow to the school!"

"You'll catch your deaths!" exclaimed Mrs. Clearwater. "Get your clothes off and on the radiators to dry this minute, you hear?"

"White teachers can't get through the snow to school," said Franklin. "Us little black kids can!"

"White teachers aren't from around here," muttered Mrs. Clearwater. "They got a longer way to go."

It was then, while Mrs. Clearwater was taking off her galoshes again, while Ugly Mary (after she had placed her pants on the radiator to dry) crawled into her corner with her book, while Arthur, Franklin and Randolph were wringing out their clothes over the kitchen sink, while there were children playing inside the apartment and children playing outside in the street and children playing on the stairs between the inside and the outside, that a woman appeared in the apartment's door.

Invisible to those who zoomed past her and around her, in and out, up and down the stairs, she was the first person sensibly dressed for the frozen tundra Robby had seen. Her boots were tall and thick and encrusted with snow. Her skirt was a heavy tweed, hemmed with snow. Her coat was quilted and belted and ran from her knees to her throat. Her gloves were lined leather. An enormous scarf was wound twice around her neck; the ends hung below her waist. On her head, pulled down over her ears, was a knitted cap. Only her nose was exposed to the atmosphere, and it was red. She carried a briefcase.

Standing in the door, soundlessly her lips said, "Seven." Her eyes widened as she looked around the room. Red and white splotches appeared on her face. Her lips said, "Eight, nine, ten." Her look softened as she spotted Ugly Mary reading in the corner, yet still her lips said, "Eleven." Upon seeing Robby her face turned entirely red. Her eyes narrowed. Her lips said, "Twelve."

Mrs. Clearwater looked up from where she was bending over her boots in the chair. "Well, Miss Maisie! You made it through the snow after all! You're a credit to your race and as regular as the curse!"

"I'm glad to find you in," the woman said.

"In what?" asked Mrs. Clearwater. She got up and brought her boots to the cupboard, dropped them in, and closed the cupboard's door.

"At home." Miss Maisie sat in the rocking chair. "Obviously I have to talk to you." She pulled off her gloves. "This is an intolerable situation. It can't go on."

"But it do seem to," said Mrs. Clearwater. "It do."

Mrs. Clearwater's accent became more inflected, Robby noticed, more rhythmical, more mellifluous. And, Robby noticed, Mrs. Clearwater smiled at herself frequently, as if at hearing the way she was saying things, as she had the night before when she had referred to the Atlantic Ocean as the Land o' Goshen.

Miss Maisie took a large notebook and pen from her briefcase and opened both for use. Snow from her boots was making a puddle on the floor.

"Really," she said in disgust, indicating Arthur, Randolph and Franklin with the rear end of her pen. "Can't you make those boys stop that?"

"Here, you bo' weevils, stop that," Mrs. Clearwater said. "Can't you see the charitable lady's here? Your clothes are dry now. Go outdoors."

"Our clothes ain't dry yet," said Franklin. "We just put 'em on the radiator one minute ago."

"Then sit still, there."

"Disgusting," said Miss Maisie. "Three near-naked boys and there's a girl sitting right there in the corner." Miss Maisie made a note in her book. "She's near-naked, too."

Mrs. Clearwater laughed. "That's all right, Miss Maisie. You put this many people in a room small as this, and there ain't much they end up not knowin' 'bout each other."

"Those boys were wrestling near-naked."

"They just warmin' theyselves up. They ain't got no fine, quilted snow-coats. No, sir!"

"This certainly will go in the morals section of my report."

"Why, Miss Maisie, you makin' another report?"

"I certainly am."

"You know what, Miss Maisie? You make up reports and give 'em in somewhere downtown where they chew 'em up in some big machine and put 'em in boxes and next day I go to the store and buy 'em back as cornflakes."

"Perhaps if you had more respect for what we're trying to do for you, cooperate a little more, we could solve some of the problems you seem incapable of solving yourself."

"What problems I got, Miss Maisie? I got my children, my health and just enough money to keep goin' to the store and buyin' your reports as cornflakes."

Miss Maisie used the blunt end of her pen again. "You must tell those boys to cover up! If you don't find their nakedness objectionable in front of the little girl, I most certainly do!"

"The only clothes they got is wet."

"Have them do something! They're exposed!"

"Here, Franklin. Get a blanket and put yourselves under it. The charitable lady says she don't want to see so much of you until you're older."

"Mrs. Clearwater, I will not continue to put up with your insults."

"I hope not."

"And if you think by insulting me and abusing me you can get rid of me, you're badly mistaken. I am a trained social worker, a city employee, here to help you, and help you we will, even if our straightening out this intolerable situation means your ending up in jail. Do I make myself clear?"

"Jail! Hunh! Wouldn't that be somethin'. Mrs. Clearwater in jail. Anythin' else you can think to do for me, Miss Maisie?"

"It's not impossible. We have enough evidence to bring moral charges against you, charges for neglect, abuse, hampering a city official in the discharge of her duty—"

"And it's not impossible I'm gonna shut my door in your face! Think of you comin' here and talkin' that way in front of my children!"

"They're not your children, Mrs. Clearwater, and we will institutionalize them all, as soon as we can complete some paperwork. Then you'll see what we do to you."

"You're gonna institutionalize us all? Lordy Lord, we're goin' to jail, for makin' do. You keep doin' your paperwork, Miss Maisie, and we'll keep eatin' it up as cornflakes, and if anybody comes up with solutions better'n what we got, I'll go to jail quick enough to praise the Lord and get some rest."

"We'll begin by your addressing me by my proper name. I am Miss Caldwell, as you well know. Miss Carol Caldwell. I have reviewed reports about you going back years. Your penchant for calling your social worker, every one of us, *Miss Maisie* has been noted with increasing irritation."

"That what your reports say? I've always wondered what you all spend the rest of the week writin' down about us."

"Whatever humor this appellation has had in your mind has been perceived by no one else, and must have worn thin in whatever mind you have."

"Lord, Miss Maisie, you've beaten me down." Mrs. Clearwater fluttered her hands in the air. "I'm cut and bleedin' on the groun'. You done put me in my place and stepped on my face. You're gonna take my children and put me in jail, and move on to make some other po' nigger wail!"

From under the blanket came giggles, and a very quiet cheer. "Yeah, Mrs. Clearwater!"

Contrary to her words, Mrs. Clearwater stood over Miss Maisie, hands on her hips, feet planted wide apart. "How come I never see no white people in Harlem except those what got jobs with the city? How come no black people got jobs with the city?"

Miss Maisie cleared her throat and looked down.

"How come they're no black social workers? You ever send me a black social worker, and I'll never call her Miss Maisie. That's a promise!"

"Jobs are available to black social workers. It's just that so few have the education—"

"So few have the education 'cause all the social workers is white! Ain't that right?"

"Mrs. Clearwater, you and I can't solve all the problems of the world—"

"Miss Maisie, you can't even solve your own problems!" Mrs. Clearwater pointed to the floor at Miss Maisie's feet. "You seem to be leakin' some."

Miss Maisie looked down at the puddle the snow from her boots had made.

Mrs. Clearwater said, "You expect me to clean that up? You

expect me to come into your house and leave a puddle? You don't expect me to come into your house at all. My children might come into the house and take off their clothes to dry and wrassle around to get warm, but they take the snow off them before they come in and they don't leave no puddles for Mrs. Clearwater to clean up. They don't come in here and insult me and threaten me with no pen and leave no puddles on my floor. You hear me, Miss Maisie?"

"I hear you, Mrs. Clearwater," said Miss Maisie. "I realize I probably did insult you, and if I did I apologize heartily. If you'd just explain where all these children came from—"

"I've explained! Not once but one thousand times. The night I found Ambrose sleepin' in a packin' case I went to the police station and explained about it, and they said, 'It's late, now, you bring that boy home and somebody from the city will be in touch with you.' "

Miss Maisie flicked through her notebook to a list. "Ambrose?"

"That was years ago! Ambrose is now gone to the Army. Within a week, he brought home Billy and John."

"Billy and John?"

"Billy's already dead in the fightin' in North Africa. The world's full of bo' weevils, Miss Maisie."

"I see. I don't think I understand."

"I been explainin' all along! And once a month some Miss Maisie's been comin' along as if she had a right, comin' right in, sittin' in my chair, askin' me the same questions, gettin' the same answers, insultin' me, threatenin' me no matter what I say, makin' up reports and it never done no good. No truck full of food to feed my children never pulled up at my door. No car never come by with clothes and blankets and enough mattresses. Nobody never gave me no cash money this close to Christmas to buy no stockin's for my children. Nobody never found better homes for my children than the one they got. All you Miss Maisies ever done is come by regular like clockwork to insult what we got, to insult what we are, make up reports and go away leavin' puddles on the floor for me to clean up."

"*Burned*," said a voice from under the blanket.

"I see," said Miss Maisie. "I see how it can look from your perspective. With the war there really isn't much room in the orphanages—"

"There ain't no perspective to it. It's a fact. It's also a fact the city orphanages are a disgrace. My minister went and looked. He said they line naked boys who've acted up some against a wall and play fire hoses on them full force! That's lovin' 'em!"

"With so many children, there is a need for extraordinary measures of discipline."

"Some fine citizens they're makin'. Hunh!"

Miss Maisie's face, even her forehead, was entirely red. She looked up at Mrs. Clearwater. "It's also a fact, Mrs. Clearwater," Miss Maisie said, "that you are a prostitute."

"Yes, ma'am!" Mrs. Clearwater said joyously. "You better believe it!"

"You admit it."

"Never think otherwise, Miss Maisie."

Miss Maisie looked down at her notebook. "Our agency has had you on file for more than ten years now. No one has ever reported seeing a Mr. Clearwater. No record of your marriage has ever been found." Miss Maisie sighed. "Yet clearly you have children here, even now, who are only five and six years old."

"That's right."

Miss Maisie sighed much more deeply. "In fact, if I just counted correctly, you have twelve children here, all roughly between the ages of five and twelve."

Mrs. Clearwater laughed. "You figure it out, Miss Maisie. You think I got more'n my share of children."

"I think you have."

"But as long as you got me down in your book as a prostitute," chortled Mrs. Clearwater, "you can't figure out which are my *natural* children, can you?"

Miss Maisie asked tiredly, "Mrs. Clearwater, which are your natural children?"

"They're all natural children, sure enough."

Miss Maisie looked at Robby Burnes. "Are all these children your children, Mrs. Clearwater?"

"They ain't no one else's."

"When I visited you last month, I counted ten children."

"You must have counted wrong."

"As of last Friday you have eleven children enrolled in the local school—all under the name Clearwater."

"They must be slow in their paperwork down there."

"There are twelve children here, Mrs. Clearwater, and we can't find birth records for any of them."

"Well, Miss Maisie, they were all born, sure enough. It's just that slow paperwork. Terrible slow paperwork. No wonder the cornflakes is stale."

"I know you have a job cleaning the Baptist church, Mrs. Clearwater."

"Bowin' low before the Lord."

"You are willing to be thought a prostitute simply to obstruct the law . . . is that it?"

"You ain't goin' to find no partial solutions for us, Miss Maisie. You ain't goin' to take some of my children and throw 'em in front of no fire hose. I'd like to see these children well cared for. You find a solution for all of us, or none of us. I needs to help these children out, Miss Maisie. Not once a month, makin' out reports. I needs to help them out twenty-four hours a day. I'm doin' the best I can."

Miss Maisie laid tired eyes on Robby Burnes. "That white boy isn't your child."

"Robert? Sure enough, he's my bo' weevil."

"Mrs. Clearwater, he is blond, blue-eyed, and he wasn't here last month."

"I got white blood in me. I can have a white child. Why, you should have seen the John who was that boy's father! He was extra-white. Even whiter than you are, Miss Maisie! Last month while you were here, Robert was 'round the corner buyin' up your cornflakes."

Miss Maisie said to Robby, "What is your name, son?"

"Robert, miss."

"Robert what?"

"Robert Clearwater, miss."

"How old are you?"

"Eight years old, miss."

"You look bigger than that. Do you go to school?"

"Yes, miss. I go to the local piss."

"What? What did you say?"

"I said, 'Yes, miss.' "

"How long have you been here, Robert, living with Mrs. Clearwater?"

"I was born here, miss."

"You don't talk like Mrs. Clearwater."

"I don't have much to say, miss."

"I mean, you seem to have an English accent."

"If I were any more English I couldn't talk at all, miss."

"What did you say?"

"I said, I have a toothache, miss."

"Why do you look so familiar to me, Robert?"

"You've seen me here before, miss."

"I've never seen you here before. But I've seen you someplace before. I'll figure it out."

A new wrestling match was going on under Arthur's, Randolph's and Franklin's blanket.

Miss Maisie pointed the blunt end of her pen at it. "Make those boys stop that!"

Mrs. Clearwater said, "Here, you! Get dressed and go out in the snow now. Before the plows come."

Happily they popped up from under the blanket and began to pull on steaming clothes.

Miss Maisie screwed the cap on her fountain pen. "Well, at least, Mrs. Clearwater, I think our little chat helped clear the air."

Mrs. Clearwater shrugged. "Air's never been smoky, in this room."

Miss Maisie picked the briefcase up from the puddle and put it in her lap. "I'll make my report and then we'll just see what shall be done."

"You won't do nothin', Miss Maisie. You Miss Maisies never have."

"Not me, precisely." Miss Maisie closed her notebook and put it in the briefcase and closed the briefcase and stood up. "I'm being reassigned—to another district. Out of Harlem, thank God. I've had just about all I can take of you black women and your unaccountable children."

"You're just earnin' a wage, Miss Maisie. I know that. We all have to earn a livin'."

Miss Maisie turned in the door and went through it and started down the stairs.

"Merry Christmas, Miss Maisie," said Mrs. Clearwater. "May all your Christmases be white."

• • •

Mrs. Clearwater chuckled and put her hand on Robby's head. "Robert Clearwater, eh?" Her hand slid down the back of his head to his neck. She gave him a gentle shake. "You like that name, Robert?"

"Yes, ma'am."

"It's a name you can remember, uh? You can say it without stumblin' over it, forgettin' parts of it."

"Yes, ma'am. You're America, ma'am. You said."

"I'm the melted pot, bo' weevil. Trouble with a pot, Robert, is that the melted part always sinks to the bottom." She laughed and shook him gently again. "Lordy Lord, I'm goin' to have much trouble explainin' you, bo' weevil. Why don't you go out and play with the other children?"

"Should I, ma'am?"

"There somethin' out there you afraid of, bo' weevil?" She turned him around to face her and looked into his eyes. "You go out and play. You have nothin' to fear with all the other bo' weevils around. Pretty soon I'll come out and see how you are."

"Yes, ma'am."

"Don't be afraid, bo' weevil."

"I won't, ma'am."

Mrs. Clearwater turned toward the sink. "I'll just get a rag, and wipe up this month's contribution from the social-workin' agency."

In the street Robby helped the others build snowmen until the snowplow came along and knocked them down. The giggle of kids pelted the back of the snowplow with snowballs. After the snowplow had gone by once each way they built snowforts on both sides of the street and had a long, wicked snowball fight.

As people came into the street from the buildings Robby noticed that many stopped and looked at him and walked along and looked back. *Lordy Lord, I'm goin' to have much trouble explainin' you, bo' weevil*, Mrs. Clearwater had said. Robby could not think about that just then. He was warm and happy and breathing hard and the cold felt good against his cheeks and even Ugly Mary came out to play. Robby busied himself protecting her in the snowball fight until he discovered her aim was much better than his and she could throw farther. It was simple, them against us/us against them, and the reality of play became the nearest and nicest and best and almost only reality. He lost his school cap in a tussle in the snow and reminded himself to look for it later.

Mrs. Clearwater, in her overshoes, left the house, went up the street, around the corner. In a while she came back, carrying a shopping bag so full the newspaper stuck out of the top of it like a flagpole.

They played Beat the Devil and dark fell on them as gently as snow had fallen the night before.

Just at full dark Mrs. Clearwater came out of the building again in her overshoes and again she walked up the street and turned the corner. When she returned she was carrying nothing.

A while later she called from the window that it was time all her bo' weevils came in. In they trooped, wet and warm and tired.

They tried to dry their clothes by wringing them over the sink and laying them on and near the radiator. Robby's knees and his cheeks were chapped and Mrs. Clearwater put some grease on them. During the long process of supper, using bowls and glasses one after the other, there were many laughs and wrestles. Francine stood on her head while others counted off the seconds for a full seven minutes. Pauley almost succeeded in teaching Blanchard, the youngest, how to wiggle his ears. Ugly Mary sat against the blankets with her skinny knees up, reading. Wellmet tried to get another cockroach race started but he could find only one cockroach. The cockroach Arthur had put in the jar the night before was dead.

They brushed their teeth and got under the blankets early because the radiators were working so hard at drying clothes the room grew cold. Under the blanket Robby kissed Ugly Mary and she kissed him back. When the light went off they put their arms and legs around each other and she went to sleep.

Robby was almost asleep when he remembered his school cap. Dark had fallen too soon and too fast for him to find it in the snow.

24

Trapped!

Robby saw his school cap first thing next morning, the instant he looked out the window. It was across the street in Tony Savallo's left hand.

Robby backed away from the window. The room was still cold but Robby was much colder.

Tony Savallo was on the sidewalk across the street, the other side of the farther snowfort. His arms were folded across his chest. Watching all the buildings at once he paced up and down the sidewalk, stepping lightly over the hunks of snow. He walked ten meters along the block one way, then ten meters back. Within two or three blocks of the railroad station, with the help of the school cap, Tony Savallo had located Robby Burnes.

"Curse my cap!" Robby said to himself.

The room was full of chatter, but Robby heard none of it. He picked his clothes off the radiator and dressed as quickly as he could, imagining terrible things. Robby was a danger to the Clearwater giggle of kids. He was a danger to Mrs. Clearwater. He had led a murderer to them. He imagined Tony Savallo bursting through the door of the little apartment and shooting everyone in sight. Robby's hands shook so much it took him forever to tie his shoelaces.

He put on his overcoat.

"Where you goin', bo' weevil?" asked Mrs. Clearwater. "You ain't had breakfast yet. Anyway, you're comin' with me today, to help me clean the Baptist church."

"Just cold, ma'am," said Robby. He shouldered his collars up around his neck and rubbed his hands together. "Just cold."

Doling out breakfast to the others she gave him a long look.

Robby went behind the brown curtain. It took forever for him to relieve himself. From his overcoat pocket he took the envelope. It was wet from yesterday's snowball battle. He tore it open. The one hundred one-hundred-dollar bills were held together by a wide elastic. He stuffed the bills back into his pocket. He tore the envelope into small pieces and flushed them down the toilet.

Back in the main room Mrs. Clearwater gave him another curious look. She was busy feeding the children. Heddy was arguing with Wellmet about Leonardo and the airplane and the Wright brothers.

Robby brushed his teeth. As he did so he moved so that his body concealed the little brown table from the rest of the room. With his left hand he took the ten thousand dollars out of his pocket and stuck it in a cereal box at the back of the table. He pushed the money down into the box so it was not visible. Then he moved back and spat into the sink and rinsed the toothbrush.

"You haven't eaten, bo' weevil," Mrs. Clearwater complained to him.

"Later, ma'am," he said.

He moved into the crowd of children around Mrs. Clearwater and vibrated with them there a moment. Heddy challenged him: "Who invented the airplane?"

"What?" Robby said. "I don't know."

Slowly he backed toward the wall near the door. He stumbled over a mattress. His fingers found the wall. Behind his back they danced along the wall until they found the doorknob. He waited until Mrs. Clearwater turned her back to help Willy put on his steam-stiffened mittens. With her back to the room, Ugly Mary was putting on her coat without dropping her books. Her movements were slow and dignified. Robby opened the door only wide enough to let himself through. Standing in the corridor he closed the door quietly.

He ran down the two flights of stairs lightly. He stood at the front door, looking through the thick window into the street. At first Tony Savallo was not in the window. Then he sauntered into view from the left. The uneven thick glass made his body seem to waver.

Robby went along the corridor to the back of the house. Under the staircase were bashed-in rubbish barrels. Newspapers and tin cans had spilled out of them onto the floor.

At the back of the corridor he found the door to the cellar open. The cellar stairs were blocked by cardboard boxes, some empty, some full of rubbish. He started down the stairs, hoping to wade through the mess. On the fifth stair down he was up to his shoulders in cardboard boxes. Some of them were not moving easily for him. With his foot he groped for a sixth stair and found none. Crouching on one bent knee, sinking in boxes, he felt for a seventh stair and found none.

Quickly, quietly, he ran up the five flights of stairs to the top of the building, and then up another half flight. At the top was a metal-sheathed trapdoor. The bolt was rusted. He took off his shoe and banged at the bolt until the door was unlocked. Robby pushed against the door with his hands and then with his hands and his head and then with his hands and his shoulders. He opened the trapdoor just enough for a few flakes of snow to fall through. On the roof the trapdoor was blocked with snow and ice.

He put back on his shoe and ran quietly down the stairs again to the front door. Tony Savallo was exactly centered in the window, facing the house. The window's distortion made him look very tall, his shoulders very wide.

From upstairs came the sound of a door opening. Arthur shouted, "No, no, Marconi invented macaroni!" There was a great clatter of feet as the children started down the stairs.

"The Wright brothers are not wrong," insisted Arthur. "They couldn't be!"

Robby dashed along the corridor again and squeezed himself in among the rubbish barrels under the staircase. He turned to face the corridor and sat cross-legged on the floor. Eleven pairs of feet thundered on the stairs over his head.

The front door opened and slammed, opened and slammed,

opened and slammed as if it were waving the children good-bye.
The last pair of feet down the stairs Robby knew were Ugly Mary's.
They were slow, deliberate. Robby knew she was reading as she
walked.

"Mr. Plane invented the airplane," said Francine. "Plain Mr.
Plane!"

Behind Ugly Mary the front door closed quietly.

Robby heard another door open, somewhere up in the building.
Then he heard Mrs. Clearwater's voice. "Bo' weevil? Robert?
Where are you, Robert? Hunh! Must have forgot and gone to
school with the others! Now what will happen . . ."

Upstairs the door closed.

Robby looked around at the rubbish under the stairwell. He was
staring at himself. He stretched his legs out into the corridor and
reached for the newspaper. It was the Monday *Evening Star*. The
photograph of himself on the front page, albeit large, had been
cropped. *The New York Star* had used less of his photograph, bigger,
in each new edition. This version ran from the peak of his school
cap to the bottom of his chin. His hand was missing from his chin,
now, and his chin looked blotted. It was as if *The New York Star*
were consuming him slowly while making his head balloon. He
leaned his back against a rubbish barrel and smoothed the newspaper in his lap.

EXTRA

$100,000 RANSOM PAID
ROBBY'S RETURN IMMINENT

BY THADEUS LOWRY

Because of the heartwarming, fulsome and wonderful
response of the readers of *The New York Star*, the $100,000
ransom for the safe return of 10-year-old Robby Burnes has
been paid.

His return to safekeeping is expected imminently.

The kidnapping of the orphaned Duke of Pladroman has
had the New York Police Department and the Federal Bureau
of Investigation thoroughly baffled. Every telephone call to
this reporter for *The New York Star* from the kidnappers has

been traced, but, because of electronic confusion, only traced back to the police station assigned the job of tracing the call.

However, once it was reported in this morning's *New York Star* that the ransom—every penny of the $100,000—had been raised successfully from the readers of *The New York Star*, this correspondent of *The New York Star* received a very special telephone call.

In metallic, measured tones the heartless kidnapper gave this correspondent of *The New York Star* precise instructions as to how to turn the money over to their criminal hands for the safe return of little Robby Burnes.

Again efforts to trace the call (with the help of the New York Telephone Company) led back only to the police station administering the trace.

Intrepid

Dutifully, with no thought for personal safety, your correspondent followed the kidnappers' instructions precisely. The kidnapper ordered that this reporter, in delivering the ransom to them, was not to be accompanied or followed by any member of the police or F.B.I.

The kidnapper's precise words were: "If there's a cop anywhere in sight when you deliver the cash the kid's head will end up in the East River and his body in the Hudson."

Carrying $100,000 cash in a brown paper bag (the publisher of *The New York Star* donated the first $5,000 to The Robby Burnes Ransom Fund) this correspondent made his way to Grand Central Station. Working through the commuters and the holiday throng this reporter reflected on how joyous an occasion is Christmas. If the joyous revellers in the railroad station only knew who passed among them, and what he carried in that brown paper bag! At what risk to himself! And for what purpose!

Your intrepid correspondent crossed Grand Central Station attracting little or no attention, and, pretending to be an ordinary person going about routine business, placed the bag containing $100,000 in locker number 1313. He closed the door without locking it, and without taking the key.

His instructions were not to wait about, but to leave the station as quickly as possible.

News

Police have just reported to your correspondent for *The New York Star* that locker number 1313 of Grand Central Station was checked before noon.

It was found empty!

The brown paper bag containing $100,000 ransom for Robby Burnes (age 10) has been taken.

Police efforts to apprehend the kidnappers of Robby Burnes have been to no avail.

The kidnappers have gotten the ransom money and have gotten away scot-free!

The nefarious voice on the telephone, dripping evil with every utterance, assured your correspondent for *The New York Star* that if ransom was paid exactly in accordance with their instructions, 10-year-old Robby Burnes would be returned to safekeeping in some unannounced location today, Tuesday.

Now we will see if there truly is honor among thieves...

The newspaper Robby read under the stairwell had darkened. A shadow had fallen across it. Robby realized he had left his legs and feet sticking out into the corridor. Robby inhaled. He took in as much breath as he could. A bulk, a person, a man was standing over him. In Robby's hands the newspaper began to shake.

"Robby?" a man's voice asked quietly. "Robby?"

25

Mort à Guerre

"Thadeus Lowry!"

"Perusing my deathless prose?"

Robby first had seen the two brown shoes near his own, then the ferule of a walking stick lower to the floor. His eyes snapped up over the vested belly, over the hanging overcoat and suit coat and over the double chins to the flushed face, bulbous nose and protruding eyes. He gulped. "No, sir. I'm reading your story in *The New York Star*."

Robby felt as if he had screamed, when he hadn't. He was breathing as unevenly as if he had screamed.

"I'll have you know," announced Thadeus Lowry, "that you are reading the second-to-last Thadeus Lowry story for that rag, *The New York Star*. After a day of breathless waiting, a dramatic pause, an update by that hack, Ronald Jasper, reporting there is no news from the police on Robby Burnes, my last story about you shall appear in tomorrow morning's *Star*. The very last word."

"Oh?"

"I've already written it."

"What's it about?"

"Your safe return."

"Have I returned safe?"

"Of course," said Thadeus Lowry. "After a latish breakfast, which we call brunch here, dreadful word, of course, but an appetizing enough pastime—"

"But, sir, I haven't returned safe." Robby scrambled up from the rubbish and out from under the stairwell. "That man standing across the street—Tony Savallo—is going to shoot me. How did you find me, anyway, Thadeus Lowry? How did you know where I was?"

"Never mind about that now." Thadeus Lowry seemed as perturbed at the thought of Robby Burnes being shot as at the thought of having to rewrite his copy for the early edition. "What do you mean Tony Savallo is going to shoot you?"

"I saw him shoot a man Saturday night. In the street. I was in Tony Savallo's truck and I saw him through the window, and he saw me, and he's been chasing me, he shot at me twice—"

"Tony Savallo." Thadeus Lowry reflected. "So Tony Savallo shot Ginsy O'Brien."

"He shot *someone*, sir."

"He's shot lots of people. It's what he does."

Thadeus Lowry stepped to the front door and looked through the distorting glass. Robby peeped over the lower edge of the window frame.

"Odd I didn't notice him when I came in," said Thadeus Lowry. "Yet I did observe your legs sticking out from under the stairwell. It does go to prove," sighed Thadeus Lowry philosophically, "that one is inclined to see only what one is looking for." He turned away from the door. "That is Tony Savallo, all right."

"You know the Savallos, sir?"

"I've known Guido Savallo for years. We were both members of the 1928 crime commission. He had some remarkably instructive insights as to how crime is organized, I must say, but was extremely reticent about specific names and dates. A very theoretical fellow, he seemed. Tony Savallo I've been observing lurking about since he made his bones at the tender age of sixteen."

"Do you know him to speak to, sir?"

"I wouldn't speak to him."

"You wouldn't, sir? Nothing you might say—"

"He's a hit man for his Uncle Guido."

"A hit man?"

"He murders people."

"I know, sir."

"By the dozens."

"No one to talk to, sir? You talk to everyone."

"Conversations with Tony Savallo have a way of being short and terminating with a bang."

"He really wants to kill me, sir."

"He has every reason to." In the front hall of the apartment building Thadeus Lowry frowned for a long moment. "Young man?" he finally said. "You're in trouble."

"I know, sir. Is my return imminent?"

"Perhaps to your Maker."

"You see, Tony Savallo doesn't know which building I'm in. He found my school cap in the snow, so he knows I'm somewhere here."

"Playing cat to your mouse, eh? The minute you show your whiskers he grabs you by the neck and bangs you against the floor until you die? That it?"

Robby felt Thadeus Lowry's analogy in the back of his neck. "He has a gun, sir."

"Ah," said Thadeus Lowry. "So he simply blows your head off."

The simplicity outlined by Thadeus Lowry caused a stab of pain between Robby's eyes. "Yes, sir."

"Permit me to reconnoiter." Thadeus Lowry reconnoitered by walking a small circle in the front hall. "Is there a telephone in this building?"

"No, sir. I don't think so."

"But a Mrs. Clearwater called me last night, saying you could be picked up at this address."

Robby remembered Mrs. Clearwater leaving the building twice yesterday. The first time she returned with groceries and a newspaper. The second time she returned with nothing. "She went out, sir, to make the call."

"I see. Where's the back door?"

"There isn't one. There's a cellar door. It's stuffed with rubbish and the cellar stairs are missing."

Thadeus Lowry pointed up the stairs with his walking stick. "Door to the roof?"

"Blocked with snow and ice, sir."

"Fire escapes? Are there fire escapes?"

Robby recollected what he had seen from the front and back windows of Mrs. Clearwater's apartment. "No, sir. I haven't seen any fire escapes."

Thadeus Lowry's face was grim. "Some church owns these buildings," he said. "Doubtless they want their tenants to get a taste of hellfire before they perish. This place is a firetrap."

"A people trap, sir."

"Yes. More to the point: a people trap. Well, Robby, no point in our cowering under a stairway, as it were."

"No, sir."

"This is rather like how your father and I met. I think. We were both cowering under a stairway, so to speak. In France."

"Yes, sir."

"Makes a nice story, anyway. *Mort à guerre.*"

"Lovely story, sir. I enjoyed it."

"Never mind, Robby. I'm brave enough for both of us."

"That's good, sir."

"Now, I'll tell you what to do, Robby." Thadeus Lowry took Robby by the elbow. His voice became lower, somber, confidential. "I want you to go to the front door, open it, start out. Pretend you see Tony Savallo for the first time. Act surprised. Dash back in here. Slam the front door. Run and hide back here again, underneath the stairway."

Robby looked up at Thadeus Lowry. "And if he shoots me, sir, in the meantime?"

Thadeus Lowry nodded wisely. "Then we'll have to think of something else."

"Please, sir."

"I assure you, Robby. I've thought it all out. This is the best plan. It's called drawing the hare, or something."

"It's called putting me out for bait, sir."

"The only way. After all, it is you he wants to shoot. Who wants to shoot at a tired old journalist?"

"Almost everybody, sir."

"Now, now, Robby. It's our only way. Duty, Robby." Thadeus Lowry urged Robby forward by the elbow. He stood back, waiting for Robby to precede him down the corridor. "Duty," Thadeus Lowry admonished.

Robby's knees, despite all the healthful exercise and fresh air they'd had, didn't feel very strong to him at the moment. As articulately as thin, wobbly, clattering joints could, they wobbled Robby to the front door.

He put his hand on the knob. Robby remembered the last time he had followed Thadeus Lowry's instructions. Not only had he not found a school, he had been kidnapped, threatened with dismemberment, pursued and shot at since. "Thadeus Lowry?"

"Right behind you, Robby."

"I'm awfully glad you're brave."

His hot hand twisted the doorknob. He opened the door a crack and felt the cold air against his perspiring face. He opened the door more.

There was something in Robby which absolutely prohibited his looking across the street. He could *feel* Tony Savallo; he didn't need to *see* him. If Robby were going to be shot, he felt the event would be bad enough without his being an actual witness to it.

Robby kept his eyes on his feet. He put his right shoe onto the packed snowy surface of the top step. He shrieked. He considered he had gone far enough. He pulled in his foot, stepped back into the hall, and slammed the front door.

He turned around in the hall.

Thadeus Lowry was nowhere in sight. He had disappeared. The large, fat man with his huge coat and his scarf and his walking stick had vanished from the front hall!

"Whup!" said Robby in a hoarse whisper.

He rattled down the corridor toward what he knew was a dead end. His feet moved more side-to-side than frontward, as if he were trying to run up a steep hill. His knees vibrated so that his teeth shook. His posterior felt that it was behind him, somewhere behind his knees, rather than where it should have been.

His forward motion was negligible. He was only halfway down the corridor when he heard the doorknob rattle again. Suddenly the roar and scrape of a snowplow filled the front hall.

Robby lost what little control he had over his legs. His knees shook and rattled him around so that he was facing the front door.

Tony Savallo was inside the open door of the building. His feet were spread apart and his knees were bent. His arms were in front of him, more or less straight. He was pointing his gun at Robby's chest. One of Tony Savallo's eyes was closed. The intensity of the look in his one open eye made his squint almost comical to observe.

"Oh!" said Robby.

Thadeus Lowry stood beside Tony Savallo.

Thadeus Lowry had stepped out from behind the open door. His side was to Robby. In Thadeus Lowry's hand was the gun he had taken from Tootsie's nephew, Minnie's boy, Richard. Thadeus Lowry's gun was only centimeters away from Tony Savallo's head.

"Oh!" said Robby.

One of the guns went off.

Robby said, "Oh!"

Tony Savallo's head went on to his right shoulder as if folded. His left foot left the floor as if scalded. His right knee buckled as if hit from behind. His body fell to his right, hard, as if smitten by the full weight and force of justice.

Subsequently, Robby believed the efficiency with which Tony Savallo was executed would have been appreciated by Tony Savallo. It did not make a mess.

But at the moment Robby looked down at his own chest. His own hands. His own feet. His skin was sweated as if he were in deepest jungle; his body shivered as if he were in frozen tundra. But there were no holes in him; he did not bleed. He was intact and standing.

"Oh!" he said.

He could hear doors opening throughout the building.

Thadeus Lowry was bending over Tony Savallo, who lay on his side in the front hall. Voices from upstairs and outside were beginning to shout. "What was that?" "A gunshot!" "No, no, the snowplow backfired!" "Call the police!" "What happened?" Thadeus Lowry took Tony Savallo's own pistol from his right hand and stuck it into the pocket of Tony's green windbreaker. Then Thadeus Lowry put the pistol he himself had used into Tony's left hand. Carefully he fed Tony's index finger through the trigger bracket. Without causing the gun to fire again, Thadeus Lowry squeezed Tony's hand around the gun.

The front steps of the apartment house were crowded with people, as were the steps leading to the second floor.

Thadeus Lowry stood over Tony Savallo's body.

"He shot himself!" Thadeus Lowry declared. "I was the first one here! The poor boy shot himself!"

"He shot himself," said the people on the top step of the apartment house. And the word was passed down the steps. "He shot himself," said the people on the bottom step of the staircase leading to the second floor of the apartment house. And the word was passed up the stairs.

Magisterially placing his walking stick at a dignified angle to himself, Thadeus Lowry again declared, as if he had *heard* the news and was merely confirming it: "He shot himself."

Mrs. Clearwater was coming down the stairs through the people. "Hunh! Hunh! Hunh!" People moved aside for her great girth, as it was descending and made weightier by gravity. "The po' bo' weevil! What happened to that bo' weevil?"

"Robby?" said Thadeus Lowry.

Robby stepped forward, but as he did so he watched Mrs. Clearwater kneel on the floor by Tony Savallo. She let herself down on one haunch. She picked up Tony Savallo's head and brought it into her own lap. Gristle spilled from Tony Savallo's head onto the floor, and onto her skirt.

Passing her, Robby saw her red, torn carpet slippers, their toes aspiring toward Lordy Lord, and he loved her.

"Lordy Lord," she said, cradling Tony Savallo's head in her lap. "What they done to you, bo' weevil?"

"Robby."

Robby Burnes stood with Thadeus Lowry in the door. "He shot himself," Thadeus Lowry said.

Robby wobbled down the front steps of the building, through the people.

"Yes, yes," Thadeus Lowry assured the people. "He shot himself."

On the sidewalk, Thadeus Lowry said, "This way. I have a taxi waiting at the corner."

Immediately he proceeded to stamp along the sidewalk. He used his walking stick through the chunks of snow in a perfect rhythm as if it were a lovely spring day, birds chirruped from every bush, and they had just been to see an exhibition of roses growing.

Robby wobbled along behind.

"Violent country," Thadeus Lowry proclaimed. "Violence everywhere. Never get used to it. Barely stick your nose out the door and you're witness to untoward violence. Still . . ." Robby caught up to him by sliding down a mound of snow Thadeus Lowry had had to circumnavigate. Thadeus Lowry was smiling to himself: a retired journalist who discovered there was one more story he must write. "All grist for the mill."

They came to the corner where a taxi waited, its motor running. The driver's face was wizened as it watched Thadeus Lowry. Robby wondered if the driver's face was wizened before Thadeus Lowry had first gotten into his cab.

Robby slithered over a snow pile and trudged into the backseat of the taxi.

Thadeus Lowry made his lap in the street and backed into the cab. He landed cater-cornered on the backseat.

"The Waldorf-Astoria," he instructed from that position.

The driver with the wizened face said, "Close the door, willya, Mac?"

"My feet are still in the street."

Struggling, Thadeus Lowry collected his feet into the cab. He constructed himself on the backseat, feet on the floor, hat firmly in place, walking stick propped between his legs. He looked forward. The taxi did not move. "Waldorf-Astoria," Thadeus Lowry repeated to the driver. "We have an appointment."

The car slithered forward, not going by the building in which Mrs. Clearwater and Heddy and Franklin and Wellmet and Arthur and Ugly Mary lived. Through the window Robby saw down the street that two police cars had drawn up in front of the building.

"Cheer up," Thadeus Lowry said. "No good looking green about the gills. We'll have a brunch tucked away in some quiet corner of the Waldorf-Astoria. Discuss old times. Compare notes. Celebrate my retirement from the world of affairs."

"Will I get breakfast, sir?"

"How does kippered herring, bangers and strawberry marmalade sound?"

"Like something you made up, sir."

Thadeus Lowry reached in his overcoat pocket and withdrew Robby's school cap. He handed it to Robby.

"Very careless of you," Thadeus Lowry said. "Losing that. What would your father say? My dear friend, your father, the Duke of Pladroman . . ."

26

"Allow Me to Explain."

"**A**llow me to explain," said Thadeus Lowry.

Thadeus Lowry and Robby Burnes were tucked away in a quiet corner of the mammoth Waldorf-Astoria. It was shy eleven o'clock in the morning. It was Tuesday. Robby had been in America a week shy one day.

A waiter craned over them.

"A double extra-dry martini," Thadeus Lowry said to the waiter. "I just shot a man through the head."

"Very good, sir," said the waiter.

"After you bring that," said Thadeus Lowry, "let the boy order. Although how he can eat anything, I don't know."

The waiter withdrew.

"But first," Thadeus Lowry said to Robby, "if you'll excuse me, I must phone in a story." Sitting forward in his chair, Thadeus Lowry pinched the skin on the bridge of his nose between index finger and thumb. "No rest for the weary. Thought I'd done my last story. Yet here I am, in a state of retirement, responding to journalistic duty . . . Let me see . . . *The murderer of Ginsy O'Brien was found dead before ten o'clock this morning in the vestibule of an*

*apartment building in Harlem. The gun with which he shot himself
was discovered in his hand. Ballistic tests will prove that a second gun,
found in the pocket of his green windbreaker, is the very instrument of
death which executed Ginsy O'Brien on West 26th Street last Saturday
night."* Thadeus Lowry opened his eyes and blinked at Robby.
"How do you like that?"

"All right, sir, but—"

"No 'but' about it! *Apparently distraught by his recent foul deed,
the crime of murder, Anthony Savallo, age 23, apparently took his own
life."*

"There is a 'but,' sir."

"There is no 'but' that anyone will notice."

"You took one gun out of his right hand and put another gun in
his left hand."

Thadeus Lowry stared at Robby. Thadeus Lowry stood up from
the table.

"He was right-handed, sir. You put the gun in his left hand."

Thadeus Lowry's protuberant eyes protruded even more. "How
many perfect crimes do you expect me to perpetrate in a week?" he
demanded. "I shot him in the left side of the head! I had to! The
door opened to his left!"

"Won't the police notice, sir? I mean, a right-handed person
shooting himself with his left hand?"

"Not if I tell the story first!"

The waiter appeared with his tray. Thadeus Lowry sucked the
martini off the tray as easily as a vacuum cleaner sucks up peanut
shells.

"People always believe what they read in a newspaper," Thadeus Lowry said.

• • •

While Thadeus Lowry was at the telephone dictating his most
recent pack of lies, Robby ordered kippered herring, bangers, eggs
scrambled and fried, fried tomatoes and fried potatoes, toast,
strawberry marmalade, orange juice, milk and tea. His order
arrived with a double gin martini.

Robby was eating quietly when Thadeus Lowry returned.

"God love a goose," said Thadeus Lowry, eyeing the various
plates in front of Robby. "Is eating all that good for you?" Thadeus

Lowry did not slide into his place at the table. He drew his chair back, settled on it, more or less threw a line to his martini, and berthed. "Ah, well, we have to wait anyway. I've ordered a photographer to come around and take your picture. To run with my final story tomorrow. Concerning your return to safekeeping." Thadeus Lowry's eyebrows knotted in genuine concern. "You really shouldn't look too well fed," he said. "I mean, in the photograph."

"I won't, sir."

"I mean, the color is beginning to come back into your cheeks."

"I'll try to look pale, sir." Robby continued eating. "After breakfast."

Ignorant of the happy ending Thadeus Lowry already had written for Robby, nevertheless Robby thought there would be a happy ending, however fictitious. Hoping to glance a glimmer of his forthcoming glee, Robby thought he would try the gambit of polite conversation.

"You said you're retiring, sir?"

"Yes," said Thadeus Lowry. "Superannuation. After long, hard years of sterling service, I have quit the newspaper."

"I'm sure your work will be missed."

"But I've quit with a bang."

"I'd say so, sir."

"You've been reading me?"

"Yes, sir."

"What do you think?"

"I think I'm eight years old, sir."

"What did I write?"

"Ten, sir."

"A typographical error, my boy. A typographical error. Those damned printers can't get anything straight." Thadeus Lowry leaned forward over his elbows on the table. "Allow me to explain. Thursday night I didn't have a story. No one knew you were missing. *Chérie* thought you were out being a jubilant delinquent in some schoolyard. I had had an exhausting day out tramping around the city looking for a story to write. I was sitting at my desk at *The New York Star*, keeping my eye on that bastard who keeps shoving his desk up against mine, when the phone rang."

"The man with the 'icy, metallic voice,' sir?"

"As a matter of fact, it was William O'Riordan, one of New York's finest."

"Will'um the policeman, sir? You knew who it was?"

"Do you think I'd listen to anyone who hadn't identified himself properly?"

"Of course not, sir."

"Can't have just anybody calling the newspaper with a story, you know."

"Of course not, sir."

"One must always be sure of one's sources."

"Yes, sir."

"William told me you were at home with his sister, Marie, and his brother-in-law, Frankie Savallo, stuffing down lamb *Parmesan*, and that they'd all appreciate it if I would consider you kidnapped."

"You believed him because he was a policeman, sir?"

"Of course. If you can't trust the guardians of law and order, whom can you trust?"

"I wonder that myself."

"It was a moment before I grasped the full meaning of what he was saying. At first I worried that it was their intention to knock me, of all people, up for some cash, and you know that would have been impossible."

"Yes, sir."

"It would have been against my principles to pay ransom, even if I had the cash, which, of course, I didn't."

"I understand, sir."

"One must have one's principles. But then I grasped the pristine beauty of his idea—raise a subscription for your life from the public! Wring their hearts out, fleece them, all the while selling newspapers! Perfect! I wish I could take complete credit for the idea," clucked Thadeus Lowry. "But I can't." Thadeus Lowry drained the rest of his martini glass. "Ransom of one hundred thousand dollars: They were quite decided on that. It seemed a bit much to me, but I decided to take it on as a literary challenge worthy of my talents. How quickly could I raise one hundred thousand dollars from the public on a sentimental matter?" Victoriously, he smiled across the table at the matter of sentiment. "Four days! Would you believe that?"

"No, sir."

"Well, I did it! A fantastic testament to my literary ability! Do you realize how many dollars that comes out to per word?"

"I couldn't guess, sir."

Neither could he, apparently, as he next said, "Actually, yesterday morning, while the world thought I was going to Grand Central Station with my brown paper bag stuffed with cash, having made absolutely sure I was free of police observation, instead I sauntered around for my usual midmorning visit to The Three Balls."

"The Men Only, sir?"

"What? Yes. There I met Officer William O'Riordan."

"The man who had led 'a degenerate, degraded life far outside the law?' "

"We had a great laugh. So I gave him the fifty thousand dollars—"

"Fifty thousand dollars, sir?"

"Of course."

"Weren't there one hundred thousand dollars, sir?"

"Of course. I took half. That was the deal. We arranged that Thursday night."

"While I was 'cowering in some cold corner, starved and beaten, a knife at my throat?' "

"But that wasn't true," said Thadeus Lowry. "You should never believe your own press."

"But it became true! I spent the night in a rubbish barrel! I upset everybody in an hotel! Tony Savallo chased me all over the city. He shot at me twice!"

"Tush, tush, Robby. I daresay you saw parts of New York you'd never have seen otherwise."

"I saw underneath a lot of places."

"You survived. You're all right, aren't you?"

"I may be coming down with a nose cold, sir."

"From all that breakfast you're eating, I expect. Consider my retirement! Fifty thousand dollars. Why, Robby, this frees me to do all sorts of things! Perhaps I'll go into public service, run for Congress. Or I could buy a small country newspaper, build it into an empire!"

"Oh, no, sir."

"Why not?"

Robby looked through the window. On the sidewalk people were scurrying with Christmas packages. "I don't know, sir."

"Of course," said Thadeus Lowry, again apparently hearing some distant bell of duty, "what I really should do is write a book."

"Oh, yes, sir. You've hit upon it."

"I've hit what?"

"The answer, sir. Your writing a book. You type so fast, sir."

"The inside story of journalism," Thadeus Lowry mused. "How it really works, by the man who knows. The honesty, the integrity, the talent men and women bring to it, the long hours, the hard work, the sparse rewards. It would make a million."

Outside on the sidewalk, Santa Claus was setting up his money pot on a tripod. Robby was surprised. The last time he had seen Santa Claus he was on his back in a gutter being beaten by an enraged taxi driver. Looking more closely, however, perhaps more closely than he would have before, Robby observed that Santa's whiskers were not really a part of Santa's face. They were the whiskers of a fat man, slipping up and down a thin man's face. And in the sunlight, the snowy, flowing hair was a bit too gossamer to have been spun by time.

Robby Burnes said, "That Santa Claus is a fake."

Thadeus Lowry looked through the window. Quietly, he said, "Never believe anything, Robby. Including this."

Thadeus Lowry shifted uncomfortably in his chair, and signalled the waiter for another drink. "Yes, that's what I'll do. Write a book and make a million. I'll send you a copy."

"Send me a copy? Where am I going?"

"Oh, yes," said Thadeus Lowry. "I haven't told you that yet."

Robby waited to be told.

Thadeus Lowry said, "You have a grandaunt, in Scotland."

"I have?"

"You didn't know?"

"I was beginning to disbelieve it."

"You also have a lawyer living luxuriously in a suite upstairs—suite 1776—in full anticipation of your imminent arrival. Name of Carp. Firm of Pollack, Carp and Fish, London."

"I have, sir? I mean, he's here? In this hotel?"

"Who else can afford this hotel save an employed lawyer? The Waldorf-Astoria has floors and floors permanently reserved for other people's lawyers."

"Has he been here all the time?"

"Arrived Friday. By plane. Apparently your old grandaunt got wind of your family's current events belatedly, climbed aboard her escutcheon, whistled into London and pulled a lot of wigs. Raised all the circles of hell, according to Carp. Dispatched him on the next plane coming west to bring you back dead or alive."

"Dead or alive?"

"Just an expression, Robby. Anyway, he arrived Friday, bought a newspaper at the airport, saw you were among the missing, checked into a suite upstairs, and has been eating gloriously ever since."

"Eating! Was he no help at all?"

"Between meals he kept insisting things be done properly, phone calls traced, that sort of thing. That was all right, of course, as William O'Riordan would only call me from the police station."

"I'm going home!"

"By plane. This afternoon. Seems a very unsafe way to travel these days, but fly you shall. You'll be home in time for Christmas, Robby. Ah, here's the eminent picture-taker for *The New York Star*."

The entrance of the photographer caused a stir. He was stopped in the door and made to explain his camera to the headwaiter. He arrived at the table flanked by waiters.

"Hullo, Burnes," the photographer said. "How does it feel to be thadeuslowried?"

Robby stood up and shook hands with the photographer. Then he shook hands with the headwaiter and the other waiters.

As the photographer took pictures of Robby, other people crowded around, shook his hand, asked him to write his name on slips of paper. They congratulated him on his return to safekeeping, and several mentioned how glad they had been to send *The New York Star* a dollar or two toward his ransom.

On the slips of paper Robby wrote: *Robert Clearwater*.

The photographer left. The crowd thinned. Robby turned back to the table.

Thadeus Lowry was gone.

The headwaiter was speaking quietly to Robby. "I hate to bother you with this, Your Grace, but the gentleman who was with you left without paying the bill."

"What?" smiled Robby. "He didn't even tell you a story?"

"He didn't say anything, sir. He just left."

Robby took the gold sovereign his father had given him out of the breast pocket of his jacket. He looked at it before giving it to the headwaiter. "Will this be all right?"

"That will be fine." The headwaiter took the sovereign. "Sorry to bother you."

"Quite all right," said Robby. "You've just been thadeuslowried. One gets used to it."

•   •   •

A very, very thin man in a three-piece suit answered the door of suite 1776.

"Mr. Carp?" Robby asked. "I'm—"

"Yes, yes, my boy," the man said. "Have you had luncheon yet?"

"No," Robby beamed, "I haven't."